CROSS WAVES

MIND HACKERS SERIES: BOOK TWO

AMANDA UHL

Published in the United States by Amanda Uhl, LLC.

Cross Waves. Copyright © 2020 by Amanda Uhl
www.amandauhl.com

ISBN: 978-1-952581-00-7
ISBN: 978-1-952581-01-4

Cover by Christian Betulan
www.coversbychristian.com

In loving memory of my mother, Caroline.
And to my mother-in-law, Janice, and all mothers everywhere.

AURA COLOR CHART

Characters:

> **Geneva Ericksen** — Rose
> **Rolf Jorgensen** — Green
> **Cynthia Torra** — Buttercup yellow
> **Julia Jorgensen** — Violet
> **Nonna Jorgensen** — Olive Green/Black
> **Carl Ericksen** — Cornflower
> **Nate Ericksen** — Teal
> **Danny Ericksen** — Royal Blue
> **Percy Withers** — Amber
> **Peter Brooks** — Arctic Blue
> **Dr. Grimshaw** — Apricot
> **Kaitlyn Girard** — Yellow-green

Traits:

> **Death** — Pink
> **Illness** — Bright Pink
> **Secrets** — Gray (can be varying degrees)
> **Unbalance/Drunkenness** — Sienna
> **Worry** — Dull Red

Healing — Orange

Growth — Green

Passion/Lust — Purple

Anger/Fear/Action — Bright Red

Revenge — Dark Red

Knowledge/Wisdom — Yellow

Truth/Honesty/Sincerity — Turquoise

Evil Intent/Murder — Black

Confusion/Crazy/Illusion — Brown

Hope — Light Blue

Regret/Sorrow — Mauve

Suspicion/Jealousy — Navy/Dark Blue

Pride/Faith — Green-blue

Calm/Peace — Blue

Dream — Beige

Determination — Coral

Triumph/Excitement — Lime

GLOSSARY OF PARANORMAL TALENTS

Hacker — An individual capable of manipulating brain waves to read minds and change thoughts. Hackers must be physically near their target to manipulate brain waves; however, they can hack into minds from a distance aided by a trainer. The majority of hackers are male.

Trainer — An individual capable of manipulating molecules and magnifying energy waves. Trainers can increase the power and reach of a hacker, enabling them to manipulate brain waves at a distance. The majority of trainers are female.

Beacon — A trainer or hacker with the ability to disburse energy waves, momentarily rendering a talent useless. This ability only works when in close physical proximity to a target and for several minutes. Beacons are extremely rare.

Dream Talent — A trainer or hacker with the ability to magnify delta waves associated with deep sleep. Dream trainers are capable of placing someone in a dream state.

They also have predictive dreams. Dream hackers can enter the dreams of another.

Tracker — Trainers and hackers who have the ability to track individuals or objects by sensing their energy.

Dark Master — Trainers or hackers with the ability to manipulate energy that vibrates at the lowest frequency, called dark energy. Dark energy is attracted to living tissue and can absorb matter. Dark Masters are feared because not only is dark energy lethal to any object it comes in contact with, but it is believed Dark Masters are incapable of loving another. Dark Masters who use their talent frequently often become psychopaths and go on killing sprees. They have extraordinary abilities, including being able to track their victims and to change their body chemistry to walk through objects, including walls. This talent is extremely rare.

Illusion Talent — Trainers or hackers capable of creating situations and interactions that look real but are not.

PROLOGUE

Five-year-old Geneva Ericksen stopped at the bottom of the stairs. Why did she have to take a stupid nap? Naps meant sleeping in her bedroom with the black walls.

She grabbed the railing and put one foot on the first step. Behind her, the kitchen door banged shut, and she turned to look. Mama came into the dining room, carrying the pink tea kettle.

She should never have told Mama and Daddy she saw colors. If she hadn't told them, they wouldn't have gotten scared. If she hadn't told them, they wouldn't have called men from the government to come to her house to talk to her. If she hadn't told them, they wouldn't have painted black over her Winnie-the-Pooh wallpaper to stop her from seeing the colors.

Mama poured herself a cup of tea and set the teapot on the table. Mama was the prettiest and smartest lady in the whole wide world. She said too many colors were bad for little girls like Geneva. But the colors couldn't come through black walls. That's why her bedroom had to be painted.

"What's the matter, sweetheart?"

"Can I have a story, please?"

Mama smiled. "Okay, honey. Go pick one out. Bring it down here—we'll read it on the big chair."

Geneva raced to her bedroom, turned on the light, and got her favorite book from under the nightstand by her bed. The pages were ripped and scribbled on in places, but she didn't care. Mama had read the story to her so many times she knew most of the words. Cinderella's stepmother and sisters were mean to her, but the handsome prince loved Cinderella. She became a princess. Geneva wanted to be a princess, too.

A pretty pink color came through her bedroom walls like fog. A cold feeling moved from her head to her feet. Where did the color come from? Why did it make her feel all strange inside—all cold and shivery like when she got out of the bathtub? Excited and scared at the same time. The government men were wrong. It didn't matter if her bedroom walls were painted black. The colors always found her.

Geneva flew down the stairs to tell Mama about the color in her room. But she remembered Mama didn't want her to talk about it. Mama saw colors, too, but not when she was a little girl like Geneva. Mama said the colors were energy, and Geneva had a powerful psychic gift. Too much power for one little girl. The government men would take Geneva and lock her away if she kept talking about seeing colors.

Mama pointed to the overstuffed recliner in the family room and smiled. "Cinderella, again? How did I know you were going to choose this book? Let's get comfortable, sweetie."

Geneva climbed onto the cozy yellow chair and waited

for Mama to sit next to her. She opened the book. Cinderella was scrubbing the floor. Cinderella was pretty. Cinderella had long, straight blonde hair like Geneva and Mama.

"Once upon a time, there lived an unhappy little girl," Mama read the first line from the story.

The doorbell rang. Mama looked up. "Now who could be dropping by in the middle of the day?"

Geneva didn't know who was at the door, but she felt all strange inside, like there was a balloon in her belly. Mama must have felt something, too, because she looked worried. The bell rang again.

"It's okay. Look at the pictures. I'll be right back."

Geneva watched. Something was wrong. Something was really wrong. The balloon in her belly got bigger and bigger. Mama opened the door. Waves of black color swept into the room. Two men dressed in dark clothes and wearing Halloween masks came in. One of the men held a gun in his hand. It was pointed at Mama. He shut the door behind him.

Geneva got off the chair. She couldn't stop the goose bumps that started at her head and raced to her toes. Her skin tingled, reminding her of the time she'd accidentally touched the electric fence on Grandpa's farm.

The man pointed his gun at Mama. "Where are the crystals?"

Geneva sprang forward, wanting the comfort of her mother.

Mama held her hand out. Her voice sounded high and scared. "Stay back, Geneva."

Geneva stopped in the middle of room, but the balloon in her tummy didn't stop. It kept growing.

Mama fetched a small bag from the cupboard next to

the fireplace and handed it to the man with the gun. He gave the bag to his friend, who put it in his pocket. The man with the bag opened the door and left the house, but the man with the gun stayed inside. He aimed his gun at Mama.

Mama cried out, her voice trembling. "You have what you came for. Don't hurt us. Please."

Geneva's heart beat faster and faster. "No, no, no!"

The man with the gun looked at her and back at Mama. "Shut the child up."

"It's okay, Geneva," Mama said. "Go to your room."

Geneva's hands tingled. She would not go to her room until she was sure Mama was okay. The bad man still held the gun in Mama's face.

Colors rushed toward Geneva from every corner of the room. Great big balls of rainbow color. The balls surrounded her, spinning faster and faster, like the merry-go-round she rode with her older brothers at the carnival. They spun so fast they were a blur of color. She opened her mouth to breathe, and the colors came inside. Her body shook hard. The balloon popped. Rose-colored fog blasted out of her and sped toward the bad man. She couldn't stop the scream that followed. It kept coming and coming and coming.

She didn't stop screaming even after the gun went off.

Rolf Jorgensen jogged up the wide stone steps leading into the CMU, the U.S. government's Cognitive Mind Unit. The discreet brown brick building, sandwiched between a pawn shop and a Chinese takeout, had been headquartered in this dreary section of Cleveland for as long as he could remember. Who would guess it housed some of the most psychically gifted and telepathic mind readers in the nation?

He entered the single oak door, keeping to the shadows in the narrow corridor by habit. Bypassing the rickety elevator, he took the stairs two at a time. Adrenaline beat an urgent passageway through his veins, and his heart pounded out an unsteady rhythm. Only his iron control kept him moving forward at an even pace.

Within minutes, he arrived at his boss's office. Eyeing the familiar number 301 stamped in bold black letters on the grainy wood surface, his gaze traveled down the hall and back to the nondescript door. No light shone from under the gap near the floor, and logic said the room was empty. Rolf knew better.

He didn't bother to knock, just pushed the door open, the worn hinges letting out a familiar groan. The blinds over the windows, which overlooked a parking lot, were drawn. He stepped inside and allowed his eyes to adjust to the dark.

"Take a seat," Peter Brooks rasped. Rolf's boss hunched over his massive desk, his graying head in his hands. The dark suit he wore was wrinkled, rather than its normal crisp lines, as if he'd slept in it for days because he couldn't take the time needed to change his clothes. The clock on his desk read 2:04 p.m.

Rolf kicked the door shut behind him. "Why are you sitting in the dark? What's the matter with you?" Maybe managing the immense talents in the CMU was taking a toll on Peter. After all, the hackers under his leadership were responsible for guarding the minds of some of the brightest scientists and leaders in the world. His boss's stress level must be immense.

"Nothing a few aspirin and sleep won't handle." Peter lifted his head and winced. Weary lines crisscrossed his forehead. His weathered skin held a gray cast. "What took you so long?"

"I got here as fast as I could." Rolf selected a mint from the candy jar on Peter's desk and popped it in his mouth. "Where's the fire?"

"It's complicated." Peter motioned to a leather chair in the corner. "Sit."

The click-clack of high-heeled footsteps echoed down the corridor outside the office. Only one woman on the team pounded the floor like that—Geneva Ericksen, the most powerful female trainer in the ranks of the CMU. Every hacker required a trainer. They magnified brain waves, allowing hackers to infiltrate the mind without being physically near a target. But he wished he could avoid this particular trainer.

He swallowed the mint and frowned, almost missing the wince in Peter's gaze. "This better be necessary." Rolf stepped around the desk and lowered himself into the chair tucked in the corner of the room, facing the door. Once settled, he drew his energy inward and listened as the heels stopped outside the office.

The door flung open, and there she stood, all five feet two of golden mightiness. Power shimmered in the air. His gaze traveled from the top of Geneva's sleek blonde head, passed over her slim form in a navy-blue dress, and stopped at her hot-pink heels. A familiar and unwelcome excitement curled in his gut as she stepped inside the room, leaving the door open behind her. Paper clips vibrated in a canister on Peter's desk, a sure sign Geneva was feeling intense emotion, probably anger.

"I won't do it."

"Be seated." Peter came from behind the desk and closed the door. "And stop the jiggling, would you? I've got a migraine."

Geneva remained standing, her small hands fisted against each hip. She took a deep, harsh breath, held it a moment, then two, before releasing the spent air on a controlled exhale. The paper clips stilled. "Give me someone else. Anyone else. I'll take your newest recruit if you'd like. Just keep Jorgensen far away from me."

"I'm afraid that's impossible," Rolf said, stretching his legs in front of him and drawling the words since he knew it annoyed her. On instinct, he probed her mind and found a weak spot in her mental safeguards.

Her wide gaze settled on his. He caught the flash of fear

and irritation flitting across her face. Her eyes narrowed and focused. A picture of a donkey's ass appeared in his mind.

He clenched his jaw but managed a smile, refusing to acknowledge the mental imagery she sent. A gate slammed into his brain, forcing him to withdraw from her thoughts. An icy pain burned a pathway down his spinal cord. But it was worth it. It was always worth it. He fixed a grin on his face and waited.

Peter turned on his desk light and sighed, the sound slow and heavy. He squinted, pinching the bridge of his nose. "I've never understood the animosity between you two. You worked well together on the Willard case. At least, you survived intact."

Geneva stuck her nose in the air, reminding Rolf of an annoyed Cupid. "We were part of a team. And I wasn't paired with Rolf. He's impossible to work with." Gauntlet thrown, her gaze locked on Rolf's, challenging him to disagree.

"As you well know, your former partner has retired," Peter said to Geneva. "You need a new one, and...your test results came back today."

Her gaze flicked from Rolf's to Peter's. "And?"

"You two are a perfect match."

Rolf frowned and uncurled his fingers. He didn't need any government-run tests to know they'd be a match. He'd known her talent resonated with his since they were kids.

"Bullshit," Geneva said.

Rolf pressed his twitching lips into a firm line before a smile slipped free.

Peter glanced at the pens, rattling in the canister on his desk, then back to Geneva, his brows raised. Geneva flushed. They all knew there was nothing more detrimental in their line of work than an out-of-control talent.

She waved a hand, and the pens stopped moving.

Peter took a sip of water from the glass in front of him. "The government doesn't make mistakes where psychic talent is concerned, Geneva. And even if I agreed with your statement—and I don't—the other mind hackers capable of channeling your energy are...nervous around you. Rolf, on the other hand, is not."

"So, because he's crazy, I get to partner with him? This is ridiculous." The desk light flickered as power surged through the room.

"Is it?" Peter asked.

The hair on Rolf's arms rose and his stomach dropped. Energy tunneled to the surface, attracted to her light. He ground his teeth together and took a measured breath, tamping it down.

Geneva flicked her hands in an upward motion. The light dimmed then returned to its normal level. Rolf let his breath out slow and easy. The tingling in his gut relaxed.

"I know neither of you are happy with this development," Peter said, "but it's for the best. Your country needs you—I need you—to set aside your differences and act like adults. As of today, you're partners, so get used to it. I think you'll both have a vested interest in your first assignment."

"What first assignment?" Rolf asked.

Peter opened a Manila folder on his desk. "What do you know about the legend of the crystals?"

Geneva stiffened. "They exist."

Peter shuffled the papers in the folder. "Correction. A few exist. The ones your mother found. The ones someone murdered her to steal."

Geneva shielded her eyes with her hand. Her anxiety hit Rolf's skull like a mallet. A phantom ghost of power brushed against his chest. He sucked in air. This was what made it so dangerous to work with her. Whenever she was upset, it wreaked havoc with his ability to control his own energy. He flared his nostrils as he'd been trained. This allowed him to release the air in his lungs in slow and even increments, eliminating the excess energy building inside him.

"Yes, and the one my former partner used to restore his wife's memories," she said, finally sitting in the chair. "I witnessed him activate the crystal. He said the stone had been in his family for decades."

Rolf shifted his weight on the chair. Despite her air of confidence, Geneva had never fully recovered from her mother's murder more than twenty years ago. A murder she had witnessed. He bit the inside of his cheek to keep himself in check and forced his brain to reason. Peter had brought up her mother's death for a purpose. This entire meeting was a test of her control. The recent examination must have proven Geneva's talent was stronger than the higher-ups reckoned.

Peter tapped a pen on the desk. "That's the only other crystal we've cataloged. Some say there are more, each with special properties, allowing them to absorb and project psychic talent. Many have searched long and hard for them without success."

Rolf clenched his muscles to keep himself from moving and pretended his insides weren't as jumpy as a grasshopper. "What do missing crystals have to do with me needing a new partner? And why did I need to rush here to learn this? Seems to me you could have put it all in a text."

"When's the last time you talked to your sister?"

He stilled. Dark energy stirred in his belly. "Friday morning," he ground out. "Why?"

"She's missing."

2

PARTNERS

An iceberg of fear punched a hole through Rolf's gut. Automatically, he stood, reaching for his cell phone to check his recent texts and calls. Nothing from his sister. He moved toward the door but paused in front of Peter's desk. "Why the hell didn't you say so as soon as I got here?"

"Because you would have taken off."

"Right." He turned to leave.

"Stop. I want Geneva as your partner on this. She can trace your sister's energy trail."

He thought about ignoring his boss's order. It was his sister they were talking about, after all. He didn't need Geneva and her extraordinary tracking ability to find her. He could draw on his own power. But it would be risky, to say the least. He sighed and turned around.

"When was the last time you communicated with Julia?" Geneva asked Peter, tilting her blonde head.

Rolf recognized the pose. Geneva saw something in Peter's energy the rest of the world couldn't. That extrasensory gift to see and read a person's aura made her unique, even among their kind. Automatically, he searched for a weak spot in Peter's defenses and found none. No surprise there. The safeguards protecting his boss's brain had been reinforced.

"Late Sunday afternoon," Peter said. "She'd been dreaming about an unsolved murder."

"You're leaving out an important detail," Geneva said. "What is it?"

Peter swiveled his chair toward Geneva. "She dreamed of your mother's murder."

Geneva froze. Static electricity flashed around her body and disappeared.

The ball of energy inside Rolf twisted and churned, excited by her distress and the power she generated, which threatened to blow the roof off the place. Despite the risk to himself, Rolf moved to Geneva's side and squeezed her shoulder. Heat sparked between them like he'd slid his shoes across an invisible carpet before touching her. He snapped his hand back. "Breathe."

Her blue eyes met his for a moment before moving back to Peter's. Tears moistened her long lashes. "My...my mother? Why didn't you tell me right away?"

"She begged me not to." Peter rubbed one hand at his temple and fingered a paper in the folder with the other. "Julia had no choice but to investigate your mother's death. You know what it's like for a dream talent. They don't choose their dreams. Dreams choose them."

Rolf tugged a hand through his hair. "Who's she paired with?"

"Percy Withers."

"My idiot cousin? Why the hell would you pair Julia with Percy? He can't fight his way out of a paper bag.

Explains why she's gone missing in such a short space of time. He could never protect her."

"I paired her and Percy because they both asked me to."

"Well, that doesn't make any sense. Why would Julia *ask* to be paired with Percy? She doesn't like him any better than I do."

"Julia dreamed Percy could help her."

"Where was she last seen?" Geneva asked. Two small crease marks formed between her eyes. Besides being his sister, Julia and Geneva were best friends.

"I suspect Julia's in Phoenix, Arizona. Cell phone records indicate she contacted a jewelry store there on Saturday."

"A jewelry store?" Geneva tipped her head to the side and pursed her lips.

"Why would Julia not tell me what she was doing?" Rolf asked, his voice tight. His gut clenched. His sister always told him when she was assigned a case. Why had she kept silent on this one? "I would have helped her."

"She knew you were guarding the POTUS from mind hackers in China. Speaking of which, I assume you successfully safeguarded the president's mind before coming here?"

Rolf nodded. "Of course."

Peter cleared his throat. "Julia didn't want to pull you away from such a critical assignment for a lead she wasn't sure would amount to anything. She had doubts about her dreams. Told me she kept getting mixed messages." He turned to Geneva. "And she didn't tell you because she's protecting you. She didn't want to put you through the anguish of reliving your mother's death if she was wrong."

He thumbed through the papers in the folder, pulling a photograph from among them. "That's why I allowed her to go with Percy. It was supposed to be a simple follow-up on a dream sequence. I blame myself for their disappearance."

Rolf studied the picture. An assortment of crystals was displayed in a jeweler's case.

"Julia found the missing crystals?" Geneva asked, her tone harsh.

"I don't know. She cut off contact with me shortly after she arrived."

Geneva splayed her hands on the desk. "Get me on the next flight to Phoenix."

Peter nodded and held up a white envelope. "I've chartered a flight for both of you." He swiveled his chair toward Geneva. "Time is of the essence. The longer she stays missing, the greater the likelihood she won't return. Stay together on this." He pointed at her. "You can track Julia. And you're a human lie detector. But you can't hack into minds or change thoughts. You need Rolf for that."

"And you"–Peter swiveled toward Rolf–"need a strong partner to enhance your power. Both of you have a vested interest in a successful outcome. You'll work better together than apart." His eyes issued a warning. "It's time you got over your irrational dislike of each other."

"Fine. What time is the flight?" Rolf snagged the envelope from Peter at the same time Geneva did. Their fingers brushed and tangled, and his gaze collided with hers. Goose bumps tickled his skin. Raw power hit all six of his senses, setting his body on fire. He tugged on the envelope. She resisted, but he had a better grasp on it, and it slipped through her fingers.

"Seven p.m.," Peter said. "Details are there, including a hotel reservation in Sedona if you need it. Pack your bags and get to the airport—Burke Lakefront."

"On my way." He dug his nails into his skin until he broke the surface.

"Wait!" Geneva called, standing.

He turned at the door, raising an eyebrow.

She settled her hands on her hips. "I know it's your sister, and you think you're in charge, hotshot, but we're partners now. We should talk about this first. Develop a plan."

The dark energy cut a line to his heart. He tightened his hands around the envelope but couldn't stop them from shaking. "We'll talk at the airport. Meet me there at five."

He yanked the door handle and fled the room like demons from hell were chasing him.

3

ROLF

Where the hell was Julia?

Rolf studied the airline clerk and fought the panic surging in his veins, testing his self-control. He gritted his teeth and reached into his coat pocket, forcing his power back inside where it could do no harm.

A touch softer than butterfly wings brushed his arm. *Geneva.* The citrusy scent of her perfume filled his nostrils. He looked down at her hand and took a breath.

He grabbed his wallet, pulled it out, and gave his driver's license to the clerk. Next to him, Geneva did the same. The top of her head didn't quite reach his shoulder. Light glinted off each golden strand of her hair.

He blinked and shifted his gaze toward the windows. The situation was fraught with tension. Julia investigating a murder on her own without telling him. Partnering with his cousin, the weakest member of their team. What was his sister thinking?

He scraped a hand over his five o'clock shadow. How

would he ever be able to muster the control needed to find her?

Outside, a small airplane taxied to a stop. Crew members in blue jumpsuits surrounded it.

"Two for Phoenix?" the clerk asked, pulling Rolf's gaze back to the counter.

He nodded.

"Right," Geneva said.

"Looks like your flight's on time." The clerk checked a list and presented them each with a plastic ticket. "You can grab a seat over there." She pointed to a series of green padded chairs facing a glass window overlooking the runway. The sun began to move toward the horizon, casting late-afternoon shadows on the tarmac. "Help yourself to beverages or snacks in the lounge."

"Thank you." Geneva took off toward the waiting area, dragging her suitcase behind her.

Rolf followed, watching the gentle sway of her hips. Between his worry for Julia and the tension between him and Geneva, the flight ahead would be torture. No doubt about it.

He found a seat in the far corner from hers and pretended to read a newspaper he grabbed from the chair next to him. All the while, he could feel her energy seeking him out like a pulsing, living being. Despite his better judgment, he squinted at her from the corner of one eye. She watched him, an annoyed glare on her face.

She opened the gates of her mind. *"What is your plan to find Julia? I can tell by your aura you've concocted something I'm not going to like in that stubborn brain of yours. You might as well come on over here and tell me, so I don't waste precious energy communicating this way."*

He took his time folding the newspaper and setting it on

the seat next to him. He wasn't eager for another go around with Geneva, but he did need to let her know the course of action he'd decided on. He stood and ambled toward her, stopping when he was a foot away.

"We'll go to Bell Rock first. It's an energy vortex, close to the jewelry store Julia contacted. You know how Julia likes to visit vortexes to strengthen her talent, since they magnify our power. It's a good possibility she spent some time at this one. We'll go at midnight when no one else is around to see if you can pick up a trace of her energy."

"I can't go there."

Rolf barely controlled a shudder at the image flooding her mind. An intruder lay on the floor of her childhood home in a pool of his own blood. Geneva's thought. Her memory. Her gut-wrenching horror. Her power had gotten so out of control, she hadn't been able to stop from killing the intruder. But not before her mother had been murdered.

Rolf shoved his hands in his pockets. "I'll go alone."

Static flickered between them. "Don't be a fool. You'll never find Julia on your own."

"I'll find her." Power surged in the atmosphere. He breathed in—a silent peace offering. Geneva was right. He did need her and her talent. But not to track Julia as she believed. His own talent could handle the job easily enough. No, he preferred to use her tracking ability because drawing on his own was too risky. The more he used his gift, the more unstable he became.

Overhead, a speaker crackled, and the airline attendant announced their charter. Rolf turned and gestured toward the airplane. "C'mon."

She grabbed his arm and stepped in front of him, her luggage blocking his path. "Rolf."

A tingling sensation ran across his spine, and heat

flooded his senses. The hair on the back of his neck rose. He looked over her shoulder—anything to dampen her churning emotions, anything to maintain his self-control, anything to calm the impatient beast.

"You do understand when I go to this vortex there's a good chance I won't be able to manipulate the energy I generate, and I'll blast you into outer space?"

He stepped backward. He'd spent too many years keeping his distance to screw up now.

Her eyes stabbed into him. "Vortexes mess with people like us. Julia said their energy makes her dreams more vivid. Who knows what effect it'll have on me? Despite what you think, I don't want to kill you or anyone else who might be in the vicinity."

He kept his eyes on hers. "I'm hard to kill. Besides, you won't."

Geneva wrinkled her nose, moving a small sunburst of freckles with it. "How could you know that?"

"Simple logic." He took a breath. She smelled like the sheets his grandmother Nonna hung out to dry in the summer when he was a child. All sunshiny, fresh, and pure. "If you were going to kill me, you would have done it already."

Waves of frustration, anger, and something more—something closer to sadness—jumped from her mind to his. A vision of himself, dressed in black and seated on his motorcycle in front of The Last Chance bar, appeared in her thoughts, then vanished. He remembered the moment well. She'd been eighteen and stubborn as hell. She'd asked him for a ride on his motorcycle. He'd refused.

Rolf clenched his jaw and shoved his hands back in his pockets. That was the night a drunken asshole attacked her, and he'd been forced to intervene. He'd nearly killed the man. The event had driven him to the edge of his control. At least that was his excuse for kissing her. Eventually, he'd come to his senses. Told her to go home and play with her Barbie dolls.

She curled her lip. "I don't *need* you to go to the vortex with me. I'll pick up the trace and let you know where it leads."

His heartbeat thumped out an uneven rhythm. He squelched the knot in his chest at the thought of her tracing Julia on her own and encountering danger. "No way you're going to a vortex alone. End of story." His voice sounded clipped and cold, even to him. He stepped around her and moved toward the line of passengers.

Something shifted in the atmosphere, and the door in her mind slammed shut, blocking him from her thoughts. Blocking the enemy.

He rubbed his aching forehead. Although he knew Geneva was highly trained, he couldn't jeopardize her safety. He didn't care how bossy he sounded. He continued moving toward the boarding passengers, not waiting to see if she followed.

As if she sensed his churning thoughts, she marched by him, swinging her carry-on bag in front of her like a weapon. Twin spots of red covered her cheeks. The familiar rush of her vibrations surrounded him.

The attendant asked for their tickets. They entered the small aircraft with a dozen other passengers taking the same charter, and Geneva took the seat closest to the window, leaving him the aisle. He settled his large frame in the small space and did his best to seal his emotions from her ever-prying psychic antennae. He checked the time on his cell phone, then raised his gaze to hers. A thunderstorm gathered in her eyes, but he didn't look away. "I take it you're coming with me."

She glared at him. "I'm not doing this for you, I'm doing it for Julia. I won't be responsible if you get hurt."

Rolf couldn't stop a laugh that came out sounding harsh. "Look on the bright side. If you kill me, you won't have to partner with me anymore, will you?"

4

TEMPTATION

Geneva must have dozed off on the small aircraft because the next thing she knew, a hand shook her awake.

Rolf.

His touch lasted only a fleeting moment, but the solid strength in his palm sent an annoying tingle of awareness through her body. If only he didn't resemble a Greek god. She tried not to look at his six feet four frame and the hard muscles that bulged in his arms, a result of his rigorous daily workout regimen.

"We're landing."

She glanced his way, her gaze gliding over his thick, dark hair, impenetrable as the expression in his icy blue eyes and hard jawline. Their gazes caught and held, and an ache formed in her chest. A shiver chased down her spine. The man broadcasted danger whenever she looked at him. She'd be a fool to ignore the message.

The pilot came over the loudspeaker, breaking the connection between them. In minutes, the wheels of the plane touched the runway. She turned on her cell phone to check the time—7:42 p.m. in Phoenix.

Neither spoke as they collected their luggage and rental car. She grabbed the keys before Rolf did, but he held out his hand. "I'll drive."

She stiffened. "I've got this."

"You need to track Julia, and you can't drive a car with your eyes closed."

Although she hated to admit it, he was right. She was eager to trace Julia, but she'd need to concentrate on the energy in the atmosphere, and that worked better with her eyes closed.

"Fine," she bit off, handing him the key.

"We've got at least a two-hour drive to Sedona. See if you can find her." He didn't wait for a response, opening the driver's side door and climbing behind the wheel.

She might have balked at his authoritative tone, but the green in Rolf's aura shifted, exposing spots of red. He feared for Julia as much as she did, although he tried to disguise it. She got into the car and squinted, watching the odd combination of colors surrounding him. What else did he hide behind his impassive exterior?

She rested her head against the seat back. Rolf started the car, and the engine surged to life. He navigated out of the airport and onto the main highway with all the finesse of a professional race car driver.

Geneva closed her eyes and focused her mind on the shifting energy in the atmosphere. Colors ebbed and flowed, bombarding her senses. She latched onto a shade of violet that most closely matched Julia's aura and followed the strand until it disappeared in a sea of color.

The hills surrounding them seemed to laugh at her

futile efforts, magnifying the energy and causing a rush of color to speed toward her. She slowed her breathing to defuse the power. To bring order to chaos. When she was finally able to open her eyes to glance at Rolf, they were no longer moving.

He had pulled the car onto the side of the road and shut off the engine, his large hands hugging the wheel. The orange-red sun slipped toward the Arizona skyline. His eyes glinted, glowing coals shining in their depths. The energy she'd manipulated must have stirred his psychic senses.

"Get anything?"

"No, too much interference. How long was I out?"

"Too long." He started the car, and they moved back onto the highway.

Was he upset with her? If he was, he didn't show it, but she caught another flash of red, reflecting his worry.

"You'll get used to the new energy levels. Give it time."

Geneva sniffed, tilting her head to look out the window. Anything to avoid looking at Rolf and the turquoise color exploding within the red of his aura. *Sincerity*. Flattering, but she'd never let him know it. "I'll try again in a bit. Maybe I'll do better later."

They spent the next hour in silence until they pulled into the hotel's crowded parking lot. The moon rose, casting a glimmer of light on his dark features. She opened the car door and headed to the trunk to retrieve her luggage. As quick as she was, somehow he was there before her, setting her bags on the pavement, the muscles in his long arms flexing.

She reached for her suitcase, and their fingers brushed. Heat rippled along her frazzled nerve endings, and she pulled her hands back with a gasp. Did he feel it, too, the warmth?

Penetrating blue eyes caught and trapped hers in their icy depths. Despite everything between them and the distance in his gaze, she still found him attractive. She hated that—hated the knowledge he could invoke such powerful feelings in her with an accidental touch and a single glance. Hated the way he made her feel, all feminine, fragile, and fearful.

A rainbow of color flickered along his broad form and disappeared in a rush of energy, which seemed to take forever to dissipate. She should do something, say something to break the silence between them. But she couldn't think of a single word. All she could do was stand there, breathing in the fresh, woodsy scent of his cologne, imagining the taste of his lips on hers and remembering the first and only time they'd ever kissed.

Geneva gripped the suitcase so she wouldn't do something stupid—so she wouldn't stomp her feet and howl and then fling herself against his hard chest and ravage those firm lips. Hadn't he made it clear more times than she could count that he disliked her? She blinked, breaking the spell he cast, and tugged on her suitcase, practically jogging across the pavement in her haste to get away from him.

Despite her strong lead, by the time she entered the lobby doors, Rolf was only a few paces behind her. She dragged her luggage to the front desk. The hotel clerk greeted them with a generous smile that soon turned into a frown and then an apology.

"I'm sorry. Our computers have been down all day, and I'm only finding a reservation for one room in our system. I have a single room reserved with two double beds."

"There must be some mistake. We have a reservation for two rooms," Rolf said.

"I'm sorry, sir." The clerk shook her head. A sincere

turquoise color oozed from her chest. "The national gem convention's in Phoenix, and we're booked solid. There's only the one room available. Do you want it?"

"No." He tightened his lips. "We'll find somewhere else."

"I'm afraid you won't find anything." The turquoise color morphed into a dull red, indicating the woman's increasing anxiety. "This is the largest gem convention in the nation. Thousands of collectors flood Phoenix. Every hotel in Sedona and other nearby cities is booked. You two are lucky to have the room you do. Are you sure you want to give it up?"

Rolf passed a hand through his hair. "Yes."

"No." Geneva bit the words out between clenched teeth. Something about Rolf's willingness to give up the room so he wouldn't have to be near her ate at her self-control. Did he have to be so repulsed by her? Besides, he could speak for himself—she needed sleep.

She flashed the clerk her brightest smile. "I'll take it."

"Excellent."

The clerk held out a packet with two key cards for room 304. Geneva grabbed the cards and headed toward the elevator.

Rolf caught up to her. "What the hell are you doing?"

"We need to find Julia. I'm not spending the evening searching for a hotel room."

"We can't share a room."

"Why not? There are two beds. You'll be safe."

"It's not my safety I'm worried about."

"We have no choice unless you want to sleep in the car. I don't. Tracking burns energy. I need to be well-rested for any hope of success."

She jabbed the up arrow and waited for the doors to open.

"Fine. I'll sleep in the car." He turned to go.

She rolled her eyes. "Suit yourself, hotshot. But you're not going to get a good night's sleep in that small car." Why did she goad him? He was right—they shouldn't share a room. At the rate they were going, she might murder the stubborn jackass while he slept.

The elevator dinged, the doors opened, and she stepped inside.

"You make a good point." Rolf followed her, tripping her heartbeat into fast mode.

They faced the doors, watching them close. Neither spoke. Colors bounced off the confined space as their energies merged and multiplied. She tightened her hand around her suitcase and slowed her breathing.

They stopped on the second floor. The doors opened and a young woman entered, ogling Rolf and ignoring Geneva. He nodded and his lips tilted up in a come-play-with-me smile. Anger burned in her veins.

"Smile any wider, Romeo, and it'll reach your ears."

Rolf's attention shifted toward Geneva, and he raised an eyebrow. *"She was dumped by her boyfriend last week."*

Geneva looked from Rolf to the woman. Sure enough, the woman's aura was tinged with mauve, the color of sorrow. How embarrassing to miss the sign—Rolf must think her jealous. She wasn't, of course.

The elevator stopped on the third floor. They stepped off, dragging their suitcases behind them. The woman stayed on the elevator but gave Rolf another sweet smile. The door shut behind them, and they followed the signs to room 304.

Their room wasn't big, but it did contain the promised beds, a large window overlooking the parking lot, a desk, and a small couch. Rolf checked his cell phone. "We have some time to kill. I'm going to grab a drink in the bar."

He turned to leave as if he couldn't get away fast enough. Geneva glared at his backside. "Don't you think you ought to avoid liquor if we're going to a vortex tonight?"

God, she sounded like a nagging wife. Rolf had his hand on the doorknob, and Geneva expected he'd leave without answering. But he didn't. He turned to look at her. His chiseled features glowed in the lamplight, giving him a maniacal look.

She couldn't catch her breath as silence stretched between them, broken only by the sound of her beating heart. What was he thinking? Was he amused by her comment? Or had she angered him? She couldn't help but feel a sharp ache in her chest at the thought of adding fuel to his already bad opinion of her. Outside, an ambulance blared its noisy siren, startling her and forcing her to take a step toward him.

"Join me."

She narrowed her gaze. Was this some kind of game? "I need to freshen up. I'll meet you in the lobby in a bit."

He scanned her body. "You look fine to me."

Had Rolf given her a compliment? Did he actually want to grab a drink with her? She opened her mouth to respond, but he had already stepped into the hall.

"Meet me in the lobby at eleven. Don't be late."

The door banged shut. Geneva stared unmoving for a few minutes after he left, studying the trace of purple color that followed his retreating form. The color of lust. Her imagination. Had to be.

She took a breath and forced her limbs to move toward her suitcase. She'd not be placed off-balance by Rolf pretending to want her company. He didn't like her, had not wanted to share a hotel room. Used every chance he could to remind her how much she repelled him.

So, what did the purple color mean?

5

BELL ROCK

M*idnight*

"AFTER YOU." Rolf gestured to the open door of their rented Toyota and tried not to look at Geneva. Earlier tonight, he'd invited her to have a drink with him in the hotel bar. What the hell had he been thinking? Thank God she'd had the good sense to refuse his invitation.

He shoved his hands into his pockets, which seemed to be the safest place for them. She'd pulled her golden hair into a knot on the back of her head, and little wisps hung on either side of her face. He supposed she thought the bun would keep her hair out of the way, but instead, it made her look angelic. He shifted his feet. "Hurry."

"Maybe I should try tracking Julia from here first."

He hardened his voice. They didn't have time to waste deliberating. "It's a twenty minute drive. You can track her along the way. C'mon." They should arrive at the vortex well before midnight and start the trace as soon as possible.

Geneva flashed him a worried look.

He ground his teeth. "Get—in—the—car."

"Okay, okay, I'm trying to think this through. I'm anxious to find Julia, too." She did as he asked, thank God.

Power heaved inside him, her anxiety over visiting the vortex intensifying the toxic energy. "Buckle up." He swallowed hard and hurried to the driver's side, where he got behind the wheel and revved the engine. He waited until her seatbelt clicked and then stepped on the gas, the vehicle roaring into motion.

Her hands flew to the sides of her seat. "Slow down. We can't help Julia if we're dead."

"What are you picking up?"

"Your anxiety. It's overpowering. Can you dial it back a little?"

He let off the gas and drew in a breath, releasing it slowly through his nose until his heartbeat settled.

"That's better." She sniffed, resting her head against the seat and closing her eyes. "I'm tracing Julia now. If I don't open my eyes in ten minutes, wake me up."

He narrowed his eyes and frowned, but she'd already closed her own, so his look was wasted. What the hell did she mean, wake her up? Didn't she wake up on her own? His heartbeat jig-jogged around in a mad beat. He glanced at the clock on the radio and began counting.

Sixty seconds. What did she see? His talent lurched forward inside him, and he gritted his teeth. He focused on the road ahead to keep his power contained.

Eight miles later, he stopped at a red light, eyeing the clock again. She'd been under seven minutes now. He tapped his fingers on the wheel, glancing at her still form while he waited for the light to change. *Eight minutes.* Shouldn't she be waking up? Did she even breathe? The light changed, and he moved forward. *Nine minutes.*

"Enough." He poked her side. "Geneva, wake up."

Her body lay still as a corpse. Adrenaline drove a spike through his heart. He stomped on the brakes and veered off the road, then jammed the vehicle in park. He leaned across the seats and shook her shoulder, hard.

She didn't stir.

"Geneva, wake up. Now." No reaction. His heart did a wild dance, and power broke loose from its chain, rising toward the surface of his mind.

He unsnapped his seatbelt, gripped her shoulders, and focused on her mind, searching for a hole in her defenses. He found one and blasted through it.

A thousand twinkling lights sparkled and stunned his senses. They rotated through her mind in quick succession: deep oranges, vibrant reds, soft yellows. Her heartbeat drummed in time with the steady glow of the lights. She gasped for oxygen.

"Let go." He took control of her mind, forcing air into her starved lungs.

She gasped, the sound scraping his insides raw. A sharp ache pounded his temple. Inside her mind, the lights dimmed. Her power shifted, some part of her brain recognizing the intrusion as she came to consciousness. The dark colors took on shades of gray.

"Rolf?"

His heart leaped in his chest. *"It's about time. What the hell happened to you?"* He clutched her shoulders and pulled her toward him. "My God."

Geneva jerked in his arms, probably stunned he held

her. But he couldn't let go. Not yet. Not until he knew she was safe.

She cleared her throat. "There were so many colors." Her voice sounded weak...shell-shocked. "I couldn't make them stop. They kept coming at me, over and over. I tried to dilute them, but...I got lost. I couldn't figure out how to resurface."

Fear thickened his throat. He pulled her closer. He clenched his jaw and tried to keep his worry and anger inside, but they wouldn't be contained. "Don't you *ever* do that to me again."

"Mmmfh." Geneva twisted in his arms. "Let me go." She managed to lift her head from where he'd smashed it into his shoulder. "What's the matter with you? Why are you shouting?"

Rolf loosened his grip but did not let go. Energy surged and writhed toward her light, a mad bid for freedom. Heat exploded through his body, and he tilted her chin until their eyes met. "You could have died."

Geneva blinked at him, her haunted eyes twisting his stomach inside out. Her voice, when it came, sounded like she'd run a hundred miles. "I'm not dead. Why are you so upset?"

A hard rap sounded on the window next to him, breaking their connection. He hid his irritation and turned toward the noise to catch the gaze of a young policeman, who stared through the window, wielding a narrow flashlight. The beam swept their faces and the interior of the car.

Rolf rolled down the window.

Hands all over her.

He squinted at the officer. He believed he'd interrupted a lover's spat or a make-out session.

Geneva sat straighter in her seat and smoothed her hair.

She must have caught the essence of the officer's thoughts from his aura.

"Everything okay in there, ma'am?"

"Yes." Geneva nodded, her voice calm. "I felt a little faint. I'm fine now."

"Good." The officer jerked his head toward Rolf. "Sir, I'll need to see your driver's license."

Rolf dug in his pocket, pulled out his wallet, and handed the officer his license.

The officer studied it for a second before returning it to him. "Where're you headed?"

"My girlfriend and I were on our way to see Bell Rock at midnight. She's always wanted to see it when the moon's full." He gestured at the sky.

"Well, you should all be careful here at night. Sedona is a pretty safe town, but it's wise to keep a close lookout after dark. We've had a rash of recent robberies in the area."

"We will, Officer." Rolf checked the time on the dash. They needed to get a move on. He used the pause to nudge the officer's mind. The energy level was so high near the vortex it didn't take much to enforce the command. Geneva squirmed in her seat next to him.

Without another word, the officer touched his hat, turned, and made his way to his vehicle. Rolf waited for the man to pull away from the curb and head in the opposite direction from Bell Rock.

He didn't look at Geneva. If he did, he might find himself pulling her back into his arms. My God, he'd almost lost her tonight. "Are you okay?"

"Yes."

His hands clutched the wheel, although they weren't moving. He focused on a point in the distance. "Has this happened before? Your getting disoriented in the colors?"

She shrugged like it didn't matter. Like her safety wasn't important. "Once or twice. It's worse because of the vortex, I'm guessing. Don't worry. I'll be more careful next time."

A hot coal of fear burned a hole in his belly. A muscle ticked in his jaw. He sucked in a fierce breath. His voice rumbled. "There won't be a next time. It's too dangerous. You should have told me you were having issues tracking."

Geneva shot him a frustrated look. "You were the one who wanted me to go to a vortex, remember? I warned you what could happen."

He turned his head and fastened his eyes on hers. "No, you warned me you might blow me to smithereens. You said nothing about getting lost in the energy streams." Sweat beaded on his brow, and he swiped a hand across it. "You could have been killed. You should have stayed behind and let me handle this."

Her lips formed a thin line. "And abandon my best friend? Not happening."

"Then you can't do that again." Rolf's voice shook before he could control it. Energy flooded his fingertips, causing him to tighten his death-grip on the wheel. He had just enough control to keep it from blasting the dash into nothingness.

"Rolf, I need to trace Julia if we have any hope of finding her. That was the whole point of me coming to the vortex. Her energy is likely to be here."

She touched his thigh as if she understood on a psychic level her touch had the power to satisfy the darkness. Dark to light. Light to dark. Her hand was only there for a second, but blood rushed to the spot, and his energy settled.

"Rolf?"

He frowned at his white knuckles on the wheel. Geneva was safe. Alive. He stole a breath and then another, slowing his heartbeat into a normal rhythm. Power stilled in his gut. He turned toward her, keeping his face devoid of emotion. "You're right. We don't have much time. Hang on."

He shifted the car into drive and moved back on the highway, punching the gas pedal. The seatbelt tightened around his neck like a noose. They were heading to Bell Rock, and he'd managed to keep his secret safe for another day. Score one for Jorgensen. He almost groaned in relief.

Bell Rock was so named for the bell-shaped stone, rising in the distance, a dark giant in the night. During the day, the rock would be the orangish-red color Sedona was known for, but in the dark, the vortex looked like the rest of the landscape.

Five minutes later, they arrived at the base of the hill, and he pulled into the empty parking lot and shut off the engine. The hairs at the back of his neck stood at attention. They had reached the vortex. Did he really want Geneva risking her life even for his sister? Could he handle it if something happened to her? He curled his hands around the steering wheel.

Geneva unlocked her seatbelt, the noise breaking the silence between them.

He didn't look at her. He couldn't risk it.

"Are you ready?" She touched his arm, forcing him to turn and acknowledge her.

He released his hands from the wheel and dropped them to his seat. The car was dark—too dark to make out her expression.

"Rolf, I'm sorry if I scared you."

Something loosened in his chest. He swallowed. "You could have died back there."

She shook her head and lowered her voice. "I wasn't prepared for all the colors. I'm fine now."

He leaned toward her, his arm brushing her chest. Her sweet breath warmed his face. A sudden chill racked his body, and unable to stop himself, he breathed her in. Her power infiltrated his lungs. His gaze registered the wariness in hers before she looked away.

"This is the closest we can get by car. We'll need to walk from here," she said.

He rubbed a hand over his forehead, forcing himself to consider their options. They needed to trace Julia tonight. But after witnessing Geneva's near-death experience, could he allow her to trace his sister's energy from a vortex, knowing she might never wake up? Unless... "I have a condition."

"Condition?" She cocked her head and frowned. "I don't do conditions."

He firmed his lips and prepared himself for battle. "If you want to trace Julia, I'll need to be in your mind."

Her eyes latched on to his. "No."

"It's the only way I'll let you risk your life."

"Rolf, if something happens to me, you'd be trapped."

"I won't be trapped. I'll get you out."

"I can't let you. I can't..."

He held up a hand. "This is non-negotiable. I won't let you trace her otherwise." He held her gaze, allowing her into his mind, so she could understand the extent of his stubbornness.

She shook her head and rolled her eyes. "Fine. But only because it's Julia we're talking about. I won't waste precious time arguing."

He nodded, the pressure around his heart easing. "All right, then. Let's get started."

The second the words left his tongue, power swelled in

the atmosphere. One by one, Geneva released the safeguards in her mind.

He latched on to her energy, pushing past her brain's natural defenses to slip into her thoughts. Darkness surged through his veins at the intimacy, urging him to stake a claim in her mind. To link them together in the way of their kind. The air around them shimmered in silent expectation.

Geneva grabbed the door handle and pushed, almost falling out in her haste to exit the vehicle.

He sat there a moment, eyes closed. He should be relieved she'd had the good sense to get away from him. He should be grateful he hadn't created a portal in her mind where they could share thoughts freely. A portal was for lovers, and they were not that. Could never be that.

He got out of the car and locked the door, stretching his legs and moving toward the vortex, which seemed to understand his dilemma. With his mind locked with Geneva's, he knew the instant she began to search for a trace of Julia's energy.

The vortex beckoned with fingers of blue light. The tendrils wrapped around him, easing the tension in his body. Comforting, not threatening, reminding him of Nonna's hugs.

A movement caught the corner of his eye. Geneva walked past. He lengthened his stride until he reached her, pointing toward the vortex. Although he couldn't see it well, the giant red rock, the heart of the vortex, couldn't be far. They were maybe ten yards away from the base now. *"Any trace of Julia?"*

She shifted to face the direction of the vortex and tilted her head to the side. *"No. Strange..."*

"What is it?"

"A *warm feeling. It seems to be coming from the vortex. Can you sense it in my mind?*"

He stilled. "*Yeah. It's powerful. Let's get closer.*" Rolf touched her arm. "*Follow me.*"

He shined his flashlight toward the trail to the side of where they were standing. "*Stay close and don't move off the path. I don't want you getting stung by a scorpion. Or worse.*"

He didn't spell out what could be worse, but sent her a glimpse of rattlesnakes, javelinas, and desert cactus.

They hiked a few more yards. Geneva paused mid-stride, forcing Rolf to stop, too. She sniffed the air and squinted, her slim form tense as if the vortex represented some unknown danger.

He stepped in front of her. "*What is it?*"

"*Dream waves.*"

He flashed the light on the landscape in front of them. Nothing moved—no hint of life. "*Impossible. No human being can produce a vast quantity of dream energy in the middle of a desert.*"

A cold wind blew through the hillside, chilling his insides. A rock came loose and tumbled in front of them. His neck tingled. Tentacles of dream energy reached for him, brushing his mind, seeking entrance.

Geneva gasped. "*Don't believe anything you see next.*"

The strange energy sucked them deep into a nightmare.

6

ROLF

Next to Rolf, the landscape changed, going from rocky and expansive to a dark and narrow city street. Geneva's body morphed, expanding and exploding outward into tiny beads of light. In her place stood streetlights and a series of storefronts. Someone called his name. A familiar shape stepped from the shadows of one of the buildings.

Cynthia Torra? The blonde bombshell news reporter he'd escorted to a party or two over the course of the year he'd been hired to protect her slipped by him. Cynthia was the daughter of a prominent US senator. She showcased long legs, high heels, and a form-fitting dress on a body that could grace the front cover of *Sports Illustrated*. She flipped her hair to the side and gave him a come-hither look from wide green eyes.

"I thought you'd never get here." Her silky voice slid over him, seducing him where he stood under the streetlight.

Before he could react, she grabbed his hand, pulling him closer, her voice a sexy whisper. "You can't imagine the things I want to do to you." Her warm breath touched his cheek, and her lips were upon his, drowning out a response. Cynthia wrapped her body around him like an exotic dancer around a pole.

This couldn't be real. He'd only ever exchanged a kiss with Cynthia, and that was purposeful and in front of witnesses. Afterward, he'd made it clear to her he wasn't looking for a relationship. No, the nightmare wasn't his. It must be Geneva's. She had warned him not to believe whatever they saw before she disappeared.

Geneva! Where was she? Panic shook his slumbering talent. Dark tentacles came to life inside him, twisting and churning toward the surface. He needed to find her. He pulled away from Cynthia, but she held him in a death grip. A hum of energy vibrated on the psychic plane. *What the hell?* The vibrations were all too real.

Rolf gave a mighty heave—enough to break the hold Cynthia had on him. He peered into the darkness. Geneva must be somewhere. He cupped his hands around his mouth so his voice would carry. "Get a hold of yourself. This isn't real."

Power collected and was gathered by a single source. An electrical charge raced along the back of his neck. Time seemed to stop—a familiar silence descended. A silence fraught with danger. He aimed his voice toward the darkest section of the street.

"Control your energy, Geneva. This is a dream, remember. Don't believe what you're seeing. Your subconscious is magnifying your emotions. Cynthia is not real. Fight this."

"Babe, why are you saying these things?" Cynthia caught his arm. "I know how you like it." She blew in his ear. "We're meant for one another. You know it." She faced the darkness, pointing. "She knows it, too."

"No." Rolf tore himself from Cynthia's clinging fingers.

He strode forward until he caught a glimpse of Geneva, her smooth face pale and eerie in the moonlight. Power shimmered in the air, rattling windows next to him and shaking debris from who knows where. "Fight, Geneva."

She trembled and stared at him with helpless eyes. She raised her hands. Light streamed in and around her. The light meant she had trouble controlling her emotions. Lack of emotional control loosened her power—he'd not escape the dream unharmed. His dark gift beckoned, taunting him to erase Cynthia from existence. He clenched his jaw and sucked in a furious breath, trapping the roiling energy deep inside. He would not release the dark power. Not with Geneva in the vicinity. Not when she could be hurt. He braced himself. *What will it feel like to die?*

A crack filled the air, splitting the night sky into two equal and brilliant halves. Or maybe that was his head?

Pain followed—a crushing, aching, endless sort of pain. The kind of pain that made grown men cry. He slipped into unconsciousness, the sound of his own screams filling the darkness.

7

CRYSTAL

"Rolf, wake up!"

Geneva clung to Rolf's body, her arms and hands stretched across his chest and gripping his shoulders, preventing him from rolling off the side of the hill and suffering further injury. His chest rose and fell. She steadied herself and laid two fingers across his neck. He still breathed. He still had a pulse. She had not killed him, despite the way his body twisted and writhed before he fell. And his screams.

Dear God. She suppressed a mighty sob. His screams had pierced the dark. A stab of guilt attacked her consciousness. She'd nearly murdered him. She'd managed to deflect the worst of the dream energy but not before sending a blast Rolf's way. Where had the dream waves come from? She'd nearly unleashed her full power. Thank God she'd kept some control.

"Rolf, please." If he heard her plea, he didn't respond. His body lay still and silent.

She scrambled in the dark for the flashlight. Rolf must have dropped it when she struck him. Thankfully, it hadn't rolled far away. She flicked the switch, sweeping the flashlight beam around his body before settling on his face. Rolf's eyes were closed, and a jagged red gash ran across his forehead. Blood matted his hair and more smeared the rock his head rested against. He'd struck the boulder when he fell.

Geneva smoothed his hair and felt the large lump on the back of his skull. He let out a groan, the sound loud and reassuring in the quiet night. She released her breath in a whoosh. "Are you okay?"

Rolf opened his eyes and blinked. Pain radiated in their icy depths. "God, that hurt," he moaned, raising his hands to his head and covering his eyes.

"Thank God you're conscious. I'm sorry. I've never had to funnel dream energy so close to a vortex."

Rolf remained motionless, as if he held his head together. Geneva studied the dull, bright pink of his aura. "I'd better get you to a government hospital."

He moved his hands, and his irises glittered a metallic blue-gray. "No hospital."

"Let me help you."

She grasped his hand, and Rolf winced. Geneva closed her eyes and set herself to deaden the effect of the dream energy.

Oranges flittered across the canvas of her mind. Healing energy. *Breathe in.* Orange energy appeared in the center of her closed eyelids. *Breathe out.* The energy pulsed and glowed. *Breathe in.* More orange energy joined the image in her mind, which now had a heartbeat. *Breathe out.* Geneva transferred the beating heart from her mind to his. While she couldn't heal him, the transfer of energy would act as a painkiller and ease his recovery.

Rolf's fingers brushed her cheek. She blinked. His touch

conveyed his thanks and something more. Something unspoken. "Honey, you sure know how to take a man to the depths of hell and bring him to the gates of heaven."

Geneva pushed his hand from her face. "You're delirious."

Rolf groaned. "You won't get an argument from me there." He sat up slowly and leaned toward her ear, his breath cool on her hot cheeks. "Thank you."

The sound of his rough voice sent a tremble through her body. A solid wall of muscle surrounded her, seeming to absorb all the oxygen in the air. "You're thanking me for almost getting you killed?"

He placed his fingers under her chin and raised her face toward his. "I told you I'm hard to kill."

His eyes locked with hers, probing, intense. Geneva held her breath. Rolf's lips were so near hers, if she leaned a few inches closer and to the right, they'd meet. Like she'd longed for once upon a time. A tingling formed in her belly then traveled outward until her whole body lit up. What was the matter with her? It must be the high energy and stress of the evening. This wasn't high school.

She removed his fingers and turned her head toward the rocky landscape, away from Rolf and the unholy temptation he represented.

An odd shade of deep purple blasted from the hill now only about ten yards away, catching her attention. They weren't alone. She stood, opening her mind to Rolf, her psychic senses on full alert. *"Someone's out there."*

He rose carefully and faced the hill. Although she knew the movement was painful, he didn't make a sound. And despite his weakness and the extra drain on their energy to share thoughts, he spoke in her mind to avoid being overheard and detected. *"Who is it?"*

"I'm not sure. Probably whoever sent the dream waves." Geneva shared a mental view of the purple light and its location and passed him the flashlight.

Rolf pointed the beam toward the hill. "I don't see anyone. But I don't like this. Let's get a little closer and introduce ourselves." He took a step forward.

"Uh, Rolf, I don't think that's a good idea."

"Why?"

"I'm not sure it's human."

Rolf paused. "An animal?"

"I don't think so."

"What?"

"I don't know. The color—it's like nothing I've seen before— at least not around a person. It's strong and deadly."

"Does it want to harm us?"

Geneva closed her eyes. Deep violet flooded her senses, strong and steady. She opened them. "I don't think so, but it's difficult to tell. Whatever is generating the color contains an endless amount of energy. There's no break in the pattern and intensity of the waves."

Rolf focused on the hills, motioning behind him. "Stay here. I'll check it out. If you see or sense a struggle, get the hell out of here and call Peter." He dug in his jacket pocket for the car key.

She shook her head. "Rolf, you're weak, you've lost a lot of blood, and you've got a lump the size of a fist on the back of your head. No way are you going in there alone in your condition."

He eyed her for a long moment, his gaze intense. "Are you sure you're up for it after what happened in the car?"

She placed her hands on her hips. "Does it matter? If we're facing someone with talent, you're going to need my help."

His lips thinned, but he must have seen the logic in her argument because he pointed the flashlight beam ahead of them and turned toward the hill, his voice tight and controlled. *All right. Let's go."*

Geneva moved to catch up with his long strides. The eerie purple light shining from the vortex didn't move. They drew closer. Some of the light moved toward them in a direct line, turning the golden flashlight beam purple. They topped the short rise in the hill and stopped in tacit agreement.

Geneva watched the purple light. Friend or foe? The hue and pattern of color did not alter. If it were foe, it would already be wreaking havoc on her energy field. Instead, the waves continued moving forward at an even pace.

Rolf turned to her, his gaze steady. *"What do you sense?"*

"The energy's even. There are no spikes in the color. We should be okay to approach."

They moved forward in tandem. The energy cloud grew larger and heavier, until it surrounded them. *"There."* Geneva motioned.

Rolf pointed the flashlight beam to a small object on the ground. He bent and retrieved it while Geneva peered over his shoulder. "What is it?"

"Some kind of crystal." He turned it over in his hands, examining it from all sides. "Doesn't look like anything special."

"Let me see."

"Be careful." He handed it to her along with the flashlight.

Geneva grasped the stone in her palm, feeling the smoothness of its sides with her fingers. The energy stream died, and the color winked out. She continued to run her fingers down the sides of the crystal to see if she could reactivate the energy field. Nothing.

"Well?" Rolf's aura had lost the bright pink of illness and

had returned closer to its customary green, indicating he was feeling a bit better. He'd probably have one nasty headache in the morning, though, and a scar where his head had struck the rock.

"Whatever power it contained is gone. It's an ordinary stone." She pocketed the crystal as evidence. She would send it to Peter to have it analyzed, but she suspected the lab would verify it contained a normal amount of energy. "How did it get there?"

"A crystal with that kind of energy doesn't just appear at a vortex on its own. Someone put it there. I wonder..." Rolf stilled.

"What?"

"Whoever put it there knew it would be activated the moment a person with talent used their power. And they could have placed it there at any time, knowing that we'd probably show up eventually and activate it."

"You think the crystal was intended for me?"

Rolf nodded. "Maybe. They may have wanted you to lose control and kill me. Probably figured you would be so involved handling the dream energy and calling an ambulance, you wouldn't have time to go searching the vortex afterward. They'd have time to reclaim the crystal before we discovered it. Clearly, someone who doesn't know you well."

She met his gaze. "Rolf, because I managed to deflect the dream energy this time doesn't mean you'll be so lucky next time. Whoever did this could have been successful in making me lose control. I could have killed you." A chill rushed through her body.

"You didn't." He took the flashlight from her hands and shined enough light between them to see her face. "You okay?"

"Yes, I'm fine."

"That was some dream sequence with Cynthia. I wonder —" Rolf's eyes pinned hers in the steady glow of the flashlight beam.

Heat rushed to her cheeks. "What?"

He brushed the hair from her eyes, the rare touch doing strange things to her insides. Turquoise light spilled from his broad frame. "You got it wrong in your nightmare. I never slept with Cynthia Torra."

She tightened her lips and tore her gaze from his to look over his shoulder. But with his mind firmly entrenched in hers, there was nowhere to hide. Still, she tried for nonchalance. "Why would I care who you slept with?" She shrugged, but she couldn't deny that his words sent a tremble through her system. Rolf didn't lie. The turquoise color indicated he spoke the truth.

Rolf chuckled, the sound loud in the silence between them.

She glared at him. "The dream exaggerated my true feelings." She kept her eyes on his. "I don't give a shit about your relationship with that woman."

His gaze remained steady, unshakable. The quirk of his brows labeled her a liar. The nightmare had revealed far too much of her inner emotions, and he was still in her mind. He knew her thoughts.

"Whatever you say. I'm just glad we got it straightened out."

"Why?" she whispered, her heart beating like someone played kettle drums inside her. Why did he care if she thought he had a fling with Cynthia Torra or not? He hated her, didn't he?

His lips pursed, then tilted, widening into a slow smile that transformed his harsh features into something beautiful. "If I have to be immersed in any more of your surprise nightmares, at least they should be accurate."

The smile was so unexpected, it robbed Geneva of breath. Rolf was teasing her. Excitement bubbled in the pit of her stomach, and nervous laughter tore through her lips. Anger, she could take. Contempt, she was used to. But she had no idea how to deal with his humor.

She tore her gaze from his, disrupting whatever was happening between them. Must be the bump on his head. Rolf hadn't shared a joke with her since they were small children, running through the neighborhood in a game of tag. "The dream shouldn't have been surprising given your reputation."

Rolf pointed the flashlight toward the trail so she could no longer see his face. His voice tightened. "An illusion. I've spent more nights alone than you could possibly imagine."

She wanted to deny his gruff statement, but more turquoise pulsed inside his aura. More energy than normal. She stood transfixed. He allowed her to see he spoke the truth. She took a step forward and stumbled on the uneven ground. Was this some sort of sick game?

He turned and grasped her arm so she didn't fall down the rocky slope that led to their car. "Watch yourself now." His hands were strong and capable—protective, even.

Like everyone else, Geneva had heard the rumors about Rolf and Cynthia. What a cute couple, her coworkers said. Don't know what he sees in her, Julia confided. In a rare moment of disgust over the brother she adored, Julia showed Geneva a newspaper clipping of Rolf escorting Cynthia to a fancy party.

Whatever their relationship, it didn't appear platonic. But how else to explain the turquoise color she'd seen in his aura indicating he spoke the truth?

8

TRUTH

W hat the hell was he thinking? He should have let her believe the lies told about him. The lies he'd fanned to life and deliberately magnified. The lies kept her safe.

Rolf punched his pillow and tried without success to fall asleep. His head pounded, and he had a hard time finding a comfortable spot. Geneva had insisted on dressing the wound on his forehead—another form of torture.

He turned to his side and listened to her breathing in the bed next to him. She wasn't sleeping. Her panic settled in his mind as if it were his own, a strange offshoot of his talent. Even as children, the dark inside him yearned to meld with her light. Where others saw only toughness, Rolf understood the deep fears she battled. He eyed Geneva's dark shape in the other bed. He longed for inches between them instead of a nightstand with a Gideon bible. He longed to wrap her in his arms and comfort her. And that was precisely the problem. She wasn't his to comfort. She could never be his. Not if he wanted her safe. And he did. More than anything.

When they'd returned from the vortex, he'd removed himself from her mind. Now she guarded her thoughts, and out of respect for her, he wouldn't attempt to breach her defenses. Yet, he couldn't help wondering what thoughts required such a strong defense? Did she imagine the worst for Julia like he did? Did she wonder who wanted him dead?

He turned on his back. Energy simmered deep inside where he kept it sealed. His hidden talent could find his sister if he let it, but it would swallow his heart and soul with it. Turn him into a raging psychopath who would kill the ones he loved the most. And that he could never allow.

He pulled air into his lungs and rolled to his other side —the one farthest from her. It was becoming harder to control his true nature. He shouldn't use his talent. The more he used it, the greater the danger he'd lose all compassion for humanity. But the vortex had Geneva's talent off-kilter, so he might have no choice. One thing was certain, if he did draw on his power, Geneva couldn't be near him. He didn't trust himself around her.

Rolf opened his eyes and stared toward the window. Where was Julia? She'd been missing almost two whole days. Who had placed a crystal in the vortex? Who wanted him dead? Where had they gotten the crystal? Most of the CMU believed it wasn't possible to charge crystals, but he now had concrete proof they were wrong.

Their cell phones buzzed in quick succession, causing adrenaline to surge through his body, scattering his thoughts. Rolf scrambled for his on the nightstand beside his bed. From the other bed, Geneva grabbed hers. He squinted at the screen, grimacing as he read the text from Peter.

2:42 a.m. Prepare for the calvary. Geneva's brothers are on their way. Estimated arrival time, 0900 hours.

Rolf had reported what had happened at the vortex, and now Peter was sending in reinforcements. He suspected a larger plot and wasn't taking any chances.

Damn. Rolf grimaced and set the phone back on the nightstand. Like everyone else, Geneva's brothers—Nate and Daniel Erickson—believed the rumors he'd circulated. They thought he was a womanizer. They'd not be happy to find their beloved sister sharing a hotel room with him. Hell, they probably didn't like Geneva sharing a car ride with him.

He lay on his back and stared at the ceiling, trying to ignore the rustling in the other bed as Geneva repositioned herself. He pictured her as she'd looked earlier tonight on the hillside, hovering over him, her concerned gaze landing on his wounded forehead before staring into his eyes. She'd laid cool hands on his head and filled him with a white-hot heat, taking his pain away and igniting a desire so strong, he'd nearly lost control.

"Rolf?"

Her voice broke the silence, instantly rousing the darkness inside him. "What's wrong?"

"Nothing's wrong. I was only wondering...what did you mean, earlier tonight, when you said your reputation wasn't as bad as I'd imagined? Did you really mean you and Cynthia Torra... Are you saying you never slept together?"

So, that's what had occupied her thoughts. A lightness filled him. Joy. An emotion so infrequent he had a hard time identifying it. If he was any kind of man, he'd let her continue to believe the lies. But like earlier tonight, something about the vulnerability in her voice placed a stranglehold on his vocal cords, and he couldn't tell this particular lie again. "Yes, that's what I meant."

"But how is that possible? I saw the photograph in the newspaper."

He shrugged, although he knew she couldn't see it in the dark. "She kissed me, and it was caught on camera." He had allowed the kiss to happen—deliberately provoked it in front of a photographer, knowing the picture would probably appear in the newspaper the next day, where everyone would be sure to see it.

She sat up in bed. "And all the times you escorted her to events? Nothing happened between you?"

The hair on his arms rose along with the sound of her voice. To distract himself from the growing energy in the room, Rolf placed his arms behind his head and focused on the ceiling. "I was working."

She continued to gaze at him, but when he didn't respond, she sighed and lay back down. Time passed, and although he didn't read her thoughts, he could hear her mind clicking along, comparing what she had believed about him with what he had just relayed. Silence reigned, broken only by the sound of a car passing by on the street outside the window. He knew she wasn't sleeping, though. He could feel her seething emotions—sense her anger, frustration, hurt.

Her quiet voice broke the stillness, quivering with intensity. "Why do you hate me?"

His stomach retracted, his heart lurched in his chest, and the blood zipped through his veins on a mission to destroy what remained of his aching heart. There it was. The large mammal in the room with them. The biggest lie of all he'd made her believe—that he hated her. The lie she'd swallowed hook, line, and sinker and continued to believe all these years later.

"Don't pretend to be sleeping. I know you're awake."

There was no way out. No way to keep from hurting her. No way to let her believe, even for a moment, that he cared for her. That there was a fighting chance they could ever be together.

"Answer me." She sat up and turned on the light. In the soft glow, it wasn't difficult to make out the curves of her slim silhouette underneath the white T-shirt she wore. She didn't have a bra on.

He held his breath, unable to look away. His heartbeat stopped and then slammed hard in his chest.

"Rolf, don't you remember how it used to be? We were friends once. I looked up to you. You were my protector. I always knew I could turn to you when there was trouble. What happened between us? What did I ever do to earn your dislike?"

Nothing. She had done nothing.

The slight tremble in her voice was nearly his undoing. He had to fight every ounce of his will not to go to her but instead to move his body up and out of bed and begin packing his things. He had to get out of here. *Now.* Away from the temptation she represented. He couldn't trust himself to stay a minute longer. Her brothers understood it on a psychic level, even if they didn't fully understand who or what he was.

He found his suitcase, threw his toothbrush inside, zipped it.

"Where are you going?" She stood too close, smelling like fresh air and heaven.

Rolf gritted his teeth and didn't respond. He couldn't. She touched his arm, and he was done. He turned so fast, she tumbled into him. He caught her before she fell. Her small hands gripped his shoulders, and her soft chest pressed against his own. And there was that damn smell again, reminding him of the apple trees that grew in a long line on Nonna's farm. He could feel her curves through the thin T-shirt she wore.

Let her go.

His mind shouted the warning, but his body didn't listen. His hands held her close, and his lungs breathed her in. *Mine.* Dark energy shifted, moved, swirled inside him. The man in him would deny the bond, but the dark knew better. It claimed her for its true mate. Urged him to meld his mind with hers—to create a link so they could share thoughts freely. Dear God, it grew impossible to resist this connection between them.

Geneva must have also felt the shift in energy, but this time, she didn't push him away. No, she stayed put, a warm invitation.

"Rolf. What's the matter?"

"Nothing." He gritted his teeth and clamped down on the darkness with all his might. He grabbed the car keys from her hands, thrust her from him, and headed out the door.

"Rolf, wait."

He didn't respond. He couldn't. Her brothers were right to hate him.

9

JULIA

Geneva tossed and turned in the double bed, sleeping on and off until morning. When she awoke, she lay on her back and gazed at the ceiling with burning eyes and wondered if Rolf had managed to sleep comfortably in the small car. She hoped he spent the night like she did, restless and aching and empty.

For a moment last night, she'd had the insane idea he desired her. Had found herself anticipating his kiss as if the attraction between them were mutual, and all she could think about was the feel of his lips on hers. My God, she'd practically thrust herself upon him. She cringed at the memory. He didn't want her in that way. It had all been a fantasy of her own making.

She swallowed the dryness in her mouth and checked the time on her cell phone. Eight in the morning. She shut her eyes, but her mind circled the evening's activities like birds of prey. They'd missed something. Some important piece of the puzzle. Painful exhaustion cramped her muscles. She couldn't stop thinking about the last twenty-four hours—their flight from Cleveland, arrival at the hotel, visit to the vortex, the nightmare.

Someone had wanted her to kill Rolf. Someone had known or anticipated their arrival at the vortex. Someone had infused a crystal with an exorbitant amount of dream energy. Enough energy to bring her worst nightmare to life. Enough energy to cause her to lose control. There were plenty of dream talents in the CMU. The stored energy could have belonged to any one of them. But Julia was in Arizona. And before Geneva had been swept into the nightmare, she'd sensed something familiar about the concentrated energy.

She snapped her eyes open, sat up in bed, and peered into the room, searching for answers. Julia had been forced to—somehow—charge a crystal with a massive amount of her energy.

Geneva flung off the covers and headed to the bathroom, her thoughts a chaotic mess. Only one other person had ever charged a crystal—at least that she had witnessed—her former partner, David Jenkins. Desperation had driven him to try it—his future wife lay dying. The stone was special—had been in the Jenkins family for decades. Geneva would not have believed it possible if she hadn't witnessed the incredible feat. David had used the crystal to store his wife's memories and then restore them later, bringing her back from a near-comatose state.

She caught her reflection in the bathroom mirror. Her eyes looked wide and bruised and fearful. If David's family had a special stone, then why couldn't there be similar stones out there? And if David charged a crystal, why couldn't Julia? All it took was a strong talent, and Julia certainly possessed the power to manipulate massive quantities of dream energy.

Despite her misgivings, for the first time since she learned of Julia's absence, hope that her friend lived stirred in Geneva's heart. If she was right and Julia had charged the crystal, perhaps whoever held her kept her alive, maybe even nearby.

She scrambled for her clothes. She needed to find Rolf and tell him what she suspected.

Her mind followed the trail of his energy to the parking lot, spying his green glow. Her heartbeat thrummed against her ribcage. Rolf wasn't alone. The green was joined by two powerful and familiar colors—teal and royal blue—her brothers. They were two hours earlier than expected. Why?

She grabbed the pair of shorts and T-shirt she'd tossed on the chair. Her brothers wouldn't hurt Rolf. Regardless of what they thought of him, Rolf was still a vital member of the CMU. But her brothers had always been a bit overprotective of Geneva after losing their mother at such a young age. And Rolf had a reputation with the ladies. They wouldn't be happy Peter paired them for this mission.

She flung on her clothes, slipped into her tennis shoes, and dashed toward the elevators.

10

BROTHERS

Rolf stepped outside the Toyota and stretched his arms above his head with a yawn. He rolled his neck from side to side, ignoring the cheeky Ericksen brothers leaning against the trunk of the rental like they owned it.

"Any leads on your sister?" Nate strolled toward him, the sleeves of his shirt rolled up. He was the taller and broader of the two brothers, with a mafia boss face. His looks complemented the suspicious glint in his blue eyes. Danny, the younger brother, followed a few steps behind. His blond looks, so much like Geneva's, hid a sharp intelligence and a talent for sniffing out trouble.

"Not much. A crystal."

Nate stilled, his hands on his hips. If this were a western, Rolf imagined Nate would reach for his guns. The brothers hadn't liked Rolf ever since he'd been selected high school quarterback over Nate. Their dislike of him had strengthened when Geneva asked him out, and he'd refused. But that was many years ago, when they were fresh out of high school. What sealed the deal was more recent news—Peter's announcement Rolf would become lead hacker on the team. The brothers didn't trust him. He couldn't say he blamed them.

"What kind of crystal?"

Rolf spread his legs wide and crossed his arms, keeping his thoughts contained. He didn't care for them, either. But they were Geneva's siblings, and that made all the difference. He shrugged. "It may have had special properties."

"You mean it doesn't now?" Danny asked.

"Right. It contained dream energy last night when Geneva and I encountered it. It doesn't any longer. We'll need to have it tested to know for certain."

"What happened to your head?" Nate asked, pointing to the gash covered by white gauze and the crisscross of Band-Aids, he'd gotten from the hotel's front desk. "Get in a fight?"

"I hit a rock when we were under the influence of the dream energy."

"Where's Geneva?" He peered inside the vehicle like Rolf had her dead body stashed in there.

"In the hotel. There was only one room available. She slept in the bed. I took the car."

Nate lifted an eyebrow. "Such a gentleman." Only a slight twinge of sarcasm clung to his words.

"I try."

"Good, let's keep it that way," Danny said.

Rolf stiffened. "I don't deal well with warnings."

"Tough," Nate said, coming up next to Danny and pointing his finger at Rolf. "This is our sister we're talking about. Not one of your floozies. I get you need her help to find Julia, but that's all you'll get from her. We'll be watching you, Jorgensen."

Rolf held himself in check. Barely. Pain radiated from the lump on the back of his head to his temples. Lethal energy boiled and bubbled about to spew forth, swallowing everything in its path. Swallowing the brothers. Never had he been so close to the breaking point. The dark in him craved a fight. It would not let the brothers stand between him and his growing attachment to Geneva. It surged against the gates of his mind, threatening to break loose and destroy them.

"I would never harm your sister." His voice came out as a low rumble. He kept his eyes focused on Nate, repeating over and over in his head, "Control, control, control," like some kind of hypnotic chant. The dark monster reared its head and snapped its jaw. Heat shimmered in the air around them. Beads of sweat formed on his forehead and the back of his neck. He prayed the brothers would be smart enough to leave.

Nate must have sensed some of his mental state because he frowned. Still, he didn't move. "Good. You have a sister. You can understand how we feel a little protective of ours."

"Yes, I do." Rolf's hands shook with the effort to control the lethal darkness. He shoved them in his pockets. "And she's missing."

...never lay his filthy hands on her.

He stilled. The words floated in the air between them, straight from Nate's mind to his. He flared his nostrils and took a sharp breath, but it wasn't enough. Dark energy seethed and twisted inside him, tunneling toward the surface.

He stepped forward. Nate stepped backward. A slight figure stepped between them.

"Rolf, what's going on?" Geneva gave him a puzzled look. She lay a small, pale hand on his chest, as if she understood on a psychic level only physical contact could tame the raging beast.

For a moment, Rolf stared, not seeing or hearing anything. Then her features came into focus, the dark energy settled, and reason returned. He jerked away from her touch, stepping backward and turning away. "Nothing," he managed.

Geneva stared at him for a minute before turning to her brothers. "Why are you here so early? I wasn't expecting you until closer to nine."

The brothers looked at each other, obviously exchanging thoughts on a path that excluded Geneva.

"They don't like us paired together," Rolf said.

She wrinkled her nose, her frown deepening. Irritation appeared in her eyes. Or maybe the image came from her mind? He was never quite certain how he sensed her feelings. He just did.

"It wouldn't do for you to succumb to my considerable charms." Rolf tried for a smile, but he was pretty certain he looked like the big bad wolf. He certainly felt that way.

"What?" Her mouth formed a circle of horrified surprise. She rounded on her brothers. "Julia is missing, and that's all you can think about? Her disappearance is much more important than whether Rolf and I are getting it on or not."

Rolf coughed to cover the sudden smile that formed on his lips. Her brothers shot daggers at him. Geneva's eyes met his for a second, embarrassment at her brother's involvement in her personal life reflected in their blue depths and flushed cheeks. God knows what she read in his gaze.

She turned to her brothers. "I've something important to tell you. Rolf and I encountered dream energy last night...or early this morning."

"Rolf mentioned that and his injury." Nate's eyes shifted between Rolf and Geneva. "Where was this?"

"Rolf and I went to Bell Rock, a vortex in Sedona, at midnight, thinking I might be able to trace Julia's energy there, since she often visits them when she travels to Arizona. As soon as I got started, we encountered a powerful dream energy."

"What happened?" Danny asked.

"It threw me into a nightmare. Let's just say I had to work hard not to cause an explosion that almost killed Rolf." Geneva turned to him. "I didn't recognize it at the time, but Rolf, I'm certain the dream energy belongs to Julia. She charged the crystal."

"An old wives' tale. It's not possible to charge crystals," Nate said.

"Yes. Yes, it is, Nate. I don't know how it's done, but my former partner, David Jenkins, did it once. I saw the crystal he charged with my own eyes. I watched him use it."

"Julia is here, then." Rolf was careful to keep the surge of joy coursing through his system under wraps.

"Not necessarily. The energy could have been stored in the crystal some time ago, I suppose."

"But why would Julia charge a crystal to make you kill her brother?" Danny asked.

"A million-dollar question," Rolf said. "Julia wouldn't. Someone made her do it."

"Or tricked her," Nate said. Rolf remembered Nate had a soft spot for Julia.

"Yes, a possibility."

Geneva's cell phone pinged, indicating a new text.

"So, what do we do?" Nate asked. "Do we have any other clues?"

"No, but we'll start with the gem show at the Phoenix convention center," Rolf said. "It's a long shot, but if someone is searching for the legendary crystals they may show up there."

Geneva nodded. "We can ask around to see if anyone has been looking for rare crystals. Perhaps we'll uncover something."

Rolf's cell phone buzzed. He pulled it from his pants pocket. Awfully early to get a phone call from his dad.

Next to him, Geneva tensed, her psychic antenna tuning in to his anxiety.

"Rolf, Nonna's in the hospital."

"What happened? Is she okay?" His gaze flicked to Geneva and away. Automatically, he sealed his emotions from her. His heart skipped a beat or two, making up for lost time. Nonna had raised them after their mother divorced their father and left her kids to fend for themselves. She baked their favorite foods, read them stories, and held them whenever they were hurt or missed their mother.

"She passed out in her garden, and apparently was there all night. The neighbor found her this morning and called an ambulance. She's awake and feeling better today, and the doctors say she'll recover, but I wanted you to know. Have you found your sister?"

"Not yet. I will, though. I promise. Call me back if anything changes with Nonna. As soon as I find Julia, I'll be on the next flight."

"All right, son. Keep me posted. I'll be worried until I know you're both okay."

"I'll get in touch." He ended the call.

Rolf, what happened?" Geneva asked as soon as he stuffed his phone in his pocket and turned to look at her.

"It's Nonna. She's in the hospital, but my dad says she'll be okay."

Geneva gasped. She knew how much Nonna meant to him and Julia. "An accident?"

"She collapsed in her garden and lay there overnight. The neighbor found her this morning and called 911."

She placed her hand on his arm, warming the numbness in his heart.

"You should leave now, Rolf. Don't worry about a thing. My brothers and I will go to the gem show and see what we can uncover. Make sure Nonna is well. You'll never forgive yourself if something happens to her and you're not there.

"We can't go with you, Geneva." Danny stared at his phone. "We've got a level one emergency. Peter just sent a text. He's ordered Nate and I to Cleveland—all hands on deck. It appears North Korea hacked into the brain of Futurcom's CEO and stole critical information on the company's newest prototype. We need to get it back. He's got a helicopter waiting at the airport."

Geneva waved a hand like a shepherd scattering the flock. "Go. All of you. You can rejoin me as soon as you're able.

"There's no way you're going alone," Rolf said. "I'm coming with you."

"Rolf, there's no need."

"There's a need, all right. There's a need for me to find whoever has Julia and Percy and wring their necks."

11

NONNA

The car engine roared to life as Rolf stepped on the gas. Geneva flashed him a concerned look from the passenger seat, but he pretended not to notice. The ache where he'd hit the back of his head reached around his skull to pound both temples.

They'd not wasted any time getting showered and dressed and back on the road after the Ericksen brothers departed for the airport. Despite his need for action, he couldn't help but think they were heading into a trap. Something about the crystal ending up in the vortex didn't sit right with him. It was too much of a coincidence he and Geneva happened to stumble upon it.

He swerved into the left lane, but the sudden move did little to alleviate the snarling Phoenix traffic, compounding his frustration. Nonna had been healthy when he'd seen her a week ago. How could her health decline so fast?

He jerked the car back into the passing lane. All he wanted was to board the next plane to Cleveland and see Nonna, but first, he needed to find Julia and Percy.

Geneva sighed, and he slid her a glance before looking

back at the road. She stared out the window, but he could almost hear her thoughts. She believed his frustration stemmed from having to spend more time with her. She couldn't be further from the truth. She had no idea the lengths he'd go to protect her.

He found his sunglasses and put them on, narrowing his gaze on the road in front of him. How could he explain the odd tingling in his gut that warned him of danger? That told him the lives of those he cared about the most were threatened? He didn't understand it himself. He just knew Nonna's fall was no accident, Julia was missing, and he couldn't leave Geneva alone right now.

"You'd better slow down, or we'll wind up in an accident."

So she was back to lecturing. He didn't look at her; he didn't have to. He knew what he would see—forehead creased, lips pursed in distaste, eyes frosted over. When she looked at him like that, he wanted nothing more than to pull her into his arms and kiss her until the lie he'd maintained and reinforced melted away and there was nothing but smiles and honesty left between them. Then he'd claim her as his.

Mine, mine, mine. Rolf's heart beat hard against his chest, and dark energy swirled in time to the dangerous rhythm. He gripped the wheel and wrestled the beast. A whole minute passed before the pounding in his ears lessened, his breathing slowed, and his hands loosened their death-grip on the wheel. He'd won the battle this time, but for how much longer?

He wiped a sweaty palm on his jeans then readjusted his grip on the wheel all the while keeping his eyes on the road and away from hers. The timing of the phone call about Nonna was too perfect.

The niggling thought settled in his mind, increasing his anxiety. What were the chances Nonna would be taken to the hospital at the same time the CMU had a level one emergency, calling Geneva's brothers back to headquarters?

By the time they pulled into the convention center parking lot, fear slashed against the walls of his iron control. He suppressed an involuntary shiver, forcing his body through the motion of putting the car in park. The dark monster stirred and stretched, sensing trouble.

"You're worried."

He didn't bother to deny it. "Yes. Something about our situation doesn't feel right. Do you sense anything?"

She cocked her head to the side and closed her eyes. A few seconds later, she opened them, shaking her head. "Seems normal. There are still far too many colors, though. We'll have to go inside."

He nodded, clutching his cell phone with cold and clammy palms. "Okay."

They exited the car and headed toward the convention center entrance. He sniffed the air and paused at the double doors. He glanced at Geneva, and their gazes locked. Something shifted inside him, and his hands trembled slightly. In that moment, he didn't shield his fear. If something were to happen to her, he wouldn't be able to control the beast, and no one would be safe from his anger. "Stay close."

She frowned at the order but nodded. Then he opened the doors and followed her inside.

GENEVA STEPPED PAST ROLF, looking around at the crowds of people that filled the building. They clustered around rows and rows of merchandise for sale from thousands of sellers.

She blinked at the tables filled with stones and gems and moved forward, Rolf close on her heels.

He touched her arm. "Wait here. We'll have to buy tickets to go inside. I'll be right back."

He motioned for her to stand in the corner, and then he took off toward a line of people that snaked to a ticket window. The line seemed to be moving, but she shifted from one leg to the other. Why was she on edge? Being around Rolf was getting to her. He was hiding something important. She could feel it.

Automatically, she closed her eyes and scanned the room with her psychic senses, past the red light pouring from Rolf—so unlike him—and into the larger room. Colors assaulted her—green like trees in springtime conveying growth, blue like skies in summer relaying hope, gold like sunflowers in autumn speaking wisdom. Far too many colors to make sense of them. She'd need to get closer.

"See anything unusual?"

She opened her eyes. Rolf towered over her, the red light shifting around him, indicating his increasing anxiety.

She shook her head. "That was fast. You got the tickets already?"

"Yes."

He must have hacked into the minds of dozens of people to convince them to let him cut in line. She squinted at him. What had Rolf so on edge? He wasn't the most patient hacker, but even he would normally conserve his energy for more dangerous activity.

She didn't have time to dwell on his strange behavior further, because Rolf stepped forward and handed the attendant their tickets. She followed him through the turnstile into a large room with hundreds of tables spaced about a foot apart. People were crowded around each one, rifling through stones and bargaining with sellers.

"Try tracing them again." His face was expressionless; his energy contained. This was the Rolf she was used to.

She nodded, took ten steps forward, and closed her eyes, pushing her mind past color after color, farther, farther, farther, until she hit the remotest corner of the massive room. Amber waves floated in the air. Percy Withers's energy? Something was off... As she focused, the color grew deeper and harsher than when she'd last encountered Percy's energy. The waves became shorter, almost as if someone else's energy mixed with Percy's, manipulating him. Another talent? What was another talent doing at the gem show?

Fear rocketed through her system. Whoever manipulated the energy was strong, and they intended to inflict damage. *"I think Percy might be here, but we need to move. Now. Something's not right."* She pushed the thought at Rolf and took off, not waiting to see if he followed.

"Wait," he shouted behind her.

She didn't stop running. The colors were too strong to stay still. They needed to get to Percy now. *"Someone's manipulating him. Hurry."*

Energy spheres rushed Geneva from the four corners of the room, hovering so close she could no longer see in front of her. Rolf's energy. He must have stopped and channeled his enormous power into the room, knowing she could use it to prevent whatever was about to happen. She slowed to a jog, filled her lungs and emptied them, pulling his energy inside, slow and easy, to prevent herself from blowing the roof off the place.

Then she ran again, intent on reaching the opposite side of the building so she could intervene with whatever evil was in progress. She was too far away to determine what kind of negative energy surrounded the amber waves, but she followed the strands. She took two strides forward before her mind met with another color, a dreamy violet. *Julia?*

Now she ran full out. She heard a shout as she tore down the aisle. The crowd parted as if by magic. Rolf's magic. Geneva didn't turn to look at him, but she knew he was right behind her, using the power of his mind to force strangers to step aside, making a path for them. His efforts allowed her to move forward at a faster clip, but it forced him to slow down.

Large, brown energy balls rushed the space in front of her, buzzing and twisting in a frenzied, diabolical dance. She frowned. This wasn't Rolf's energy, but there was no time to analyze. She'd need all the power she could get to stop whatever was about to happen. Geneva sucked them inside. She tore through the crowd of patrons now, anxious to reach Percy and Julia and the strange energy and stop whatever was about to happen. An ache formed in her side, but she didn't quit racing forward, almost tripping over other patrons.

There...by a cardboard box, Julia crouched in an awkward position, searching for something. Geneva twisted and sprinted, but now it was harder to make progress around the crowd of people. Rolf must have lost sight of her.

But she didn't have time to worry because she was much closer now. Almost close enough to intervene. Julia rose from the first box and moved to the next table, where she squatted and rifled through another box.

Energy shifted and sparkled in the air, drawing Geneva's attention to Percy, who stood on the opposite side, a considerable distance away. An odd yellow-green-brown surrounded him, blotting out the normal amber color of his aura. *Someone else's talent.*

Excitement raced through her veins. *Breathe.*

Julia no longer dug through boxes. Instead, she talked with a tall man in a yellow security jacket. He grasped her arm and said something. Geneva moved forward, but she was still too far away to hear the conversation. The guard pointed to Julia's backpack, and she held it out and open. The guard rifled through.

More power wafted through the room, causing the hair on the back of Geneva's neck to stand at attention. Negative energy. She glanced at Percy. He stood close to Julia, who took a step backward. He grasped her arm and said something. He pulled a hand from his jacket pocket, a glint of metal catching the light. A knife? Geneva's heart lurched in her chest. What was Percy doing with a knife, and why was it pointed at Julia?

Geneva pushed past the people in front of her, hypnotized by the long, skinny blade flashing in Percy's hand. Julia appeared to be equally mesmerized, her eyes wide with horror. The object grew larger until it filled the space in front of them. Geneva ran at full speed, but there were too many people. She wouldn't get to Julia in time. Over the noise of the crowd, a bloodcurdling scream vibrated the air.

"Percy, no, please. Help!"

Geneva flashed a glance to where the security guard stood, but the spot was empty. Where was he? Percy lurched forward, grabbing Geneva's attention. Julia scrambled backward to avoid the sharp point of his knife. In her haste, she slipped and fell.

"Someone help me," Julia screamed.

Percy raised the knife above his head. Fear dug grooves

in Geneva's mental armor. She pushed and prodded at the crowd, but it was no use. She needed Rolf. Where was he?

"Please help."

Now she was almost upon Percy bent over Julia. Geneva hurtled the energy at him. The crowd parted, and Rolf rushed toward her. "No, Geneva, stop. You'll kill him."

Geneva glanced from Rolf back to Julia and Percy. Where were they? Where was the knife? All she could see was the security guard in the yellow jacket. She drew back on the ball of energy hurtling toward the nonexistent figures. Too late. The guard dropped to the floor. Dropped like the man who shot and killed her mother. Dropped like...dead. Oh God. Not moving. Dead. Dead. Dead.

What had she done? What the hell had she done?

A tremor shook her body. Icy fingers gripped her heart. Blood. So much blood. So much damn blood.

"She did it. Grab her!" A spectator pointed at Geneva.

A pair of long arms circled her chest, holding her in place. Geneva followed the arms into the face of a stoic security officer.

"I've got her." The officer grabbed her hands behind her back and pulled out a pair of handcuffs.

"Let her go."

The voice sounded deep and guttural, almost beastly. It took her a moment to realize the voice belonged to Rolf.

The officer's arms dropped from hers, and instantly, another pair of more powerful arms held her. Rolf's arms. His voiced settled in her ear, no hint of roughness.

"Steady now. You were targeted with illusion energy. Julia and Percy are not here."

12

ESCAPE

So it happened. She'd hurt someone, maybe killed him. An innocent civilian. A security guard, who had been knocked cold and carted out on a stretcher, blood dripping from his forehead onto the floor. Like the last time, but she was no longer four years old. They would—should—punish her.

Geneva shivered, but not from the air conditioner pumping out frigid air in the convention center. She hadn't meant to harm him. She'd thought she was saving Julia from Percy, but that hadn't been real. It had all been a horrifying illusion.

Rolf's arms enfolded her into a hard chest and welcome heat. The familiar scent of leather and pine surrounded her.

"I killed him."

"No, you didn't. He'll recover. We gotta get out of here."

"I can't just leave him." Her legs trembled, and she might have stumbled if Rolf didn't keep her upright.

"A facial wound, that's all. See the EMT over there?"

Geneva peeked over Rolf's shoulder to spy a man leaning over the stretcher. "Yes."

"He's already ascertained it's not serious."

"You hacked into his mind?" At a distance, hackers needed a partner—a trainer like herself—to enter the mind, but not when they were physically close to a target.

Rolf nodded. "Now will you come with me?"

"What about the police? They'll have questions."

"Don't worry about the police. I'll handle them."

"Rolf, we're not above the law. If I've injured this man, the CMU will know it. They'll want me evaluated. You heard Peter. They're concerned about my latest test results."

"What happened here isn't your fault. I told you it was an illusion. They won't hold you accountable."

"Maybe not, but I know the truth. This man has a family, maybe children."

"Geneva, we need to leave now."

In the end, it wasn't Rolf's justification that made up her mind to leave the convention center. It was the red color rolling off him in waves and the unusual dark splotches that kept flashing in and out of his aura. He was having difficulty controlling his energy.

"All right," she said and turned to face the security officer, who towered over her. Rolf's earlier command had worn off. He held a pair of handcuffs in one hand. "Ma'am, you're under arrest."

"Excuse me, Officer," Rolf said, the dark light around him intensifying. "She's coming with me."

The officer glared at Rolf, but before he could argue, power erupted into the air. For a moment, Geneva thought Rolf's mental command wasn't going to work this time. But then the officer's eyes drooped, and his expression went slack, and he nodded. "Right."

They didn't waste any more time then. The thought Rolf implanted under such circumstances would only last so long, and if other officers showed up, even if he used her energy, he wouldn't be able to hack all of them at the same time. He grabbed one of her hands and practically dragged her back through the cluster of people and out the front doors.

"Rolf, please, I need to catch my breath."

"Do it at the car. We have to call Peter and explain the situation. Then we need to find Julia and Percy. What just happened in there was a targeted attack. Whoever set the illusion wanted you to lose control."

Despite Rolf's punishing pace, she managed to follow him to their rental car. It took her a second to catch her breath, and in that time, he managed to start the engine and call Peter. He put the phone on speaker so he could drive and then peeled out of the parking lot.

"Have you found Julia?" Peter's voice sounded calm. Normal. He didn't yet know what had taken place.

"Not yet. Someone knew we would visit the gem show. They used illusion energy on Geneva." The red halo surrounding Rolf grew until it covered him.

"Is she okay?"

"She's fine. She's sitting next to me. You're on speaker... there's been a small accident."

"I don't like your term, small. That usually means someone screwed up royally. What happened?"

So much for Peter's calm voice. Geneva could imagine him sitting up straight and tapping his fingers on his desk.

"I thought Percy had a knife and threatened Julia—an illusion," she said. "It was only a security guard, and he didn't have a knife. Percy and Julia weren't actually there, but their energy was, I swear it."

"You killed the guard?" Now Peter's tone sounded worried.

"No."

"Well, that's a major relief. Why didn't you start with that first?"

"An injury only. A scratch. It will heal," Rolf said.

"Geneva, it's unlike you to mistake someone's energy. You'll need to get checked out at Corvey."

Her stomach did a triple somersault. The Corvey Institution in Chicago was where the CMU brought drained talents and burnt-out hackers to be evaluated for continued service. Her heart pounded, and no amount of deep breaths would settle it. She'd spent time at the Institution as a small child—a nightmare she preferred to forget.

"No." Rolf growled the word.

Something in his voice had her turning to look at him fully. He stared straight ahead so she couldn't see into his eyes, but a muscle in his jaw jumped, and the color coming from him was more a grey shadow than red. Where was the customary green color in his aura? *Weird.*

"Geneva can't risk using her talent if she's having trouble maintaining control. Corvey is the best place for her."

"She's not going there."

There was the growl again. His voice vibrated with animal-like intensity—this time, she imagined the rattle of a snake before it struck. Instinctively, she placed a hand on his arm. His skin was hot, his muscles taut. Maybe he was getting sick?

"Give me a good reason why not," Peter said.

"Whoever did this has Julia and Percy. We have to act quickly, and I need Geneva to find them. Their lives depend on it."

Something loosened in Geneva's chest, and she realized she'd been holding her breath for most of the conversation. Rolf wanted her with him. His weird reaction was because he needed her. To find his sister and Percy, not because he cared about her.

"Geneva, what do you have to say?"

Now Rolf did glance her way. The look in his eyes was filled with such intensity. There was fear there, yes, but there was something more, like her answer decided whether he lived or died. *Crazy.*

She blinked and cleared her throat. "I'm fine. I want to stay with Rolf and find Julia and Percy."

There was a pause, and Geneva's pulse raced as she waited for Peter's decision.

"All right. You'll stay on the case for now. But it's risky. The entire program depends on your ability to keep a low profile. We don't want this reaching the media. If you're having any problems at all, you need to tell us. We'll get you help. Understood?"

"Yes, of course."

"Good. Let me remind you we can't afford mistakes. If there's one more incident, it won't matter if it's an accident. The decision of where you go won't be mine to make."

13

CABIN

Rolf ended the call with Peter, but he didn't speak or acknowledge her, just continued driving, staring at the road ahead of him. At first, Geneva was too preoccupied with reconstructing the accident and wondering if she could have prevented it to care. But after they'd been driving north for a long while, she realized they'd passed Sedona and hadn't gotten off the exit for Flagstaff.

"What are we doing?"

He glanced her way long enough for her to register the distant look in his eyes. "Giving you time to recover."

"I'm fine. Where are we headed?"

"A place I know. You'll be safe there."

"Safe? We need to find Julia and Percy."

"We will."

Geneva sighed. Sometimes she thought Rolf was deliberately dense. "Why would you think they're in Flagstaff?"

"I don't."

Irritation burned a pathway through her veins. "Enough with the secrecy, already. I'll try and trace them."

"There's no need."

"Why not?" Did he think they'd magically appear?

"A hunch. I'll tell you more once we get there."

She sighed and looked out the window, as Rolf pulled into a long driveway with a rustic little A-frame log cabin at the end. The front was all windows. Someone had chopped firewood and stored it under either side of the small porch. A hot tub sat off to the side. Any other time, she would have appreciated its quaintness, but not while her best friend was still missing. "Does anyone live here? It looks empty."

He parked the car in front of the porch. "It's empty. But it's stocked with food, and there are linens and towels in the closet. C'mon, let's get inside."

It didn't take them long to walk up the short steps and open the keypad at the front door. The inside had all the charm of the outside. A table with bench seating sat in one corner. In the other, a couch and overstuffed recliner were clustered around a coffee table in front of a stone fireplace. A marble chess game sat on the coffee table. She placed her hand on a fluffy white blanket draped on the back of the recliner. If they weren't so desperate to find Julia, she'd like nothing better than to curl inside its warmth and nap. "This place is nice."

She turned to see Rolf shut the door and flick on a lamp. "Yes."

If she didn't know better, she'd almost think he enjoyed having her here. But she did know better. "Who's the owner?"

"Me."

Somehow she'd guessed it as soon as she spied the chess pieces on the coffee table. Rolf was an avid chess player. "I'm not going to ask when you bought a cabin in Flagstaff."

"I bought it a few years ago. Julia's not the only one who likes to come to Arizona."

"Why are we here, Rolf?" She focused on his aura. It seemed normal, but a whisper of red signaled he was on edge.

"We're waiting."

"Do you really think whoever has Julia and Percy is just going to show up here?"

He smiled, and the sight was so unexpected for a moment she couldn't breathe. "Yes, I do."

She narrowed her gaze, but that didn't stop him from moving toward her.

"What...what are you doing?" Her pulse pounded, and heat raced up her spine.

He grabbed her hand and tugged her toward the recliner. "Getting you comfortable." He pushed her gently down onto the recliner, then grabbed the blanket and tucked it around her. Did his hands linger a moment too long? The unexpected gesture nearly had her melting.

She narrowed her gaze. Had he read her mind earlier? Is that why he covered her in the blanket? Or maybe it was her own wishful thinking. She drew her energy inward.

He took the couch opposite, stretching his long legs in front of him.

She leaned forward. "Rolf, why do you think Julia and Percy's kidnappers will follow us to this remote cabin?"

He rubbed the back of his neck and then ran a hand through his dark locks. He looked tired. Apparently, neither of them had gotten enough sleep last night.

"I think they want you. Or more accurately, they want your talent."

She tried to speak, but her voice cracked, so she whispered. "Why?"

"Whoever's behind the attacks knows your ability is off the charts. That makes your talent a very valuable commodity on the black market. If they can store it in their crystals, they'll have buyers—lots of them."

She clutched her hands in her lap. "You think they can force me to give it to them?"

"Yes. But first, they'll have to kidnap you. And to do that, they'll need to get through me."

"Is that why they kidnapped Percy and Julia, then? For their energy?"

"It's what I suspect. The energy used in the crystal we found in the vortex was Julia's, and she wouldn't have voluntarily let them store it in a crystal."

"But the energy at the gem show was illusion energy. That's not Percy's talent."

"No, it's not." Red light and green warred within Rolf's aura.

"They've kidnapped someone else, haven't they? Someone with illusion energy."

Rolf grimaced. "Probably."

"So, what do we do now?"

"Stay here. Make supper. Recuperate. If I'm right, they'll show up, and we'll be ready for them."

ROLF SCOOPED spaghetti and meatballs onto two plates and set them on the table. All the while, he fought a terrible weight in his stomach. What would happen if he wasn't able to protect Geneva? What if his plan incited the monster inside him? What if he got so out of control, he couldn't stop from hurting her?

"Rolf."

He came back to the present with a start. She must have been talking to him for some time. He pretended he'd been listening. "What?"

"I asked when you learned to cook like this?"

He shrugged, getting up. "Since I bought this place. There are no nearby restaurants. Water?" He held up a pitcher of ice water.

"Sure."

He stood next to her and poured water in her glass and managed to resist the urge to bury his face in her soft hair. Instead, he set the pitcher down and took the seat across from her. What he didn't say was how many times he wondered what it would be like to have her here. And here she was. But it was only temporary.

She twirled the final bite of spaghetti on her fork, closed her eyes, and savored it. "Mmm...homemade sauce. This is delicious." Her eyes popped open before he could look away. "What's for dessert?"

You. He took a breath. "You always did like your sweets. I think I can dig up some chocolate ice cream in the freezer. Will that work?"

She smiled, and the sight had him gripping his water glass. He set the glass down and went to dish the ice cream before he said or did something foolish. By the time he returned, Geneva had moved to the front window and was staring at something outside.

He set the ice cream on the table and went to look at what had her so fascinated. An elk had wandered from under the pine trees surrounding the house and stood in the driveway. Its giant rack was tilted back, and it looked at him as if it knew him.

"She's staring at us. You don't suppose our kidnappers figured out how to control animals, do you?"

He laughed. "It's a he. Only males have antlers. And anything is possible, but I doubt it. There are a lot of elk in this area. They often wander close to the cabin."

She turned suddenly, her chest lining up with his. Far too close. Power swirled inside him, a funnel cloud of desire. His mind automatically found an opening in her brain waves and latched on.

"What other animals do you see around here?"

Her eyes were soft with curiosity and excitement. A piece of hair curled slightly to frame her face. How he would love to brush it away. Her lips opened slightly, and he caught a glimpse of straight white teeth. If he leaned down just a little closer, and she tilted her head up ever so slightly, their lips would meet. He could almost feel their softness.

"Rolf?"

He cleared his throat. "Elk, mule deer, coyotes...the occasional black bear or mountain lion, if you're lucky."

She rolled her eyes, but it only made her look more adorable. "That sounds like my worst nightmare."

Pink stained her cheeks, and he didn't have to read her thoughts because he knew them. "I've been in your worst nightmare, and as I recall, there were no wild animals present. Unless you count the human kind." He chuckled softly, and then he did reach out and touch the strand of hair that tempted him, moving it from her cheek.

Electricity arced between them, and the blanket dropped from around her shoulders.

"Rolf, I..." She placed a hand on his shoulder.

Their gazes locked. Step away. He should move. Now. It was the right thing to do. "What is it?"

"I'm going to find out if the elk is real."

14

TRAPPED

Geneva used the distraction of the elk to fight her attraction to Rolf. She only planned to concentrate on its energy for a moment—just enough to verify it was a real animal and not some sort of illusion or dream image planted by Julia and Percy's captors. But the moment she shut her eyes, the animal's energy proved elusive, spiraling away from her the more she tried to chase it down.

Greens turned to blues, blues to grays, and grays grew light until they nearly disappeared. *Follow me, follow me, follow me.* The elk disappeared into the gray mist.

She and Rolf were children, running in a field of daisies. He handed her a bundle of flowers because he knew how she liked them.

"I'll tell you my secret if you promise not to tell anyone else," he said.

"I would never tell anything you told me."

He hung his head as if he were embarrassed to meet her eyes.

"What's wrong, Rolf?"

"My mom left us. My dad says she won't be coming back."

"Where did she go?"

"Florida. She has a boyfriend."

He reached down and plucked a daisy, then removed its petals one by one. "She said she couldn't take it anymore. She doesn't like being around us. She wants to be around normal people."

"I'm sorry, Rolf."

He toed the grass with his foot. "She's afraid of me."

"What did you do?"

Rolf shrugged, looking up at the sky. The sun had disappeared behind dark clouds. "I don't wanna talk about it. C'mon, there's a bad storm coming. This way. To the woods."

Follow me. Follow me. Follow me.

"We're not supposed to go into the woods. If we go there, we'll never come out again."

But Rolf wasn't listening. He took off running and disappeared into the darkness. She shouldn't follow him into the woods. Her mother and father had warned her. But what choice did she have? She always followed Rolf. She followed him everywhere. She'd follow him to the end of time if she had to.

"Rolf, wait up. Please. I'm coming. Don't leave me."

Now she was running, running, running, clutching the bouquet of daisies and breathing hard. She couldn't lose Rolf. He was everything to her. She paused at the edge of the woods to catch her breath and find her courage. There was no turning back now. She plunged into the darkness after him, but her foot struck a piece of wood, sending her backward, her bottom smacking the hard ground. In front of her, pieces of wood slammed into place, forming a giant barrier.

"No, no, no." She got up and ran to the chunks of wood

nailed together, striking them with her fists over and over and over until her hands stung. The wood didn't budge. She couldn't follow Rolf. He was in the dark woods, and he would never return. He was lost to her.

Tears streamed from her eyes, and she wiped them away and then looked at her hands in horror. They were covered in blood. She'd whacked the barrier so hard, her flesh was torn. She slumped to the ground and folded her head into her knees. She wouldn't go back without Rolf, and she couldn't move forward. She would stay here forever.

A sound reached her ears, almost a murmur. She ignored it at first. But it wouldn't be ignored. It grew louder, building in intensity, almost like a person's voice. She lifted her head and looked at the field of daisies. No one was there. No one could reach her. She was alone, and night was coming fast.

"Geneva."

"Rolf?" She stood and peered at the barrier, but the sound hadn't come from inside. No, it had come from far, far away. So far, it stretched beyond the field of daisies.

"Come back, Geneva. Please."

Rolf sounded distressed. She turned and moved across the field, first walking then running toward the sound.

"But you ran into the woods?"

"Come back to me. Please."

She fell on the slick grass, but she got up and kept running toward the sound of his voice. Then the grass ended, and there was an open chasm. Before she could stop herself, she stepped into it. Into nothingness.

Falling, falling, falling.

Her stomach curled into her lungs as a feeling of weightlessness took hold. She would land at the bottom of the chasm and die. There was no way back.

Strong arms snatched her mid-fall. "Open your eyes."

Her mind obeyed, and she blinked, staring into Rolf's hard face. His eyes were dark with a fierceness she couldn't understand. His skin held a dull red cast before she realized she was seeing the energy inside him. He was consumed with worry, but he held it inside, keeping it from transferring to her.

"Don't look down. Don't look anywhere else. Stay focused on me."

"How did you find me?"

Even as she asked the question she knew. She had gotten lost in the colors. They were in the landscape of her mind. Somehow Rolf had hacked into her brain and was guiding her back to consciousness. He had taken a tremendous risk for her. Any transfer of emotion and he'd be stranded in her mind with her. Unless someone found them in the remote cabin and woke them up, their physical bodies would waste away from starvation.

"Control your fear."

The sharp sound of his voice snapped her to awareness of their dire situation. Automatically, she took a breath, calming her heartbeat.

"Look at me. Look only at me. Listen to the sound of my voice."

She did as he asked, and they ascended at a crawl. Inch by precious inch. Sweat beaded on Rolf's forehead. What tremendous control he must be exercising to move them forward. His eyes looked more black than blue. A vein stood out on his forehead. The grays grew sharper, bolder. Colors reached for her, first blues, then greens, then yellows. And then they landed on solid ground.

Rolf let out a groan and crushed her against his chest. At first, she thought her body was trembling uncontrollably before she realized the shaking was coming from Rolf. The buttons on his shirt pressed against her cheek. His body felt solid and warm.

She opened her eyes. He lay against the window of the cabin, cradling her in his arms like he'd never let go.

"You okay?"

He didn't answer, and when she pushed against his arms, they didn't budge. Her heart pounded furiously, and her lungs tightened. "Rolf, please, I can't breathe."

He moved slightly, enough for her to realize he was alive and could hear her. The shaking stopped, but he didn't say anything. And honestly, after the hell they'd endured, it was comforting to be held. *Heaven*.

Thirty minutes passed, or maybe it was an hour before his arms loosened, and she could pull far enough away to look at him. A cloud of darkness seemed to shroud his body. His eyes looked stark and empty, and that scared her worse than anything.

"I'm sorry, Rolf. It's never been this bad before. It happened so fast this time."

"You don't understand." His voice sounded gravelly.

"I do. I got lost in the colors, and you had to hack into my mind to save me. You created the barrier that stopped me from going into the woods. You found me and brought me back, even though you could have been trapped. I...thank you."

"The elk was an illusion, created for the sole purpose of attracting your attention. As soon as you opened yourself up, you were hit with dream energy. A double whammy. You didn't stand a chance. It's my fault. I should have thought of this."

Rolf groaned, and the sound was both mournful and angry. He held his thumb and pointer finger together until there was only a narrow pinprick of light between them. "You were this close to slipping from my grasp and being lost forever. If that would have happened, I..."

"You would have died. You shouldn't have gone in after me. It was too risky."

"This isn't about me." His eyes were so dark blue, they could swallow her whole. "This is about you. You can't use your talent again. Not until you get checked out. Not until we're sure you're okay. What happened tonight can never ever happen again."

The truth was a bolt of lightning, striking the weakest part of her. Oh God. "You think I should go to Corvey."

15

TRUTH

"It's your choice whether you go to Corvey or not. I won't make you do anything you don't want to do. But if you decide not to go, then you must promise not to use your talent like that again.

Fear carved an icy pathway through her veins. "What about Julia? If I don't track her, how will we ever find her?"

Rolf's gaze caught hers, stubbornness etched in the hard lines of his face. "We'll find another way."

"The thought of stepping into Corvey again gives me the creeps."

"You won't go alone. It won't be like when you were a child."

Rolf still held her in his lap, but now she felt the awkwardness of their position. And her brain was beginning to function again. She grabbed his arms. The lamplight flickered, and her heartbeat thundered in her ears. "Rolf, whoever created the illusion of the elk planned to kidnap me. They must have some way of bringing me to consciousness like you did."

"I don't think they intended to send you into a coma."

"You don't understand. They're probably outside now waiting for us to leave. They wouldn't expect you to hack into my mind and save me. They'd think you do the logical thing and rush me to a government hospital. That's when they planned to grab me and probably kill you."

Rolf held her hands. "It's okay. I took care of them."

"How?"

"When you first went under, everything seemed normal, but something was off about the elk's appearance, so I went outside to investigate. The animal disappeared when I approached, but there was someone there. They took off into the woods before I could get a good look at them. I found a crystal where the elk was standing."

She expelled the breath she'd been holding. What Rolf didn't say was he didn't follow whoever it was because he worried about her. She'd ruined their plan to find Julia and Percy with her lack of control.

Rolf tilted her face until their eyes met. "It's my fault, not yours. I knew you'd gotten lost in the colors before. I knew these kidnappers had the ability to create illusions using crystals. I should have understood what was happening and stayed with you. But I didn't realize until I went outside and found the crystal. By then, it was...almost too late."

His voice dropped, and she shivered, although she could swear the temperature in the room went up a notch. Tears filled her eyes, but she refused to let them fall. She was acting babyish. Rolf was probably growing tired of her.

He grimaced, and in one smooth motion, he lifted her in his arms and settled her on the couch, tucking an afghan around her. He sat next to her and pulled her into his arms, pressing her head next to his heart and stroking her hair. She could hear the steady thump of his heart. She must be worse off than she'd imagined, for him to hold her like this.

His voice rumbled under her ear. "Whoever this is knows too much about us. They have Julia. I suspect they interrogated her. They knew I had a place here. They knew about your talent."

She should let him go, but it felt so good to be held and stroked like she was his. Like they were a real couple and not just partners who'd survived a traumatic event. Like he truly cared about her. "They used crystals."

"Right. They created an illusion of the elk to lure you to use your talent to investigate the animal. Once you did, they were ready with a dream crystal."

"But how did you know what was happening with me? That I was lost in a dream?"

Rolf shifted his weight under her. "I'm not sure. Instinct maybe. What is it?"

She pushed herself from his chest. Rolf was only being kind by holding her. And she was a fool to believe his touch meant anything more. "I'm okay now. You can let me up."

His whole body stiffened. "I'd rather not."

"You don't have to play the gentleman."

"For an off-the-chart talent, you don't have a clue, do you?"

She studied his face and the normal green color surrounding his body. Her heartbeat kicked into overdrive. "What are you saying?"

The green color shifted and morphed into a royal purple —the color of passion. She managed a breath. The fierce look in his eyes was enough to have her coming apart in his arms.

His face descended until his lips were inches from hers. She could feel his breath on her face. Smell his sweat and piney aftershave. Automatically, she reached for him, her fingertips touching his cheek and the scrape of his five o'clock shadow. He kissed her palm, the heat sending shivers down her spine.

He groaned as if the sound was torn from some secret place inside him. "Geneva Erickson, I have wanted you for as long as I can remember. I have spent the past eight years doing whatever I had to do to keep you safe. But tonight, when a single breath or thought could have torn you from me... My God, I can't do this any longer. I can't protect you from me. I need you too damn much."

"But..."

"But nothing." His lips covered hers, warm and sensual and delicious, drowning out any protest. His tongue swept the roof of her mouth and her teeth. Energy raced along her nerve endings, tingling, burning, growing into a raging fire. She placed her hands around his neck and pulled him closer.

She kissed him with all the years of pent-up desire and frustration, reveling in the feel of his arms and inhaling his cool breath and the minty scent of him. White-hot power erupted from her hands and blasted toward the ceiling, nearly singeing the hair on the back of his head and causing her to pull back in alarm. He flinched, but she couldn't take the time to apologize. She pushed herself from his arms, gasping. "I'll hurt you."

She focused on the energy, drawing it from the ceiling to prevent the wood cross beams from bursting into flames. Out of control. My God, they had to stop, or she'd kill him.

He smiled, and the sight nearly stopped her heart. "Sweetheart, I'm not afraid of anything you can do. Ever."

"Rolf, this isn't a joke. You heard Peter. My talent is off the charts. Everyone's afraid of me. And now... Tonight..." A hot rush of tears flooded her eyes, distorting his features. "I'm too dangerous."

He smoothed each corner of her eyes with his fingertips, wiping the tears away. "I'm a selfish ass. We won't do this right now. You've been through enough today. We need to make sure you're okay. And we need to find Julia and Percy. This can wait."

"But I don't understand. You hate being near me."

"Never. I hated my loss of control around you. But I've never hated you. I acted that way to protect you."

"To protect me? From what?" All the hurt she'd felt over the past eight years came rushing to the surface. Colors danced in front of her eyes in frenzied circles, and she clenched her hands and fought for breath. "You were my best friend when we were kids, and suddenly we became teenagers, and you wanted nothing to do with me. On my eighteenth birthday, I finally dredged up enough courage to tell you how I felt, and you hurt my feelings so bad, I wouldn't come out of the house for a month. My brothers and dad wanted to kill you. And every time our paths have crossed since, you made it more than clear how you felt. You certainly didn't want to partner with me on this mission."

"I know, and I'm sorry for it. I said what I did to keep myself from taking what I shouldn't have. I thought I was strong enough to stay away. But the truth is I'm a selfish bastard. Tonight has shown me you could be snatched from me in an instant. And I need you too much to ever let that happen."

He didn't say he loved her. Only that he needed her. Still, after believing he hated her for far too long, the words sank into her heart and filled the scars he'd left there like a healing balm.

"Rest now." He moved her back against the pillows, tucking the afghan around her shoulders. "I'll get a fire going. We'll talk about this later."

He turned his back and opened up the grate on the stone fireplace. An array of colors flickered around him. On the surface, he seemed okay, but the colors in his aura gave her an intimate view of how he struggled to control his emotions. Rolf needed the break from the conversation as much as she did.

He stacked kindling and paper in the grate, lit a match, and threw it on the pile.

They'd find Julia and Percy, wherever they were being held, she vowed. She'd go to Corvey and figure out what she needed to do to get her talent under control. Then she'd show Rolf what he'd missed out on for all these years.

16

DISCOVERY

R olf crouched in front of the stone fireplace, lit a match, and tossed it onto the small pieces of kindling he'd crisscrossed on top of each other. Nights were chilly in Flagstaff, even in the middle of summer. Building a fire would not only keep the cabin warm but give him much-needed time to regain control of his emotions.

The kindling erupted into flames, reminding him of how he'd erupted earlier tonight, nearly destroying everything he'd worked so hard to master. He kept his back to Geneva, but he knew exactly where she'd positioned herself on the couch behind him. His mind sought hers, even as he fought against it. He wouldn't rush her. He could at least give her that. She needed time to understand and accept him for what he was before they established a portal. Once they linked their minds, there would be no going back.

He added another log to the fire and watched as the kindling sparked and flamed around it. The fire gave off heat, but none of it penetrated the ice around his heart. He'd nearly lost her tonight. When he'd seen the figure flee into the woods outside the cabin, he'd nearly given into the raging darkness inside him. Nearly allowed it to destroy his humanity. The only thing that had stopped him was the knowledge Geneva was inside the cabin alone and could be in grave danger.

He studied the flames and admitted what he'd denied for far too long. He had to link with Geneva to contain the dark inside him. There was no way around it. He wasn't strong enough to protect her from what he'd become. When he'd forced his way inside her mind, he hadn't thought he could call her back from her dream state. Yet somehow the dark in him tracked the last bit of her light and stopped it from disappearing altogether. He'd bound her to him and refused to let go. Then he called until she heard his voice and listened. If she hadn't...well, he'd hate to imagine what would have happened to both of them if she hadn't.

"Rolf, what is it?"

Her soft voice slid over his skin, warming it. He took a breath and turned. She leaned toward him, the blanket sliding from her shoulders. Silky blonde hair fell around her face, framing it. She smiled tentatively, but when he didn't smile back, it melted away.

"Have you changed your mind already then? Are you worried what happened tonight will happen again? I gave you my word. I'll go to Corvey. I won't try to trace Julia and Percy."

"That's not it."

"What then?"

He had to tell her. To describe his cursed gift and hope she'd not desert him. To make himself vulnerable as he'd never done before. To risk losing her and his sanity. His cell phone buzzed, and he pulled it from his pocket, glancing at the screen. "It's Peter. I should take this." A small reprieve.

She nodded, and he answered the call.

"You can call off the chase. We've found Percy and Julia."

A surge of relief tunneled through Rolf's veins, and some of the weight on his shoulders lifted. "Are they okay?"

"Yes, they were discovered wandering outside our Cleveland headquarters an hour ago, dazed but unharmed. They have no idea what happened to them while they've been gone. We're sending them to Corvey for evaluation."

"Any leads on their kidnappers?"

"Negative. They remember nothing. Their minds have been wiped."

"Their minds are reinforced, aren't they?"

"Yes, but even reinforced minds can be wiped clean. It's extremely rare, but I'm aware of at least two instances in my time with the CMU."

"What's the last thing they remember?"

"Boarding the plane in Cleveland. Whoever did this didn't leave them any chance of discovery, I'm afraid. They've suffered a trauma and should be evaluated at Corvey to make sure they'll make a full recovery. Speaking of which, how's Geneva?"

Rolf's gaze met Geneva's. "She's fine, but we had another little episode. She was hit with a dose of illusion energy, followed by dream energy, both activated from crystals I suspect were planted by Julia and Percy's kidnappers. It was not a pleasant experience. We'll go to Corvey. I'll make sure Julia's all right while I'm there."

"I'm not going to ask how your partner managed to escape harm. You can fill me in later with a full report. Get to Corvey. But be careful. Our kidnappers are still out there, and they want Geneva. Who knows what other crystals they have at their disposal."

"We're on our way." He ended the call.

"Julia and Percy are at Corvey?"

He nodded. "Yes."

"Thank God." Her pupils dilated, dwarfing the blue of her irises. The fire crackled and popped behind him as the energy in the room rose a notch. "So, it's time, then."

The fear surging through her body became his own. He came to her then, taking her into his arms. He could do this. Set aside his selfish desires. Tame the darkness for a few more weeks until she was well enough to know her own mind. Let her go if she chose to leave him.

The beast opened his mouth and gave a silent roar at the thought, but Rolf hushed it into silence. There would be time enough to tell her his secret after their visit to Corvey.

17

CORVEY INSTITUTION

Orange energy glistened outside the famed Corvey Institution, a testament real healing took place beyond its sand-colored doors. Geneva wrapped her arms around herself and fought a shiver as she stood in front of the building and eyed its unassuming doorway. The government-run psych facility was an important component of the CMU—it was where they brought drained talents and burned-out hackers after catastrophic missions or years of service. It was also where those who "went rogue" were sent for further evaluation.

Rolf pushed the door open, and she entered the wide, airy lobby by his side. Cool air greeted them. She looked around at the blue walls and vaulted ceiling and swallowed the sudden nauseous feeling in her throat. He linked his hand with hers, reminding her she wasn't alone. This time, she would not be held against her will. This time, she would be brave. This time, she had Rolf. A protective Rolf who seemed to like and care about her.

She sucked in air, eyeing several efficient-looking nurses who sat behind a long rectangular reception desk. The one closest to her, with auburn hair and a bright smile, looked up from her computer. "May I help you?"

Geneva tried for an answering smile. "Yes, I called earlier. My name is Geneva Erickson. I'm self-admitted. I've been having a...a slight issue with my talent and would like an evaluation."

The nurse eyed her with interest, before looking at the computer, her fingers tapping the keyboard. "Whoa. You're a class ten talent. What did you say your trouble was?"

Rolf stirred next to her. "She didn't. We'd like to talk to the doctor. We're also here to see my sister, Julia Jorgensen, and her partner, Percy Withers. They were admitted today."

The nurse went back to tapping keys. "Yes, your sister and her partner are on the fourth floor. That's also where you'll be staying while you're here." She nodded at Geneva. "Diane can show you to your room."

A young nurse with short dark hair, a clear complexion, and what appeared to be a ring tattoo on her middle finger appeared from out of nowhere. "Follow me." Her tone was brisk and clinical.

Geneva swallowed another shiver. She remembered this —remembered the silent hallways and countless rooms. Remembered promises the doctor who'd conducted her examination had made. Promises he hadn't kept. "Cooperate, and I'll let you talk to your father," or "Just one more test, and you can rest and enjoy a dish of ice cream." Never mind Geneva had lost her mother in a nightmare that would haunt her for the rest of her life. Eventually, her dad had been permitted to come and get her, but by then, the damage had been done.

"What is it?" Rolf entwined his fingers with hers and squeezed. Heat spread from their joined hands up her arm until it reached her heart, as they trailed the silent nurse.

She sucked in oxygen. She could do this. "A few uncomfortable memories, that's all."

He didn't look convinced, but she didn't need him worrying about her. He had enough to worry about locating Julia and Percy, making sure they were okay, and trying to find their kidnappers. "I'm fine."

She moved along, following the nurse down a long hallway until they stopped at a bank of elevators that opened as they approached. Diane waited for them to enter, following behind. The elevator moved smoothly between floors until it stopped on the fourth floor. The doors opened, and they faced rose-colored walls. Except the rose wasn't paint; it was the color of the energy floating up and down the corridor.

Rolf squeezed her hand. "What do you sense?"

Madness. "There are some seriously ill patients in this section of Corvey."

Nurse Diane stopped in front of an open room and gestured them to go inside. "Your sister is in here. I'll check with the doctor about your examination and be right back."

The nurse left, and they entered the room to find Julia propped against pillows on her bed, reading a magazine. Her long dark hair looked just as luxurious as always, but the normally serene expression on her perfectly oval face erupted in excitement the moment she saw them.

"Oh my God. Finally, someone I know." She set the magazine aside and held out her hands to Rolf, who let go of Geneva long enough to give his sister a quick hug.

"Are you okay?" Rolf studied his sister. "We've been worried about you."

"I'm totally fine. Passed all the tests with flying colors. I told Peter as much. Except for missing three days, I feel great."

He moved aside so Geneva could hug her friend. "You don't remember anything?" Geneva asked.

"I wish I did. They must have tampered with my mind to get me to cooperate, but the doctors here can find no evidence of implanted thoughts."

"What about Percy?"

"Same thing. He's next door if you want to talk to him. Think you guys can get us out of here today?"

Rolf shook his head. "Unlikely."

"Why not? If this is your idea of punishment because I started an investigation without you, I'm sorry. I won't do it again. Believe me when I say I never want to see another crystal for as long as I live."

Geneva patted her hand. "It's not you. It's me. Remember how I told you I got lost a few times over the past couple of years when trying to trace people's energy?"

"Yes, what about it?"

Geneva nodded. "It's happened twice more—both times in Arizona when I was looking for you and Percy. The second time I nearly wound up in a coma. I want to get checked out before I use my talent again."

"But I thought you completed testing last month and passed?"

"Yeah, but Peter told me I've gotten stronger. I need to know how much stronger. I need to know if I can control whatever's happening to me. I don't want to hurt anyone."

"Of course."

The nurse from earlier entered the room and looked at Geneva. "I hate to interrupt, but if you're ready, the doctor is available to see you now. He's just down the hall. Come with me."

Geneva stood and wiped her hands on her jeans.

"I'll go with her," Rolf said, coming up next to Geneva. Waves of calming blue color surrounded her.

"I'm sorry, but that's not permitted," the nurse said, her expression severe. "Having another talent in the room can interfere with our equipment."

"Tough," Rolf said, staring down the nurse. "I want to be with her."

The nurse frowned and glanced at Geneva. "We can't guarantee accurate test results if your partner is in the room."

Geneva looked at Rolf. She wouldn't let irrational fear take over. She could do this. "I want accurate results. I need to know I won't accidentally hurt you or anyone else. Please. Stay here and talk to Julia and Percy. See what you can find out."

Rolf nodded slowly, reluctance carved in the hard lines on his face. He turned to the nurse. "How long will it take?"

"A few hours at the most. I can let you know when she's finished."

"Come and get me if there's the smallest issue."

"Absolutely, I will." She turned to Geneva. "Follow me."

Geneva gave Rolf and Julia one last glance before trailing after the nurse, her heartbeat drumming in her ears. She passed two patients whose auras alternated bright pink and dark gray—a deadly combination. Psychopaths. She held her breath, carefully avoiding any contact. She didn't need crazy tarnishing her energy before the examination.

The nurse stopped in front of a beige door and turned the handle, gesturing for Geneva to enter. The room was large, with windows covered by white shades and pale green walls. There was a long counter that held a few medical supplies next to a sink, but other than that, the room looked quite homey. In the center of the room, a brown leather recliner was positioned next to a sleek coffee table, which held a fern and several magazines. A small table with two chairs sat in the corner. The nurse gestured Geneva to one of the chairs. It all seemed quite...normal. If anything could be called normal in her world.

"Make yourself comfortable. The doctor won't be long."

Geneva had only just calmed her nerves when the nurse returned with a small tray and set it on the coffee table. "Sorry, I nearly forgot. You need to take 500 milligrams of Amphersan before the tests can be administered."

"What is it?"

"Nothing to be afraid of. It's a mild depressant designed to relax your muscles and lower your inhibitions. It will allow you to fully open your talent so we can gauge the strength of your ability. Make sense?"

"Yes."

"Okay. It will take about thirty minutes for the medicine to take effect, and we can begin the tests. The doctor will be in shortly."

The nurse left the room, and Geneva took the drug and waited. She could tell as the drug began to work because her limbs felt heavy. Oranges and pinks shifted and blended in the corner of the room until she could hardly tell them apart. Or why it mattered. She closed her eyes. When she opened them, a thin man in a dark suit towered over her. For a moment, she was five years old, fighting the boogeyman.

"Hello, Geneva," the figure rumbled, his oily voice causing the hair on the back of her neck to rise.

She rubbed her eyes, her stomach twisting as if it tried to get loose—far away from the man in front of her. The man who'd held her captive for months and made her relive her mother's death until she'd broken down and bawled like the baby she was. The man with whom she pleaded but who wouldn't let her go home to her family. "Dr. Grimshaw?"

"Yes, my dear." The doctor laid a possessive hand on her shoulder.

Geneva shrank from Dr. Grimshaw's long, bony fingers, which curled against her. Her stomach twisted until she thought she'd puke. Memories flooded her mind. Dr. Grimshaw forcing her to use her talent until she'd passed out. Over and over and over again. Dr. Grimshaw, who thought it great fun to experiment on her when she was young and defenseless and couldn't say no.

"So happy you remember me. It's been a long time since we last met."

She focused on his voice. He sounded thoughtful, but Geneva knew he wasn't searching his memory banks. No, the turquoise color issuing from his mouth indicated the man knew how long it had been.

"Twenty-one years, hasn't it? A little taller, but you haven't changed much."

She blinked. "Why are you here?" The words seemed to come from a long way off. Shock probably. She swallowed the bile in her throat.

"I'm here to administer your tests, of course. The doctors here thought I would be the best choice given our history." Dark gray spewed from his lips. *Lies.* The trouble with her type of talent, she had no way of knowing if the entire statement was a lie or a portion. Why? What was Grimshaw hiding? He obviously didn't care if she knew it was a lie or not.

A throbbing began at the base of her skull. Her thoughts came slowly, but every cell in her body screamed at her to tell Grimshaw where to go. She gasped for air but only drew a shallow breath. Geneva held her hands together and rubbed, hoping to increase the circulation.

"This will go easier for you if you cooperate."

Dr. Grimshaw's voice wavered in and out. Each time he spoke, Geneva couldn't stop listening, like his words held the secrets of the universe. They didn't, of course.

Somehow, she found herself lying in the brown leather recliner. She did her best to relax her body, ignoring the shimmering energy waves around her. Grimshaw sat opposite her, crossing his long legs. He held a shiny clipboard and a pencil.

"Think back to the moment you saw Julia being threatened at the convention center in Phoenix," Grimshaw said.

Her mind did Grimshaw's bidding, recalling Percy's face as he'd raised the giant stiletto in the air. Power rushed through her system, pooling at the base of her skull. She tried to sit up but couldn't move. She lay there, allowing the energy particles to magnify as if she had no will or control over them. Sweat formed on her face and the back of her neck. She licked dry lips that tasted salty.

"I know how you're feeling." Grimshaw got up and crossed to her recliner, bending over her, his breath hot on her face and smelling of coffee and day-old bread. "You don't need to work so hard, my dear. We're all friends here, aren't we? I won't allow you to harm anyone. You're safe. Aim for the crystals. They'll draw your energy."

Geneva's eyes moved to the strange crystals resting on the table next to her. She had avoided looking at them ever since Dr. Grimshaw pulled a white bundle from one of the cabinets and opened it on the counter. Now she found herself drawn to them. One of them—the one on the right —was different, yellower than the others, its composition thicker.

Dr. Grimshaw said they needed to talk. He wanted to help her. She knew better than to believe him, but whatever they'd given her was having a strange effect. It seemed to give Dr. Grimshaw control of her mind. She'd almost done his bidding. What was wrong with her?

"You always were a stubborn patient." Grimshaw eyed her, frustration evident on his bony face. "Feisty. You never liked to listen." He pulled out a long, thin needle. "I'm confident I can help you relax."

Fear slowed her thoughts. She watched the doctor squeeze the air out of the syringe as if she had an out-of-body experience. Waves of roiling coral energy covered him. *Determination.* She knew the color well, having seen it surrounding her own face in the mirror on occasion. Grimshaw was determined to make her lose control. She had to stop him. *Rolf,* she called. *Silly.* Rolf could not hear her. He was too far away to pick up her cry. She was on her own.

She sucked in air, drawing more of the vibrating molecules inside.

"Now, now." Grimshaw patted her arm like she was a small child. "This will pinch a little, and then you'll be able to relax. I can complete the testing, and perhaps, if you cooperate, you can be released to your family. Don't you want to go home again?"

Yes, she did want to go home again. But not like this. "Don't touch me, asshole."

Her words did nothing to quell Grimshaw, who pulled at her arm. *Stop.* She shouted the words, but they were in her mind. Her body lay helpless. The doctor raised her arm in the air and tied a band around her biceps. He poked one long finger at her vein.

Rage hit her lungs with an icy jolt. Energy particles

collected in thick, heavy clouds, taunting her, begging for release. Did Grimshaw comprehend the danger? The urge to draw the particles to her was immense. If only she trusted herself not to aim and fire, killing the doctor in the process.

"Good thing you're fair-skinned. Much easier to find your veins," Grimshaw grunted, poking the needle into her skin. The sharp sting sent a wave of fear through her.

Rolf, I need you. Geneva screamed inside her head. A waste of precious time. Rolf couldn't hear her. Neither could Grimshaw.

Dark energy shimmered in a corner of the room. Geneva tossed and turned on the leather recliner, a thousand fire ants biting into her skin, injecting their poison. What was happening? What had Grimshaw done?

"Quit fighting. It hurts because you're resisting. Listen to my voice. That's it."

Despite herself, she found herself listening to Grimshaw. By the time the first fireball rolled from her palms and entered the crystal, she couldn't remember why she fought to hang onto it.

She watched as though it was happening to someone else. The hardened crystal seemed to suck the raw waves into it, expanding and contracting in front of Grimshaw's sunken eyes, bulging from their sockets. He dropped the needle he'd been holding and raced toward the door, flinging it open and dashing through. What was the matter with the man? He'd gotten what he wanted, hadn't he?

All the crystals but one shattered into a thousand slivers, and the energy waves came rushing back to their source, a tsunami of particles demanding entrance. Geneva gasped at the punch to her gut, her body jerking left, then right, reabsorbing the molecules.

18

DARK ENERGY

An electric charge raced down Rolf's spine. *"Geneva? What's wrong?"*

A small shot of dark energy rushed from his fingertips before he could stop it, melting the portion of the chair he was sitting on into nothingness. *Shit.* He sucked in air and wrapped his heated palms together, jerking the dark power inward. *What the hell?* Lucky for him, Julia and Percy were in a heated conversation and didn't notice the damaged seat cushion.

Another jolt of electricity snapped down his spinal cord. He stood and dashed toward the doorway.

"Where's the fire?" Percy asked.

"Are you okay?" Julia called after him.

"It's Geneva. Something's wrong with her."

"Wait. I'm coming with you."

Another electrical charge shot through Rolf's skull, urging him onward. *Faster, faster, faster.* The dark beast raged for its freedom, but Rolf drew on his training to bind it. He couldn't lose control. Not now. Not when Geneva needed him.

"What's wrong with her?" Julia huffed behind him. He could hear the pounding of her feet and her breathlessness.

Fire burned a path in his chest. Pain lanced his lungs. He yelled over his shoulder, but he didn't slow down. He couldn't. "She's hurt. In agony."

Two terrifying minutes passed while Rolf zipped through the corridor, praying no staff tried to stop him in his mental state, drawing on his dark talent to dictate his path. Beads of sweat formed and dripped into his eyes, slick and stinging. He swiped a hand across his face and fought for control. He couldn't lose Geneva. Not now. Just a few minutes more, and he'd be by her side.

Rolf spotted the open door up ahead. *Sixty seconds, ten.* He burst through the doorway, his eyes searching and finding Geneva's shape lying on a recliner in what looked to be an examination room. She looked small and fragile. She looked dead. But Rolf knew she wasn't. The dark energy inside him strained toward her light. He didn't take his gaze from her, heading straight to her side.

Julia followed behind him in her blue hospital gown, with Percy a few steps behind her.

"What's happened to her?"

"I'm not sure. Don't..."

Julia reached for Geneva's hand before Rolf could stop her and flinched, dropping it. "My God. It's like putting my fingers in an electrical socket. She's overloaded. There's gobs of energy around her. Almost...almost like she attacked herself."

Rolf frowned. "That's impossible."

"Not so impossible."

Rolf looked toward the door at the older gentlemen who entered. Her doctor, he presumed.

"The patient is unstable. She nearly killed me just now. I

was forced to give her a shot to calm her. Unfortunately, there's no way to divert the energy she's harnessed. It's returning to its source. I had to run for my life. We'll need to wait until the energy dissipates, or she wakes and dispels it."

"No." Rolf forced the words through clenched teeth. He would deal with the so-called doctor later. "She won't make it. Listen to me, all of you. We need to channel the energy surrounding her to another source."

Julia's voice sounded breathless. "But, Rolf, that's impossible. We'd need a stronger energy source, and we all know there's no one stronger than Geneva."

"Yes, there is."

A pregnant silence greeted his statement.

"What do you mean?" The doctor voiced the question, his tone thoughtful and clinical.

He ignored the question, his mind intent on one goal: bringing Geneva to consciousness. He grasped her hands.

Julia gasped. "Be careful. She's charged, remember?"

He didn't respond. He would not let Geneva die. Even if he revealed the one secret he'd swore he'd always keep. Even if they locked him up forever. Even if they destroyed him.

"Julia, you'll need to work to absorb as much energy as you can. Percy, Doctor, stay back if you know what's good for you."

The doctor scuttled to the doorway, and Percy followed him, but neither left the room. Rolf caught sight of Julia, her eyes wide and frightened. Her puzzled gaze paused on the wound on his forehead. She sensed something wrong with him, but by the look on her face, couldn't imagine what it could be. She would learn soon enough. They all would.

He ignored them, his mind settling on Geneva's and the large amounts of dark energy encasing her. He issued a mental command. Toxic energy blasted forth from Geneva's chest, a black cloud hovering over him.

He didn't know how long he'd stayed there, absorbing the dark energy into himself and diverting the excess harmless energy to Julia. *One minute? Ten?*

Eventually, he'd siphoned enough energy from Geneva to stabilize her. The moment she was safe, Rolf blocked the flow, cutting the energy stream. Julia did the same.

He remained, head bowed over Geneva, his breath uneven. What had it cost him to absorb and channel dark energy? Another piece of his soul? Another step closer to madness? He moved an unsteady hand toward Geneva, then dropped it to his side. If he touched her, he'd transfer the lethal waves back to her.

He flicked a glance Julia's way. She remained still, hesitant, her large brown eyes reflecting surprise, fear, awe. Whatever she read in his caused her to swallow and look away.

He cleared his throat. "Get moving. Try and reach her. Bring her to consciousness. But be prepared. She's going to have one hell of a nasty headache."

Julia nodded, and Rolf straightened, turning toward the doctor, who had re-entered the room to roll what looked like diamonds in a white towel. Rolf clenched his jaw but kept his demeanor a cold mask. "I want answers, and I want them now."

"Of course." The doctor smiled, all cool pleasantness. He pointed his long bony free hand toward the door; the other hand held the towel. "Follow me."

Rolf moved to Percy, who stood frozen in place, a stunned expression carved on his face. "You and I will talk later. You'd better have a damn good reason for getting involved in this mess."

He didn't wait for a response but flicked a final glance at Julia, whose hands covered Geneva's pale ones. Then he strode after the doctor, who headed to God knows where.

The danger had passed, hadn't it? Geneva would live. He'd not let the dark power control him. So why did he keep revisiting Geneva's lifeless body and the horrified expressions on the others' faces. All but the doctor's. He'd not been shocked or afraid like the others. No, on the contrary, he appeared almost gleeful.

19

DARK MASTER

He shouldn't have left her. Rolf trailed the doctor, guilt gnawing his insides, threatening his self-control. He sucked in a shallow breath, a desperate attempt to manage his raging temper.

Did the doctor have any idea how close he came to being covered in blackness? Every speck of kinetic energy blotted out of existence? If he did, he gave no indication. *Geneva must survive.* Her light kept the darkness at bay.

"Right this way." The doctor motioned to an empty examination room, starker than the one they'd left.

Rolf strode inside, his eyes sweeping the four corners, taking in the equipment and examination table with straps used to subdue the rowdier patients, he supposed. Rolf smiled, but it contained no warmth. Straps couldn't conquer the dark energy threatening to consume him. He turned to the doctor. "Who are you, and what did you do to her?"

The doctor blinked, his eyes wide. "My name is Dr. Grimshaw. I assure you, I did nothing I haven't done to hundreds of patients. I gave her a shot of a drug we use to calm patients when they grow anxious. She was agitated, worried about her growing abilities and the examination. The drug helped to calm her."

"What was in it?"

"It's a barbiturate. Suffice it to say, she did not handle the drug well. It caused her to lose control."

Rolf ran a hand through his hair, struggling to absorb what Dr. Grimshaw told him. "She had an allergic reaction?"

"Correct. But the fact she had such a reaction is a concern. She appears to have little control of her energy. I need to verify she's not a threat to society. Have a seat."

Rolf eyed the chair but made no move toward it. "She's not a threat."

"You have proof?"

"I've been working with her for the past several days, and the only threat she's been is to herself."

Dr. Grimshaw held his clipboard in front of him and set the towel on the table. "Geneva Erickson will stay here until we can figure out what is happening to her. If I were to release her and she were to cause an innocent person to be injured..."

Grimshaw let the thought dangle, allowing Rolf to complete the sentence in his mind. *The doctor would be at fault.*

"What's in the towel you rolled up?"

"Please, won't you take a seat?" Dr. Grimshaw gestured to a hard, metal chair, his voice modulated. "We can talk about this sensibly, can't we?"

Rolf sighed, sifting a hand through his hair again. The dark energy took its usual toll. No hacker could channel the amount of energy he'd manipulated and remain on his feet. He would crash and burn. He checked his watch. He had maybe five minutes to wrest the truth from Grimshaw, then he'd be useless for a couple of hours. He sat where Grimshaw indicated and fought to keep his eyes open.

"That was a tremendous amount of energy you expended. Who taught you to manipulate dark energy?"

Rolf grimaced, his thoughts shifting to Nonna as he'd last seen her at her house two weeks ago, making oatmeal cookies, her long, dark hair in its customary bun. He squelched the image. He shouldn't give Grimshaw any more information than necessary. "No one. I asked you, what's in the towel?"

"Oh, come now, Mr. Jorgensen. No one learns to manipulate that quantity of dark energy without some training. We both know it's a specialized skill that's rare among hackers. Who trained you?"

Rolf struggled to focus on the question. How had the doctor known his name? The room spun, and his hands automatically went to his head. He blinked and strained to keep his eyes open. *Too late. No more time.* Grimshaw said something. His mouth moved, but Rolf heard no sound. Yet, the words Grimshaw spoke rang in Rolf's head.

"Pleasant dreams, Mr. Jorgensen."

A sting of a needle pierced his arm, cutting through the fog around his brain. Rolf's eyes closed on the sight of Grimshaw grinning from ear to ear.

GENEVA CAME to with a jerk and placed a hand on her forehead, as if she could prevent it from splitting in two. She squinted at the cool violet shade next to her. *Julia.* "What... what happened?" Her voice croaked.

"Thank God, you're awake. You were out for hours."

She looked around her room at the Corvey Institution. "How did I get in here?"

"You don't remember?" Julia drew closer, her face pale.

"No, last I remember I was in Dr. Grimshaw's examination room. What happened to me?" Geneva lifted the blanket and let it drop.

"Don't try to get up. Take it slow."

Geneva ignored the warning, propping herself on her elbows. Pain radiated from her head to her toes in payment for the sudden movement. She lay back and took shallow breaths until the throbbing subsided.

"Here, let me help." Julia placed an arm behind Geneva's shoulders and lifted her, arranging the pillow behind her back. Dull brushstrokes of red color bled through the violet in her aura, relaying her worry and something more. Something closer to fear. "Drink this."

"Thanks." Geneva took the cup of water Julia handed her and drained it. "Where is he?"

"Dr. Grimshaw?" Julia returned the empty cup to a nearby table. "I'm not sure. I haven't seen him since he left the examination room you were in hours ago."

"No, not Grimshaw. Rolf.

Julia frowned and tucked her hands behind her back as if she didn't know what to do with them. She cocked her head to the side. "He's with Dr. Grimshaw."

Geneva rubbed her eyes, blocking out the colors gathering in front of her. "What happened to me?" She blinked at Julia. The red color strengthened, overcoming the violet.

Julia approached, her eyes narrowed in concern. "Rolf—he saved you. But he was steaming mad Dr. Grimshaw left you alone. They went off somewhere to talk and have been holed up together ever since. While you were out, Percy and

I were released from care. Once we knew you would recover, the nurses brought you to this room so you'd be more comfortable, and I've been with you ever since." She placed a hand on Geneva's forehead. "You're still warm, but much better than earlier. How are you feeling?"

"I'm okay." Geneva pulled the blanket off her overheated body. "I need to find Rolf." She made no move, however, to slip out of bed. Whatever had happened had almost fried her. She'd take her time getting up. She glanced at Julia, who clutched her hands in front of her. "Julia, you need to tell me what happened—why are you so frightened?"

"Do you remember being with Dr. Grimshaw—losing control?" Julia deflected with a question of her own.

Geneva ran a hand through her hair and tugged, as if it could help her remember. She'd been talking to Grimshaw —he'd wanted her to do something—something she shouldn't. He'd given her a shot. Some drug. Whatever it was had unlocked her full power. *Oh God.* She groaned, covering her face with her hands. *What have I done?*

Energy rushed toward her from the four corners of the room. She drew in deep breaths and met the waves with mental imagery. She imagined herself a rock, steady and unchangeable. Waves of energy crashed into the rock but couldn't penetrate its hard surface. Her pulse softened, slowed. She removed her hands from her face. "Grimshaw gave me some sort of shot. It must have erased my memories. I called for Rolf, and he...he—Julia, I'm worried. For Rolf." A dark, depressing heaviness covered her. "Something's wrong—I think Rolf is gone from here. We need to find him. Now."

She took a deep breath and pushed herself up, swinging her legs over the side of the bed. The room spun, coming in and out of her vision like she looked through a bad set of binoculars. She lowered her head and closed her eyes. "I may need a minute."

"I'll go look for him. You stay here and rest."

"No. I can't. Not if Rolf's in trouble."

Julia placed a cool hand on the back of Geneva's neck, soothing her aching head.

Geneva opened her eyes and breathed deep. "Tell me about the crystals. Do you know where they come from?"

"I'm not certain. I'm not even sure any more exist." Julia got up, turned on the light, and fetched Geneva's clothes from the previous day. "You'll feel better once you get out of that hospital gown."

Geneva held out a hand for her clothes, but Julia ignored it. Instead, she crouched in front of her and held the shorts out so Geneva could slide into them, first one leg and then the other.

Geneva's head thumped with every movement. God, she hated the recovery period that followed overuse of her talent. "More crystals exist, all right. David had one. I never did learn where he got it."

"Where is it now? Here let me help you." Julia slipped Geneva's T-shirt over her head.

"He hung on to it, I suppose. Once it served its purpose, it could no longer be used. It didn't look like anything special—a red, heart-shaped piece of glass. At the time, I thought him crazy. But it worked. He stored her memories, and later, when her brain was pretty much wiped, he gave them back to her. He saved her life. What I want to know is how?"

"I'm not sure." Violet energy sparked with gray.

Geneva stilled. "Don't keep secrets. Not from me."

Julia sighed and handed Geneva her sandals. "You and your psychic antennae. I'm not sure of anything anymore."

She twisted so her back was facing Geneva, the play of violet and gray in her aura at odds with her statement. Her aura shifted, becoming a solid hue once again. Geneva waited for the truth to emerge. Her friend was not good at secrets.

Julia turned, two red spots high on her cheeks. "I've been having dreams again. You know how it is."

Geneva schooled her features. "About my mother. I know. Peter mentioned it when he sent us to find you. That's why you didn't tell me what you were doing. You didn't want to upset me if your dream turned out to be a false lead."

Julia twisted her hands. "That's right. A man in my dream told me there were more crystals in Arizona. That if I searched for them, I might find your mother's killer. And then Percy got a tip the missing crystals were at the gem show. The last thing I remember, we were on our way to the airport. I'm sorry you and Rolf had to come after us."

Geneva didn't move. Many in their world thought dream talents were a teensy bit crazy. She knew better than to give a reaction that might be misinterpreted. Not if she wanted to learn what had Julia so alarmed. "What about the man in your dream?"

"He's a fantasy; he's not real. He calls himself Caleb. He comes into my dreams whenever I or someone I love is in danger."

"And?"

"He warned me you were in grave danger. Said there were more crystals that could be used in ways not intended. I didn't know whether to believe him, but he's been right before. I was worried for you. He told me that Percy was onto something. I thought if I worked with Percy to find the other crystals, it might lead me to your mother's killer. Instead, the bad guys found us, stored our talent in crystals, and then wiped our minds so we have no memory of them. At least that's what I'm told happened."

Geneva stood. The room no longer spun. "Is that what Rolf used to save me? A crystal?"

Julia opened her mouth, her aura reflecting more gray than violet. "I don't know how he did it."

Lies again. What was going on? Julia never lied to her. Unless she protected someone. Someone she loved.

Geneva moved forward. "I know you love your brother. But I can't help him unless you tell me the truth. What did Rolf do to save me?"

"He— Oh God." Julia turned, covering her face with her hands. Her dark hair spread over them, as if they, too, could conceal the truth. Her muffled voice had Geneva straining to hear. "He channeled it, the dark energy."

Geneva stilled. *Impossible.* She couldn't have heard correctly.

Julia raised her head, her eyes pooling and glistening with unshed tears. "I never suspected. He never let on."

Geneva filled her lungs and tried to move, but her legs were bolted to the floor. "You must be mistaken."

"No, I'm not. I'm still having trouble believing it myself. But I saw what he did. He pulled the dark waves out of you. He took them inside himself."

Geneva's legs half-collapsed under her, and she fell to the bed, her heart stopping and stuttering. She fisted her hands in the blanket. My God, how had she not known? "He never told me."

Pain bubbled up from the empty shell that was her heart, piercing her lungs. The blood in her veins went from hot to cold in an instant, freezing what remained of her insides.

"I'm as floored as you." Julia sat next to her and curled an arm around her shoulder. "I'm sorry, Geneva."

She should have known. There had been clues if she'd only paid more attention. The secret he refused to tell her in the dream she'd been thrown into at his cabin in Flagstaff. How women seemed to fall over themselves to be near him. How he tempted her at every turn. How he never feared her power like the others. The flashes of dark light she sometimes thought she saw around him.

She tightened her fingers around the bedding as if it could keep her insides from coming apart. Keep the frozen pieces from shattering into a million tiny slivers.

Every story she'd heard, every manual she'd read said dark masters were dangerous. There was always the risk the dark energy would consume the master, forcing death and destruction on anyone in their path. No woman with any sense would fall for a dark master.

Legend had it they could not love.

Her heartbeat raced, loosening her hard-fought control. A rainbow of colors swirled in front of her. A single thought replayed in her mind. They cannot love. They cannot love. They cannot love.

I love him.

The truth exploded in her head like a grenade. A glass on a nearby table popped and shattered. A rumbling shook the air. She sucked in a shallow breath. Hadn't she always loved him?

My God, she should have known. She understood so much now. Why he pushed her away from him. Why he always seemed so remote.

Julia grabbed her hand and squeezed. "Take it easy now. Deep breaths. We'll get through this."

Geneva willed her mind to a blank, which was kind of like putting a small, wet blanket over a forest fire. Her feelings could never be returned. Rolf could not love another. Energy shimmered in the air, begging for release.

"Are you linked?"

She shook her head, careful to avoid sudden movement. A dangerous amount of energy danced before her eyes. "No."

"How is it you each seem to know when the other is hurt, then?"

Breathe. One, two, three. Breathe. "I don't know."

"Geneva, Rolf isn't a monster. He cares for you. I know he does. He saved your life."

One, two, three. Breathe. "Yes."

"And you have feelings for him, too, don't you?"

Geneva unraveled the first energy ball until it dissolved. "Yes."

Julia wrapped an arm around her. "I dreamed of a wedding. Yours and Rolf's. Nonna always said your lives are intertwined."

Geneva removed herself from Julia's embrace. She stood, eliminating the remaining ball of energy in front of her with a careless flick of her fingers. Rolf could never love her. No wedding dream or odd remark from Nonna could change that fact. "He must be here somewhere. We have to find him."

Julia tugged on her arm. "Geneva, what are you thinking? You can't chase after Rolf. You nearly died today. You need to rest. I'll go."

"No way will I lie here when Rolf's in trouble. Stand back."

She pulled energy from the room and focused on the door lock. A sharp crack sounded. Geneva twisted the knob, and the door opened. She could lose her job and be permanently incarcerated for this, but it didn't matter. Rolf was in trouble. She wouldn't stay in this room while he was in danger.

She didn't wait to see if Julia followed.

20

KIDNAPPED

The biting pain woke him. Rolf gasped, trying to remember how he got here. He lay on a cot—he could feel the thin mattress under him and the bedding with his fingers. He tried to move, but his wrists and ankles were bound with some sort of canvas strap. This was not happening.

Where am I? A familiar darkness swirled inside him, threatening his control. He strained to see in the dark room, but whatever it was holding him prevented movements left or right. *What the hell?* Some small noise alerted him to another's presence. "Who's there?" His raspy voice sounded strange to his own ears. Did he smoke? He couldn't recall.

"Don't try to move," a woman's voice called out. "It will only hurt more."

"Who are you?" His eyes swept the space in front of him but could not make out a shape.

"I'm not sure. They never told me." The voice moved closer.

"They never—you don't have a name?"

"No. I thought maybe I had one, but I can't remember. Do you know your name?"

"Of course, I'm—" Stinging pain lanced his forehead, causing him to close his eyes and clench his fists. *I don't remember. I don't remember my own name.* He had one. That much he was certain. What was it?

Cool hands touched his forehead. "Don't try to remember. It's easier. Less painful."

He opened his eyes. "Why is it so dark? Why can't I see you?"

"The darkness deadens our abilities. When they need them, they're stronger."

"Deadens our..." That was it. The strange ripple inside him. The constant battle he fought to not let the dark energy consume him. This, at least, was familiar. He could not let the darkness out, or it would...what would it do? He gasped. Once again, pain sliced into his skull.

"Try and rest. After the exercise tomorrow, I shouldn't be exhausted. I might be able to take the pain away for a spell in exchange for conversation. It's been a long time since I've had anyone to talk to."

"You can take the pain away?" He latched onto her words.

"Yes, for a little while."

"Do you have anything to loosen these straps? My hands are tied."

"Try to stay still. And don't think. It's the thinking that makes the pain worse. They don't want you to remember."

Not remember? What didn't they want him to remember? And who were they? He didn't recall speaking, but he voiced his thoughts aloud because the woman answered like he had.

"The government, of course." The woman felt for his

hands, caressing the straps that bit into his skin. "What's your talent? You must be dangerous for them to bind you like this."

My talent? Dark energy rose in the pit of his belly, a lethal gas seeking escape. He gritted his teeth, forcing the energy inward. When he didn't speak, the woman continued. Her cool voice washed over him, calming the seething waves.

"You should sleep while you can. You'll need to conserve your strength to meet their demands."

"What do you mean? What do they want from us?"

"Our talent. They want our talent. They can't take all of it, though. If they did, they'd kill us."

The woman laughed, a high tinkling laugh. *Is she crazy?* Being in this blackness day in and day out would drive anyone crazy. He cleared his throat. "How long have you been in here?"

"Hmm, I don't know. A while, I think."

"How are you able to move around in the dark so easily?"

"I've memorized the room."

The cot shifted with her weight as she sat next to him. The feather-light touch of her fingers stroked his hair.

"Why aren't your hands bound?"

"They used to be. When they first brought me here. I tried to escape and they hurt me. They took the straps off."

"You never tried to escape again?"

"No." The woman's voice sounded low and stiff, as if she feared her kidnappers would leap out from the darkness and torture her for speaking. "I don't try to escape. I don't like to remember anymore. They killed my brother. He went mad."

He stiffened. "Your brother...? Did they torture him?"

She sighed and stood again, as if his words disturbed her. Her voice moved away from him. "I don't know. That's all I ever remembered. Trying to remember anything more is painful. I'd prefer to forget."

"Where are you going?" Irrational fear slammed into his gut, disturbing the dark energy. "Don't go, please."

"They're coming. It's time."

Panic hit him with the force of a sledgehammer. Adrenaline flooded his system. He had to get out of here. The hair on his arms rose. Dark energy moved in his belly. A door opened, followed by a blinding light. He closed his eyes then reopened them, squinting. A woman stood over his bedside. Her golden hair and heart-shaped face struck a familiar chord. Who was she?

"Hello, Rolf." The woman's lips curved into a dazzling Marilyn Monroe smile. "Don't tell me you don't remember me."

Rolf! Yes, that was his name. He blinked at the vision in front of him. How did she know it?

"Oh, come now, Rolf. Shall I jog your memory?"

A knifepoint of pain shot into his temples, forcing his eyes closed. *Don't try to remember. It's easier.* The earlier woman's words echoed in his head.

Warm breath landed on his cheek. Firm lips touched his. A memory struck with blinding clarity. *Cynthia Torra?* He turned his face away and gasped, clenching his fists, unable to deaden the jackhammer pounding into his brain. He was dreaming. Or was he mad?

When he raised his head, she smiled, her expression triumphant. "I knew the kiss would do it."

GENEVA KEPT a brisk pace through the corridors of the vast institute, searching every room she passed for Rolf. Soft footsteps trailed hers. *Julia.*

Fear was her companion, driving her forward with each step. By the time she found Dr. Grimshaw, the energy around her body had reached alarming levels.

Grimshaw was in the far west wing. She suspected it housed severe cases based on the ugly combination of sienna and bright pink streaming from the walls. He'd probably been visiting a patient, because he held a clipboard in his hands.

"Where is he?" She didn't waste time on pleasantries.

Grimshaw didn't pretend to not know who she meant, although she could tell by his aura he wanted to. "Good to see you've recovered from your little episode. If you're speaking of your partner, he's not here."

"Where did you send him?" Pencils rattled in a canister on a desk nearby.

"Calm yourself, my dear. Must I remind you, you're breaking CMU rules leaving your room and being here right now? I didn't send him anywhere. Government officials came. He's out of my league. I don't manage the dark ones."

"Rolf isn't a threat." Energy vibrated in the air around her. She waved her hands in a futile attempt to dispel it. "He's not dangerous. He used dark energy to save me. He would never have done it otherwise. Where have they taken him?"

Grimshaw's fish eyes watched her, blinking rapidly. Julia placed a firm hand on her arm and squeezed, drawing Geneva to her side, communicating a silent message. She must stay calm. If she didn't, Dr. Grimshaw could label her a threat and lock her away forever. Geneva forced air into her lungs, scattering the seething energy surrounding her.

"I don't know." Grimshaw pursed his lips and scribbled something on the clipboard. "They wouldn't release that information. You, however, are free to go. I've signed your paperwork."

Geneva raised her brows. "You're letting me go? After you nearly killed me this morning?"

"Yes, well, that was unfortunate. Clearly, you didn't respond well to our tests. I would have preferred to keep you here for observation, but the CMU has ordered your release. You're free to leave."

Grimshaw detached the paper from the clipboard and handed it to her. "Here. Take this to the front desk. They'll give you your personal items."

She glanced at the scrawling handwriting on the release form.

"Is something the matter, Geneva?"

"Yes, I mean, no, I'm fine. But...does this mean I passed the examination? That I have control of my talent? Should I no longer be afraid of getting lost in colors when I track someone's energy?"

"You were paired with a dark master. The incidents you experienced were triggered by your partner's dark energy and magnified—by the vortex you visited and later through the use of crystals. Given the unusual circumstances, it's my evaluation that you have yourself under control and aren't a threat. Would you agree?"

"Of course, she's not a threat," Julia said. "I've known her forever and lived with her for four years. She's never been a threat."

Mauve and crimson streams of color swirled in front of Geneva. Julia's anxiety mixed with the doctor's regret. He didn't want to let her go. And yet he did. *Why?*

She focused on Dr. Grimshaw. "What did they look like...the people who took Rolf?"

Grimshaw twisted his lips. "You're not planning to do any sleuthing on your own, are you? That would be foolish. Very, very foolish. The CMU might reverse its decision. You might find yourself in a four-foot cell."

Geneva refused to let his warning scare her. "You must have seen them. Were they hackers?"

Grimshaw narrowed his beetle brows. "Shall I call a guard to escort you back to the green ward?"

She shook her head. Challenging Dr. Grimshaw would not help her find Rolf. It'd only get her more of the doctor's tests. "No, that won't be necessary."

"We're leaving," Julia said. "I'll see that Geneva gets home safely. Thank you, Dr. Grimshaw." Julia motioned in front of them.

Geneva followed but couldn't stop from turning to observe the color surrounding the doctor—dark rays of mauve. *Deep regret.* Why did he let her go?

He gave her a skeleton smile. "Goodbye, Geneva. Let's not have further incidents, shall we? I'd rather not see you back here. Next time, we might not survive."

Was that a warning? What was Grimshaw capable of?

21

CRYSTALS

"What are you doing here? Where am I?" Rolf had recovered from his earlier shock.

There was a click, and light flooded the room, blinding him. Rolf closed his eyes and opened them, squinting until his eyes adjusted. Cynthia looked down on him like some sort of avenging angel, her platinum hair circling her head in a shiny halo. His thoughts spun and shifted from one thought to the next.

He cast his gaze around what he could see of his surroundings. It appeared to be a laboratory of sorts. Shiny instruments lay on a skinny table, along with a microscope and some sort of clear fluid in a series of test tubes. His eyes caught and rested on a row of gems, lying on a blue cloth. Light reflected off their surface, giving them a translucent glow. *Crystals.* His gaze met Cynthia's. She smiled.

"Yes, they're crystals. They've been fabricated to absorb extreme amounts of energy. Your energy. You're in a government-run testing facility, Rolf. You have unique abilities that could be lethal to the general population. The government will conduct a series of tests, and if you cooperate, you could be released in a week."

He studied the crystals. They appeared to be ordinary stones. "And if I don't cooperate?"

"That's why I'm here." She ran one ruby-frosted nail through his hair.

Was Cynthia threatening him? Was this payback because he'd rejected her advances? She'd made no secret of her attraction to him when he'd been ordered to protect her, inviting him home on several occasions. She was a news reporter, not a trainer. She possessed no psychic talent. What did she plan to do to him now, stab him with her pretty nails?

He might have laughed out loud if her touch didn't make him lightheaded. Did she think he'd participate in some ridiculous government tests of his talent? *Fat chance.* Dark energy rushed from his gut to the tips of his fingers. Cold seeped into his bones. A low growl escaped from his throat before he could contain it. "What do you mean?"

Cynthia ignored the question, continuing to run a hand through the hair on his forehead, her fingers cool on his hot skin. They seemed to burn their way into his brain. His stomach took a nosedive. What was happening? He squinted at her, but the angel impression remained. The glow surrounding her was real and not some figment of his imagination. *Crap.*

Above him, Cynthia smiled. "Like you, I also have unique abilities. From time to time, in situations like these, my talents are needed. Now lie still. This will only take a moment."

Rage, thick and furious, clawed at his mind, seeking escape. No way in hell would he be the government's science experiment. He didn't want to unleash the monster inside him. But if it gained his release, so be it. He wouldn't lie here one second more.

He took a breath and let the dark energy infiltrate his body. Power, thick and heady, surged through his veins seeking to blot out the enemy. For the first time in a long while, he let the dark energy flow through and out of him. It rushed through cold fingers, flooding into the room and canceling out every speck of light it came in contact with, absorbing each molecule of energy.

Pshhhhzing. The bonds holding him stretched and broke. If he were to look into a mirror, he knew what he'd see. His blue eyes would be large and black. *Merciless.* As merciless as the rage that filled his heart.

He stood, focusing on Cynthia and the odd light surrounding her. She looked radiant. A strange thought to have in the moment. But it was true. The dark energy didn't cover her—didn't absorb her light. Instead, it reflected off her. She raised her left hand and shattered the dark energy into a brilliant display of every color in the spectrum.

His legs buckled, and he tottered forward but managed to stay on his feet. She moved toward him as if she'd done nothing. "Yes, my dear Rolf. Dark energy is useless around me. A strange talent to be sure, but it comes in handy at times. Now sit."

Cynthia tapped one rainbow-tipped finger on his nose, eliminating the remainder of the dark energy in the room.

He sat.

"PETER SAYS ROLF'S being held at a maximum-security center. It's top secret. Even Peter doesn't know the details." Geneva pocketed her cell phone and dragged her suitcase behind her. The CMU feared those with dark energy. No one talked about them much, but she'd heard the rumors. Stories of dark masters who'd go on killing sprees before they were rounded up and killed by agents who specialized in that sort of thing.

She and Julia left the Institution, pausing outside in the parking lot to wait for an Uber. They'd booked rooms for the night at a nearby hotel because their flight back to Cleveland didn't depart until the next day. Percy had gone ahead earlier but promised to meet them in the hotel lobby bar. Geneva had a few questions for him.

She took a swig from the water bottle she carried with her. My God, it was hot. She felt so helpless. Where was Rolf being held? Chicago? Or perhaps someplace else, someplace far away, someplace she'd not think to look. She pictured him as she'd last seen him, worried for her and protective. He'd not wanted to leave her side, but he'd done it when she asked him. And then he'd somehow heard her cry for help and saved her, knowing it would expose his secret. The government had locked him away somewhere... alone, possibly suffering and worried. She pulled her T-shirt away from her body, but it didn't cool her.

Across from her, Julia's dark eyes radiated concern. Her aura took on a dull red cast. "Why are they holding him?"

"The CMU knows Rolf channeled dark energy—Dr. Grimshaw reported it. They're having him tested. Peter doesn't think he's being held at Corvey, though, since we're here. That leaves any number of other government testing centers. The CMU has facilities all over the country. Until the tests are complete and it's determined he's not a threat, I'm being paired with your cousin Roland."

Geneva had never been one to pace, but the movement helped to relieve the increasing pressure inside her. She needed action. Needed to get out of this relentless heat and find Rolf, wherever they'd taken him. Needed to reassure herself he was okay. Needed time alone to analyze and come to terms with her feelings for him.

She gestured toward the Uber car pulling into the parking lot. Ruby-red color followed her movements. "Let's get to the hotel and talk to Percy. We need to figure out where they've taken Rolf. We must find him."

Julia placed a gentle hand on her shoulder. "Think, Geneva. Even if we discover where he's being held, you know he'll be guarded. We'd need help to get to him, let alone find a way to escape."

Geneva studied her friend, weighing the logic of her words. She released a shaky breath. Julia was right. She waved a sweaty palm, dispelling the sea of red in front of her.

"Have you tried to talk to him? You may not be linked, but you share a special bond. He knew you were in trouble. Do you feel anything? Anything at all?"

Geneva squinted at the colored air in front of her. According to Dr. Grimshaw, it was safe for her to use her talent. She took a breath to settle her mind, then closed her eyes and opened her senses. Colors seeped into her mind. Blues, yellows, reds, pinks, oranges, greens. She sorted through each shade, looking for Rolf's energy. Lime, aqua, teal, and forest, but none of the deep green that resonated with Rolf. Rolf was no longer in Chicago.

She opened her eyes and shook her head. *Nothing*. She clenched her fists to keep her aching despair from exploding out of her. "He's not here." Her insides ached, and she shivered, unable to stop a small amount of energy from escaping. It shimmered in front of her until she sucked what she could inside with her next breath.

Julia stamped on a small fire igniting next to her foot. The heat, combined with the massive amount of energy surrounding them, proved to be a combustible combination. She grasped Geneva's shoulders. "Snap out of it. Rolf needs you. Dark energy or not, he's a good man. He saved your life. He cares about you."

Geneva blinked, unclenching her fists. She breathed in the unique scent of dry air and hot asphalt to help regain her composure. She took another slow breath and another. Her heartbeat settled, pumping out a reassuring rhythm. Next to her, Julia dropped her hands to her side.

"He was here a few hours ago. Could they have moved him out of state that fast?" Julia asked.

Geneva straightened, defying the fear coursing through her body. "Anything is possible. It's the U.S. government. They have unlimited resources." She tapped her friend on the arm, letting her know without words she had herself under control. "Let's collect your stuff and figure out what to do next. I'll let Peter know Rolf's not in Chicago. We'll recruit Percy to help us find Rolf."

They moved toward the driver, who'd pulled up at the curb. They would find Rolf, wherever he was being held, she vowed. And when she did, she'd stun his captors with one hell of an explosion or anything else she needed to do to save him.

22

PERCY

The Uber driver dropped them at Julia's hotel to regroup and talk to Percy. As expected, they found him at the bar nursing a beer.

"You've heard from Peter?" Julia asked, taking the seat to the left of him.

Geneva grabbed the one on the right and ordered an iced tea. She'd avoided alcohol ever since the "bar incident," which was what she called the night Rolf had saved her from a drunken brawl, kissed her, then sent her home like a child. Alcohol dulled her senses, stripped her control, and made her dangerous. She could never lose herself in a drink like the majority of the population.

"Yeah." Percy scrunched his face and stared into his glass as if it held answers. His aura shimmered a dull red, then gray.

"What's wrong?" Julia asked.

Geneva relaxed into the stool and sipped the tea the bartender deposited in front of her. If she wasn't mistaken, Percy was about to make a confession.

"I made a mistake." He glanced at Geneva, biting the corner of his lip, and then back to his beer.

"Does this have anything to do with the crystals we were sent to recover?" Julia asked.

"Yeah."

"Do they even exist?" Geneva wrapped her fingers around her glass.

"A few exist. I've held them. I was told there are more. They're worth a ton of money. If we'd found them, I would've earned a large finder's fee. A fortune. I could have quit my job. Never have to work another day in my life."

"You were working with someone on the side?"

Percy hung his head like a dog who was caught in the act of eating the Thanksgiving turkey. "Yeah. I'm sorry. I had no idea he would drug and kidnap us. That wasn't part of the deal."

Geneva caught Percy's eyes. Her next question was important, and she wanted to make sure he told the truth. "What do you know about where the government's taken Rolf?"

Percy blinked. "I don't. I swear it. I'm clueless." He swallowed, his Adam's apple bobbing in his neck. He looked around the bar and lowered his voice to a whisper. Geneva had to strain to catch his next words. "I don't care how many crystals there are. I never want to see the damn things again. But I don't trust the guy I was working for. Calls himself the Gemcatcher. He's dangerous."

"Who is he?"

"I don't know. I've never met the man in person."

"How did you hook up with him?"

Percy lowered his head. "On a blog post. I'd heard about the legend of the crystals from my cousin David. I researched the topic. That's when I ran across Gemcatcher.

He claimed to have discovered a few and was advertising a large finder's fee to locate the rest on a website dedicated to investigating ancient gems. You know I've a special talent for finding lost objects. I figured maybe I'd track them. I needed the money. I'd...accrued some debts."

Percy paused and took a sip of his beer. His hand trembled. "I'm not stupid, you know. On a video call, I made him show me the crystals he claimed to have found. He only had a handful. Had them hidden in a safe. One of them contained illusion energy. Two of them had never been charged and were capable of storing our energy. I don't know where he got the illusion stone or how the energy got into it. He claimed he found it that way. Said he'd figured out how to manufacture synthetic crystals, too, but they needed to be tested to see if they worked."

Percy turned to Julia, who had both hands under her chin. "When you contacted me about partnering with you to find the crystals, I figured I'd gotten lucky. I'd help you find the crystals, and in return, I could make a little money on the side. The Gemcatcher said the crystals would be worth millions to hackers outside the U.S."

"You're slime," Julia said. "You should have told me."

Percy hung his head. "I didn't know he'd almost kill Geneva. I agreed because I know how loyal you both are to the CMU. I knew you'd never cooperate otherwise."

"Go on," Geneva said.

"Peter knew I was good at finding lost objects. When Julia started dreaming about them and asking questions, he told me she wanted me to join her on the mission." Percy looked to Julia. "I did plan to help you. I swear it. I just needed the money. I figured you wouldn't need all the stones if we discovered more existed. I would keep some to sell to my new acquaintance. We'd both get what we wanted. Now I wish I'd never laid eyes on them."

Geneva slid off the barstool and grabbed her purse. She tapped Percy on the shoulder, careful to block her energy. "You do know what this means, don't you?"

"No, what?"

"Since you're good at finding things, you're going to help us find Rolf."

———

WHAT THE HELL had Cynthia done to him? Rolf dropped his head into his hands and took a few shallow breaths. One touch, and she'd drained his energy. My God, how come he'd had no idea she was one of them? And a beacon? Why hadn't Peter told him? He'd been assigned to protect the woman, for God's sake, and still he hadn't guessed. How could that be?"

"What's the matter? Cat got your tongue?"

"You work for the government?"

Cynthia gave him a throaty chuckle. "Of course not. I'm a news reporter. What would I be doing with the government?"

"Why are you here? What do you want from me?"

Cynthia plucked the long syringe from the table and pushed the plunger to remove any air bubbles. She shook her head and frowned, marring the smooth lines of her face. "You hackers are all the same. So intent on your mission, you miss what's right underneath your cute little noses."

Rolf eyed her. She came toward his bed, determination in her expression. She stopped in front of him. Rolf blinked. Her smile blended with her blonde prettiness and the strange glow surrounding her. "In the ordinary course of events, I would want nothing but your sexy self. I'm not ashamed to admit I am...attracted to you." She laughed again and ran a hand along his arm, squeezing his biceps. She seemed to be enjoying herself. "I love strong, confident men. I believed your lack of interest stemmed from her... well, let's just say my invitation still stands. But now I need more. Your talent for dark energy has made you extremely useful to me. Lie still, darling. This will be over before you know it."

Her? Who was she referring to? He tried to lift his arms, but they remained at his sides, useless appendages. *Weak.* What was he forgetting? *Her.* He gasped. Pain sliced his forehead. The agony was so intense, he barely felt the sting of the needle.

23

LOOSE ENDS

Gemcatcher peered through the examination window into the room where Jorgensen and the Girard woman were held. Jorgensen grew agitated. The Girard woman had retired to the far corner of the room. She knew better than to interfere. Cynthia leaned over and kissed Jorgensen on the lips. *Must you?* She had to know he watched. He couldn't stop his frown of annoyance. They didn't need further complications. Cynthia had always enjoyed drama. That was something they had in common. They both played well to the camera.

Jorgensen, of course, looked stunned. Who wouldn't after they'd been kissed by Cynthia? Her blonde head glowed in the dark. *My beacon.* She stamped out the dark energy streaming from Jorgensen with a flick of a finger, grasped the needle, and prepared to inject the paralyzing agent.

Cynthia never failed to amaze him. So cool and poised under pressure. Pride bloomed in his gut. Her talent only worked in close quarters and for mere minutes, but her victims didn't know it. Her movements were quick and efficient. Gemcatcher relaxed when the shot went in, and Jorgensen sank back on the hospital bed. He pressed his hands against the cool glass. This next part was critical to their success.

Dark energy streamed from Rolf's chest and arms into the synthetic crystals. He watched for an explosion, but the two crystals on the table absorbed and contained the lethal energy. Bingo! The synthetic crystals held. They'd done it. Excitement raced through his system, his heart to thumping. Now it remained to place a price on each crystal. How should he price death? He smiled. After all these years, he would have the wealth and power he craved. He had a list of buyers waiting to purchase the deadly crystals.

He tapped on the glass. Cynthia didn't spare a glance in his direction. She scooped up the crystals and left, leaving Jorgensen on the cot. The drug Grimshaw had concocted would wear off with little effect. Jorgensen would be ready and able to charge more crystals within twenty-four hours.

Cynthia looked from side to side, handed him the crystals in silence, and hurried through the hallway to the exit. He checked his watch—a little after three in the morning. At this time of night, no one would notice them exiting the vacant building. Still, it wouldn't do to take unnecessary risks. They spent little time in one another's company here. If anyone were to spot them together, it would raise questions. Cynthia would return tomorrow on her own.

He took one last look at Jorgensen, who lay unmoving, and turned toward the exit. He fingered the crystals, warm and solid in his hand, before pocketing them. By now, Cynthia had had plenty of time to leave the premises. Time for him to climb into his car and head home.

He exited the building and made his way toward the Jaguar. Cynthia had Jorgensen well in hand. It would be his task to eliminate the loose ends. Number one on the list would be Percy Withers. Now they had a solid source for the synthetic crystals, they no longer needed the real thing. Percy was dumb enough to talk. After all their careful planning, they couldn't afford any screw-ups. Besides, they needed to make sure the synthetic crystals could kill. What better target than the hacker.

He shook his head in disgust, opened the car door, and slid into the driver's seat. He pulled from his pocket an initialed handkerchief he'd had made when he'd first become a public figure. It reminded him he'd made it despite his father's dire predictions.

Gemcatcher entered the highway, admiring the Jaguar's smooth suspension like he always did. He caught a glimpse of himself in the rearview mirror. No one must suspect him. He nodded his satisfaction, rubbing his chin with one hand. Not a wrinkle marred his white shirt or his forehead.

He stepped on the gas, heading to the exit and the airport. He'd get on the next flight to Chicago and deliver surprise packages to Percy Withers and Julia Jorgensen. Once he deposited the crystals, he'd put some distance between himself and the scene of the crime. The next time either of them used their psychic gifts, the crystals would activate. Then it would be good riddance to both of them.

"OHHHHH...OHHHH!"

The moaning sound woke Geneva from a deep sleep. She sat and looked around at the still-dark room, struggling to recall her location. She, Julia, and Percy had spent the evening discussing their next steps. Rather than get her own room, Geneva agreed to share Julia's room, so neither would be alone. She looked at the bed next to her where a body tossed and turned, beige waves floated above her. "Julia. Julia, wake up!"

Julia didn't wake. Geneva turned on the lamp on the nightstand, slid out of bed, and went to her side, shaking her. "Wake up, honey, you're dreaming."

Geneva persisted until the moaning stopped and Julia's brown eyes, wide and fearful, peered into hers.

"What's the matter? What were you dreaming?"

Julia shot out of bed. Geneva braced herself. The beige dream energy surrounding Julia's body had turned cherry red. Julia let out a low, keening moan. "It's Percy. Oh God! Someone wants him dead. C'mon, there's no time to waste."

Geneva scrambled to find her jeans and slip on her sandals to chase after Julia, who was already halfway down the hall, still in her pajamas. Julia stopped at a door and pounded. No answer. A faint trickle of pink fog found its way through the doorjamb. *Too late.* Geneva placed one hand on Julia's. "He's dead."

"Oh my God!" Julia sobbed. "It's my fault. I shouldn't have left him alone."

Geneva shook her head. "It's no one's fault; least of all yours. Percy put himself in danger the moment he agreed to help the Gemcatcher. If it's anyone's fault, it's mine. I forced him to stay here and help us. If I'd let him go home, he might still be alive."

Guilt gnawed at her insides, taking a chunk of her heart with it. Geneva placed a hand on the locking mechanism and ejected energy into it, breaking the seal. She pushed open the door, expecting to see loads of pink energy. Nothing could have prepared her for what greeted them.

She gasped. Julia let out a cry. Dark energy seethed above the bed where Percy had rested—Rolf's energy. Nothing remained of Percy, not even whatever he'd been wearing. The room was cloaked in blackness.

24

FIRE

"Shut the door, hurry!"

Geneva froze in place. Dark energy raced toward her and Julia, attracted to their combined light. It couldn't be. Rolf would never harm his cousin. She knew it like she knew her own name or the color of her hair. And yet there was no doubt the seething dark energy in Percy's room was Rolf's, and it had blotted Percy out of existence, covering and absorbing his energy molecules. And it was set to do the same with her and Julia if she didn't get a move-on. She shut the door at the exact moment the long tentacles of dark energy reached for her. A tiny piece clipped the outside of her right hand.

"Ow!" Geneva grabbed her hand and leaned against the door to catch her breath. The dark energy slithered and disappeared, devouring the spot of flesh with it. Pain, sharp and intense, penetrated her foggy thoughts. She peered at the tiny hole where her skin should have been. Blood oozed from the wound.

Has Rolf been here? Had he killed Percy...snuffed out the life of his cousin? Maybe he'd turned into a raging psychopath as the legends claimed. *I saw it. He pulled the dark waves out of you. He took them inside himself.* Julia's words from the previous day haunted her, ringing in her head with a conviction she could not ignore. Rolf was a dark master, incapable of feeling or expressing love. Geneva cared for the one man who couldn't love her back. Was he also capable of murder? Had he let the dark overrule any goodness in his nature? Had he deliberately targeted Percy, hitting him with a fatal dose of dark energy?

"Are you okay?" Julia's eyes were big and wide, her face creased with concern. She pulled Geneva toward her. Not that they needed to worry about the dark energy in the bedroom. It was attracted to living tissue. If they kept the door shut, it would eventually dissipate. It was outside the bedroom it would be a problem.

Energy from every end of the spectrum gathered in front of her hissing and coiling.

"Geneva, you're scaring me. Snap out of it."

Geneva took a breath. "I'm trying." The energy ball inside her grew to alarming proportions. Sweat beaded on her forehead. For once, she wished to let loose. To not have to be the one always in control.

The light above her head sparked and fizzled, followed by the next and the next down the long hallway.

"This isn't the time to lose control. Get a hold of yourself. There are innocent people in these rooms."

Geneva registered Julia's voice as if it came from a long distance away. Had Rolf really murdered his cousin? True, what Percy had attempted was wrong, and she, Rolf, and Julia were paying the consequences. But was Percy's weakness any reason to kill him?

Dark masters were ruthless, she reminded herself. *Merciless.* Incapable of loving or being loved. It was said when they turned, they gained extraordinary abilities to track their victims, walking through walls, blotting out the existence of their victims one by one. With each death, they grew more powerful.

She groaned into her hands. "Oh God." Next to her, the box containing a fire extinguisher popped, spraying glass in every direction.

Julia shook the glass from her hair. She gripped Geneva's shoulders, speaking calmly in her ear. "Think. Rolf's being coerced. The government is using him as a weapon."

Geneva clasped her hands in front of her. "You're right. Rolf would never do this. He's being forced to use dark energy." Her breath hitched. She didn't voice her greatest fear— that if Rolf were forced to use dark energy, he would eventually turn on everyone he loved. Instead, she closed her eyes and focused on the mass in front of her, stretching from floor to ceiling.

It took a solid half-hour to disperse the energy clustered around her and return the levels to something more manageable. By the time she was through, she slumped against the door. Her muscles ached in every part of her body, drenching her in sweat. She wiped her palms on her pants. Julia tugged on her arm.

"I know you're beat, but we have to get out of here and alert Peter. There's no way he's involved with this. He can help us figure out where Rolf is being held and put a stop to what's happening. There's nothing we can do to help Percy, and if we're caught here, we'll spend hours responding to questions we can't answer. Better let Peter handle this mess."

Geneva nodded and struggled to her feet, her legs cramping. Working with such large volumes of energy built up an excess of lactic acid in her muscles.

"C'mon." Julia grabbed her hand and pulled her along

until they reached their room. She began packing her suitcase. Geneva called Peter and put him on speakerphone.

"Rolf killed Percy?" Peter's voice held traces of sleep.
"Impossible. You told me yourself Rolf's not in Chicago.
There's no way he could have killed him."

"He doesn't have to be in Chicago. The government is
manufacturing synthetic crystals. They've figured out how
to store our energy in them. They activate when someone
uses their talent. That's what Dr. Grimshaw was doing when
he tested me at Corvey. They were after my energy. And now
they've forced Rolf to store dark energy in the crystals and
used it to kill Percy."

"Why would the government kill one of its own men?"

"I don't know. I only know Rolf would never murder
Percy."

"The government understands the danger of using dark
energy. They wouldn't turn a hacker into a violent lunatic
unless there was a good reason."

"Right—and that's money. The crystals are worth
billions to other countries. The government plans to sell
them. Explains why there's so much secrecy around where
Rolf is being tested."

Worry crept into Peter's voice. "I hope to God you aren't
right. I've been working a few leads to see if I can discover
where Rolf's being held. Did you learn anything more from
Percy before he was killed?"

"Just that he was working with a guy who calls himself
the Gemcatcher."

"Who is this Gemcatcher?"

"Percy's Internet contact." Julia pulled clothes from the
dresser drawer and shoved them into her suitcase. "He has a
website where they met. He's sort of an expert on rare gems.
Percy had a deal on the side with him. He was going to pay

Percy to recover the real crystals. Gemcatcher had a couple and believed more existed."

"Did Percy find any?"

"No. At least he told us he hadn't."

"Hmm."

"What?" Geneva called from the bathroom, where she was collecting Julia's personal items.

"If this Gemcatcher orchestrated Percy's death, then he must not have needed him to find the crystals."

"Maybe he found the stones and didn't need Percy anymore?" Geneva exited the bathroom and dropped shampoo and a razor into a bag. "Maybe he was worried Percy would tell someone what he knew? I'm certain Percy knew more than he told us."

"Like what?" Julia unplugged her devices and stuffed the cords in her purse.

"Maybe something that would lead to the Gemcatcher."

"You may be right," Peter said. "But if that's the case, you're both in serious danger."

"What do you mean?" Julia asked.

"He means Gemcatcher would suspect Percy would discuss the matter with us. He won't take the chance we know his identity. He'll kill us before we can point a finger."

"Yes," Peter agreed. "He would want to eliminate anyone who might be able to incriminate him. I'd suggest you both high-tail it out of there and back to Cleveland tonight where we can keep an eye on you."

"But what about Rolf?" Geneva asked. "We have to find him."

"Right," Peter acknowledged. "But we know Rolf's not in Chicago. Whoever this Gemcatcher is must be high up in the food chain. Who knows what resources they have at their disposal? I don't like it. I'm booking tickets for the next flight out of Chicago tonight, and you both need to be on the plane. Hurry! Let's get you out of there."

Something glittered on the desk in the room, attracting Geneva's attention. *A crystal?*

Julia let out a scream, scrambling toward the door. A line of fire sprang up in her footsteps.

"What's the matter? Are you all right?" Peter's voice shouted through the phone. But Geneva didn't spend precious time answering. She dropped the phone, staring in horror at the flames trailing Julia. Fear raced through her system. Her best friend was about to turn into a puff of smoke.

25

HER

P ain surrounded Rolf, digging into his skull and tearing at the walls of his resistance. What was he forgetting? *Don't try to remember.* He blanked his thoughts and the pain lessened. He blinked, opening his eyes. The room was once again in blackness. He tried to swallow, but his tongue was dry. His legs and arms were no longer restrained, but the weakness in his limbs made him doubt their ability to hold him. He peered into the darkness but could not see Cynthia or the halo surrounding her. *Is she gone?*

"She left a while ago." The woman he had met earlier answered his unspoken thought.

Rolf turned toward the sound and cleared his throat. "Cynthia?" His voice croaked.

"Is that her name? She never told me. I call her the bright one. She's much nicer than the other."

"What other?"

"The man that comes. The angry one."

Rolf attempted to sit. Heat radiated from his palms, indicating a large expenditure of energy. What had Cynthia done to him? His head throbbed. Did he want to know?

He lay back, eyes closed, not trying to remember. Maybe it was better this way.

The woman spoke again, bringing him back to his surroundings and the pain licking his temples. "Are you hungry?"

His stomach chose that moment to let out a growl. The woman gave a high-pitched squeal. "Of course, you are! Why didn't I think of it earlier? We have plenty of food and water, if you can eat in the dark. They bring fresh food every day."

She left her chair, and he could hear the sounds of her fumbling across the room. Minutes later, she returned and handed him a plate. A few blind touches, and he recognized a sandwich. He grabbed it, taking one bite and then another —within minutes, he'd devoured the whole thing.

"Feel better?"

"A little. Is there a bathroom?"

"Of course. I'll show you the way. Watch your step."

It appeared they had all the creature comforts in their prison, except light. The woman seemed to delight in having a companion and talked often. He supposed it came from spending time alone in the dark. She chattered the whole way to the bathroom and back to his bed. His limbs refused to hold him; he had to lean on the woman to walk to and from. When she returned him to his cot, he lay for a time to catch his breath. His bladder was empty, but the pain in his head remained.

"Do you want to sleep? I hoped you'd stay awake for a while, but I know it's tiring after they visit."

"I do need sleep. My head aches."

"Oh, I can help with that. Since you came, they've lost interest in me. I'm not tired. Let me help you."

Before Rolf knew what she was about, the woman placed both her hands on his head, sending a jolt of electricity through him. He groaned. After the initial shock of her touch, the relief was immediate and welcomed. His head still ached, but it was much less intense than moments earlier. "Thank you."

"Of course. You would do the same for me."

Her hands remain tangled in his hair. Would he have shared his energy to take away her pain? Rolf wasn't so sure of it. The way he figured, he would have lost his mind in this cave long before he could be of any help to her. Still, the energy exchange had been intimate, revealing far more about the precarious mental state of his companion and her interest in him than he'd anticipated. He brushed her hands away, careful to place some distance between them. An awkward pause stretched. "How often do they visit?"

"The lady? Once a day, I think. I mean, it's hard to tell one day from the next, but it seems like once a day to bring food." She paused. "I heard the lady call you Rolf. Is that your name?"

"Yes."

"I like you. She likes you, too. That's why she called you by name."

"Is that what you think? I'm not so sure she did it out of kindness."

"What do you mean?"

"I suspect she knew my remembering would be painful. Debilitating. She wanted me off-balance so I wouldn't try to escape."

"I never thought of that. Could you have escaped?"

"Maybe. If I had known what came next, I would have tried. Have you never tried to escape the dark?"

The woman moved away from him. Rolf thought maybe she wouldn't answer. But she did. "Not in a long time. If you're caught, they make you pay. You're better off staying put."

"What happened when you tried?"

The woman's energy changed, shifted, drew inward. He grew better at reading her. Especially since she had touched him, taking away his pain. *"I remembered."*

Her sadness filled him. *"Your brother. The one they killed. I'm sorry."*

"It's okay. I'm glad I remembered him. Worth the pain."

"That's how I feel about..." He wouldn't go there. Couldn't afford the suffering the memory brought with it. Too late. *"Her."* He struggled to draw breath. Steel knives sliced into his brain, and he screamed in agony.

26

RED ALERT

Flames licked at the bedding beside Julia. Peter continued shouting from the cell phone. Geneva ignored him. She focused on the ball of fire, searching and finding the thread of energy at its center. Whoever had done this hadn't counted on Geneva being in the room. It didn't take her long to determine the pattern in her own energy waves and counteract them until the fiery flames diminished and winked out of existence.

She turned to Julia, who had been swatting at the growing flames with a wet washcloth she had retrieved from the bathroom. "Are you all right?"

"Yes." She gasped, her big, brown eyes wide in her white face. "My God, Geneva. If you hadn't been here, I'd have been toast."

"What the hell's going on?" Peter still shouted through the phone.

Geneva grabbed it from the floor where she had dropped it. "We're okay." She projected calm into her voice. "Looks like whoever did this was after Julia. At least now we know how he's doing it and who's involved."

"What do you mean?"

Geneva held the crystal for Julia to see. "It's the crystals. Grimshaw's figured out how to trap my energy in them. He apparently stole my energy and trapped it in a crystal when I was in the Institution. But something went wrong, or whoever's orchestrating this in the government got suspicious, so he let me go."

Julia stared at her, a look of horror on her face.

"Don't you see? Grimshaw's the Gemcatcher. That's how he has the crystals. And now he has Rolf. We need to find Grimshaw and squeeze the truth out of him. If I don't kill him first."

Peter's sigh was audible through the phone. "I'm afraid it's impossible."

"What do you mean?"

"Grimshaw was found in his lab at the Institution about thirty minutes ago—dead. There's no sign of foul play. He left a note. Official word is suicide. He shot himself in the head."

ROLF SAT in a chair the woman offered and peered into the darkness. He had grown accustomed to the absence of light. *Fitting.*

Anger, hot and dark, moved in his gut, promising retribution on those who would harm him. *Or Her.* The woman he had remembered.

He clung to his control with a tenuous thread. According to legend, no matter how hard he fought the transformation, the dark energy would overtake him, causing him to lose all compassion for mankind. Death and destruction would follow to those he cared about. It was his fate. Why fight it?

Why not let it fill him, strengthen him in his time of need? Despite her abilities, Cynthia could have no concept of the beast raging inside and the lengths it would go to protect itself.

He stretched his hands above his head. Ever since his companion had lain warm hands on him, his limbs did not feel so much like limp rags, either. The food in his belly helped, too. With his basic bodily necessities taken care of, Rolf could think.

He wrapped his arms across his chest and considered his options. There weren't many. Stay here in the dark and be drained of his energy daily. Or find a way to escape. He would find a way to escape. But first, he needed to determine who or what Cynthia was and why she needed his energy.

If only he could remember. *Her.* He didn't dare explore who she was, the tantalizing glimpse he'd remembered of a woman who held an important place in his life, lest the paralyzing pain return. Still, he clung to the memory like a homeless man to the first real food he's had in weeks.

His temple throbbed—a warning. What had they drugged him with, he and the woman who sat next to him and shared his prison? Was it in the shot Cynthia gave him or maybe in their food or water?

The woman stirred next to him. She never stayed silent long. "What are you thinking?"

He turned toward her voice, although he couldn't see a thing. "We will find a way to escape."

"There is no way out. I've tried. The only exit is the one Cynthia came through, and the door is steel and locked."

"We'll overpower her."

The woman made a sound of disgust. "She can't be overpowered. You saw what she can do. There's no escape. They'll kill us first."

He shook his head. "They won't kill us. They need us."

"They'll separate us." The woman's voice trembled. She clutched his arm, her grip strong. "I can't go back to being alone. I can't."

Rolf covered her hand with his own. Despite his weariness and the dark eating away at his insides, he sent her a soothing image of being home surrounded by friends. *"You won't be alone. I promise. But I do need your assistance to overcome our captors. To escape. Will you help me?"*

Her hand warmed in his. He could sense the fear pounding through her veins. She must not refuse him. He cracked the door in his mind again, giving her a taste of the connection she craved.

She shuddered. "Yes."

Satisfaction bloomed, and he allowed her a brief glimpse of himself before shutting off his mind. He drew a slow breath, lest his next thought bring a return of the crippling pain he'd endured when he'd remembered. *Her.* The slim blonde in his vision. The woman he wanted above all others. His reason to stay alive—to escape. The only thing keeping him from letting the dark overtake him.

27

WATCHED

Pallbearers dressed in dark suits wheeled a white coffin etched in gold into the Everlasting Cemetery on Chicago's north side. It had been four days since Grimshaw's death, supposedly by his own hand. Four days of grueling interviews at CMU headquarters about Percy and the doctor's deaths, frantic calls to her brothers, and desperate and useless attempts to track Rolf to wherever he was being held. Four days of a mounting emptiness and little sleep.

Hoping she'd find another clue that would lead to Rolf and to bring what little comfort she could to Percy's family, Geneva had attended Percy's calling hours in Cleveland yesterday, then caught an early morning flight to Chicago to attend Dr. Grimshaw's funeral. Her gaze caught the pile of fresh soil next to the gravesite. The man who took away her childhood was about to be buried. The pristine coffin would soon be covered with black soil.

Who was responsible for Dr. Grimshaw's death? Was Grimshaw the Gemcatcher, or was there someone else? Geneva had imagined Dr. Grimshaw dead on many occasions. He'd given her the creeps ever since she was a child, forced to endure his endless tests. She'd wished him gone. But never had she imagined his death by his own hand.

"Are you getting anything?" Julia whispered next to her. When Geneva decided to attend Grimshaw's funeral, Julia insisted on joining her. Her nightmares had accelerated with Grimshaw's and Percy's deaths, and she wanted answers. Dream talents could be endlessly patient while they wrestled with the images burned into their brain nightly.

Geneva shook her head. *"Rolf, where are you?"*

For what could have been the hundredth time, she called to him, her psychic senses on full throttle. If he heard her, there was no acknowledgment. Grimshaw hadn't been suicidal the last time Geneva had seen him. But his aura had been regretful. He hadn't wanted to let Geneva go. Did the government make him? Had government men held him at gunpoint and made it look like suicide?

The reverend recited a brief prayer, his monotone voice carrying across the bowed heads of the congregation. Geneva closed her eyes and placed her mind in the center of the colors. She searched for a thread of the unique shade of green she associated with Rolf. *Nothing.* Of course, emotions were high in the crowd. The range of colors she saw in her mind were more intense and varied. That's why she almost missed the flash of blue-black. There one moment and gone the next, lost within dozens of other, similar colors.

Had she imagined it? She opened her eyes to peer around the graveyard, her searching gaze zeroing in on a tall man in a dark suit some distance to the right and behind them. *A hacker.* She didn't allow herself to stare, of course, but bounced off the figure, pretending she didn't notice his interest in her and Julia. In the brief glance, she noticed a full head of black hair and a beard. Her gaze swept the remainder of the guests before landing on the preacher.

She inclined her head toward Julia and whispered. "We're being watched."

Julia's spine stiffened.

The suited man's eyes drilled holes in Geneva's profile, but she pretended not to notice. Did he suspect her of murdering Grimshaw? Her partners in the CMU were a suspicious lot and well-aware of her abilities. Geneva would not put it past them to have her investigated. And she had been with Grimshaw before his death. Was she under suspicion for his death?

Hurt filled her chest. She'd given the last eight years of her life to the CMU. Put herself in danger over and over again. Would she ever be trusted? Could she even trust herself? And now Rolf was in grave danger, and she had no idea how to save him.

She bit her lip. Even if she saved Rolf, he would never care for her. She swallowed the large lump in her throat, threatening to detonate, spilling into the space surrounding her. *Rolf, where are you?*

"By who?" Julia interrupted her thoughts.

For a second, Geneva forgot what they discussed. Then she remembered the man in the suit. "Don't look now, but there's a man with black hair and beard in a dark suit about five o'clock behind and to the right. He's watching us. I have no idea who sent him. Probably the CMU. They know my skills—what I'm capable of."

Julia squeezed her hand. "Why would they think you killed Grimshaw? I was with you when we last saw Dr. Grimshaw, remember? I'll testify that you left Corvey, and I was by your side the whole time."

Green-blue energy waves rolled from Julia's hands to

hers. Geneva's heart swelled. Words were meaningless. Plenty of people said one thing and meant another. Auras, on the other hand, never lied. Julia's aura indicated her deep pride and faith in Geneva. "Thanks, Julia."

Together, they watched the funeral workers lower the casket into the ground, and the assembly dispersed. They followed the rest of the guests back to their cars. All the while, Geneva did her best to ignore the intense mix of blue and black coming from the man who followed them.

DARK ENERGY STIRRED in Rolf's gut, grew and strengthened, pouring from his hands and into the crystals. One part of his mind watched. The other part hungered for violence.

Cynthia had returned. Even with the energy his fellow prisoner fed him, he hadn't been able to prevent Cynthia's ability to disarm them both. He'd never heard or seen anything like it. And Rolf had encountered a lot of unusual talents in his career. That's one thing he'd regained. A bit of memory about his former work. And his partner. The woman with the golden hair. *Geneva.* He endured the next few minutes by allowing his mind to trace and retrace his precious memory of her.

Hard to believe he'd forgotten her. Her light and beauty and grace. A familiar urge to link his mind to hers stuck hard. He ached to bind them so close together they could communicate without words.

Thank God he hadn't. She would be enduring his torment right now.

His thoughts returned to the present moment, where darkness poured from his hands, reminding him what he could never do—link her to a monster like himself. Geneva deserved more, much more than he could offer.

His heartbeat slowed and head lightened. Cynthia was a vampire, greedy for every last drop. She smiled wide, her teeth perfectly spaced and white. The only thing missing were fangs. Stealing his energy made her happy—deliriously so. Maybe this was the way it would end for him? Drained of all his energy and left to die, a shell of what he once was. He almost welcomed death.

But today wasn't the day, because Cynthia told him to stop, and his mind obeyed her. What was in the drug she gave him that allowed her to command his obedience? He watched, detached, as if he were a spectator and not the patient. Cynthia nabbed the crystals. They glowed for an instant before disappearing in the pocket of her dress. She paused, turning to him. She ran her fingers through his hair.

Her gaze flicked once toward the large mirror and back to him. Someone stood outside the window, watching. Who was it? Someone Cynthia trusted. He must be able to see inside. Could he hear them, too?

Cynthia drew her hand back and spoke, her voice so soft he had to strain to hear her. Yes, whoever was outside could hear. That's why Cynthia whispered. She did not want to be overheard. "We could be so good together, Rolf, you and me. Can't you feel it?"

She paused. What did she want him to say? Being held prisoner wasn't a turn-on. Rolf stayed silent.

Cynthia continued. "I know you want me. What if I told you that you can have me—when this is all over—when you're free. I'll come for you. We can be together."

He breathed in. Cynthia smelled like sex. The dark in him grew stronger, overtaking his humanity. Why not take what Cynthia offered? It would be an easy route to freedom, wouldn't it?

Because, his conscience argued, there was another. Another with hair the color of sunshine. Another who made him want to be better than what he was. A woman he'd protect with his last dying breath.

"Think about it." Cynthia leaned forward, pressing her warm lips to his. He didn't respond. She drew back. "We could be so good together."

She started to leave but stopped and turned around. "I'll be back." She laughed, the sound slithering over him. "Don't go anywhere."

He lay there for a time after her departure, considering. It was a dangerous game he played. Could he make Cynthia believe he'd fallen for her? Already the dark energy grew powerful. So powerful, it might overtake him. Would his memory of Geneva be enough to hold it at bay?

28

SETUP

"You're becoming too attached to the subject." Gemcatcher watched Cynthia through his dark sunglasses and dropped his menu. They'd agreed to meet for breakfast. Not unusual. When Cynthia came to town, they often met for breakfast in a different hip restaurant in D.C. to share news before the start of their busy day. This time she'd chosen a fancy café that served the best fresh-squeezed orange juice he'd tasted in some time.

"What do you mean attached?" Cynthia eyed him across the table, puzzlement written in a fine line across her forehead.

The waiter came to the table. Gemcatcher's left eye twitched. He fought the urge to place a finger under his glasses to stop it from moving. No one could see it under his shades, he reminded himself. He hated that damn twitch. He'd be glad when all this ended, and he and Cynthia could enjoy the fruits of their labor.

The waiter delivered their orders and departed. Gemcatcher shook his head and murmured so he'd not be overheard. "I see the way you look at him."

"I don't know what you mean." She stared at her scrambled eggs, ignoring him.

"Like you could devour him whole."

Cynthia blushed. She blushed, dammit. Did she have any idea how much it pissed him off?

"You exaggerate. I—I admit I find him attractive. What woman wouldn't? He's got those dark, brooding looks and angel eyes."

Now she raised one shoulder like it didn't matter. But of course, it mattered. Everything mattered. She ought to know that by now.

She opened her mouth and words came out. Silly words. She had no idea how her words made him want to heave his plate across the table.

She stuck her chin out. "He's built like a model. It's hard not to check out the goods."

He gritted his teeth. "You need to keep your head focused on the job at hand. We cannot afford any mistakes. Do you understand?"

"Yes." Her voice came out soft and submissive as he preferred.

He nodded, shook out his white cloth napkin, smoothed it over his charcoal-gray pants. "Good. You need to do the job and get out. No flirting or touching. Got it?"

"Yes."

Gemcatcher wasn't fooled. The minute his back was turned, Cynthia would be all over the hacker. She had the look women get when they're desperate for a man. He smelled it on her. When they had what they needed from Rolf, the hacker must be eliminated. Hell, Rolf was a dark one. He'd be doing a public service for the CMU.

He returned his coffee cup to the saucer. Victory was so near. He would not allow Cynthia to screw it up for them.

She took a small bite of her eggs. Not enough to keep a mouse happy. "How many more stones must we make?"

"At least fifty. Any more than that, and he'll turn." He paused and took his sunglasses off so she'd know he meant business. "We'll have to kill him. If he turns, and we let him loose, he'll track us and murder us in our sleep. But not before leaving a bloodbath in his wake. I have no desire to let a psychopath loose to come after us or wreak havoc on the world."

He tried a bite of his omelet. Soft and fluffy as expected. The twitching slowed in his left eye.

"What about the girl?"

He frowned. "What about her? That ship sailed long ago. They work together, but Geneva Ericksen doesn't want anything to do with Rolf. Word is she detests him.

Cynthia reached for her water glass and raised it to her lips to take a small sip, eyeing him over the rim. "His female companion told me Rolf retrieved a memory of Geneva, despite the pain."

Gemcatcher stilled, the terrible twitch resuming its godawful jerk in his left eyelid. He took a few deep breaths to control himself before he did something stupid, like rip the damn water glass out of her hands, attracting the attention of the other patrons in the crowded restaurant. "How is that possible?"

Cynthia set her glass on the table and leaned toward him. "It's not. No one else has done it."

"Oh, for God's sake. You're proud of him. I can read it in your eyes."

"I'm not proud. But even you will admit it's impressive."

He growled. "The only thing I'm impressed with is his ability to earn us millions of dollars. Anything more is a liability. You need to keep that in mind the next time you feel like making googly eyes at him."

He crumpled his cloth napkin. His stomach gurgled and heated. He raised his hand, and the waiter arrived with their bill. He opened his wallet, pulled out a wad of cash, and placed a hundred-dollar bill in the waiter's hands. "Keep the change." He flashed the lucky Joe his million-dollar smile.

"Excellent, sir." The waiter departed with a small bow.

Gemcatcher returned his attention to Cynthia. "Let's increase the amount we take from him on Friday. Finish the job. It's evident we need to end this fascination you have with our patient before it turns ugly. You have no idea what Rolf Jorgensen is capable of."

He adjusted his tie and rose from the table.

"You exaggerate." Cynthia grabbed her purse and stood. "Rolf would never hurt me. He was assigned to protect me. And once we erase his memories, he will have no idea he has a beef against either one of us."

"That's precisely what concerns me. If he's able to retrieve his memories despite the drug we've given him, how do we know he won't have a few other surprises up his sleeve? We can't take any chances. Let's trap his energy in the stones and be done with him."

"What about Geneva Ericksen?

Gemcatcher grabbed Cynthia's elbow, plastered a smile on his face, and escorted her out of the restaurant. "What about her?"

"He's obviously attached to her. And now she's poking around, asking questions. Makes me wonder if she's as angry at Rolf as we think she is. What if she figures out where we're hiding him? The woman's got some serious tracking skills."

They walked into the bright sunshine. Not a cloud

covered the clear blue sky. He turned Cynthia toward him to avoid bumping a couple passing to the left. "Yes, I've been thinking about Geneva. She's more resilient than I thought. The CMU, however, is now suspicious of her. Two men connected to her have died in the past week. It wouldn't take much more for the government to turn on her."

"What do you mean? What are you thinking?" Cynthia's beautiful blue eyes were filled with both admiration and something else. Something he suspected was fear. Good. Much better than the lust for Rolf she'd displayed earlier.

He smiled, the first genuine smile he'd felt for some time. "It's unfortunate everyone she comes in contact with seems to wind up dead."

29

NEAR MISS

R olf reared his upper body on his cot, his heart revving like his old Harley. "Geneva?"

He searched the space in front of him, lifting his hand to make physical contact with a form. Of course, none existed. He closed his eyes, willing a response. *"Geneva, what's wrong?*

He strained his mind for the touch of her voice. Nothing. Silence. A dream. That's all. His heart seemed to shrink in his chest. For a moment, she had been so clear, so real. God, he wanted her. His body ached for the feel of her hand on his chest, her lips on his. His mind yearned for her voice in his head.

He straightened his shoulders on the pillow and sighed, a large and ragged sound. *Wonderful.* Not only was he trapped in the dark, he was losing his mind, hearing voices where there were none. Not the time and place to go mad. He must keep his wits about him if they had any hope of escape.

"What's the matter?" The cot sunk next to him, and the

woman laid a cool hand on his arm. "Is it her? Your girlfriend?"

"No. I don't know. Maybe."

"You heard her? She spoke to you?"

He shook off her hand. "I dreamt about her. She spoke to me in my dream."

"What did she say?"

"She asked me where I hid."

"Would she come here?" The woman said. "To rescue you?"

"Yes, she would come. If she knew where to find me."

"Have you tried talking to her? If you can hear her, maybe she can hear you?"

The woman was right. The first stirrings of hope rose in his belly. He focused his mind. *"Geneva, it's Rolf. Can you hear me?"*

For a second, he did hear something—a swoosh—his lungs pushing out air. He clenched and unclenched his fists. The dream, and his constant fear for Geneva's safety, stirred emotions in his gut and exacerbated his fragile state. Energy moved on the dark end of the spectrum. His own tormented shadow. It pulled and prodded at his self-control, driving him toward violence.

The dark in him always knew and responded to Geneva's fear. He protected her. Maybe he should have linked with her? If he'd placed a portal in her mind, staking his claim, and she'd accepted the offering, their minds would link. They could talk at will. He'd be able to calm her fears and reassure himself she lived. Not sit here imagining her hurt or dead.

A muscle twitched in his cheek. Instead, he lay trapped in the dark, buried in this dark tomb with no sign of rescue.

"Anything?"

The woman's soft voice interrupted his thoughts. He had forgotten her presence. "Nothing." His voice rumbled, harsher than he'd intended.

"Maybe something's happened to her?"

The woman voiced the fear haunting his mind. She sounded hopeful, damn her. For a nanosecond, Rolf could not contain the ebb and flow of his energy. Dark tendrils rushed out and in like waves crashing the shore, denying the woman's reasoning. He grasped his hands and bowed his head. Not right. He didn't want to hurt her.

The woman jumped. "I'm sorry, I'm sorry."

A drumbeat sounded in his chest, a slow and rhythmic chant. He reared his head.

The woman fled. Did he blame her?

———

"*Geneva, it's Rolf. Can you hear me?*"

Geneva grasped the bedcovers, panting. For a moment, she thought she was still in Chicago in her hotel. Then she remembered Julia's father had called with great news last night—Nonna had fully recovered and was released from the hospital. The doctors claimed she'd had a mild stroke, although they could find no solid evidence confirming the diagnosis. Geneva suspected Nonna's illness had been caused by the Gemcatcher, but she had no proof. Julia had wanted to get home as soon as possible to see Nonna, so they'd returned to Cleveland on a red-eye.

She flicked on the light and rubbed her eyes, certain what she saw was a leftover remnant from her dream. Wisps of green energy clung to the corner of her bedroom in her Cleveland apartment, then dissolved and disappeared.

"Rolf? Is it you?"

The silence in her head mocked her distress. She scrambled out of bed, ramming her psychic senses on full throttle and leaping over a pile of discarded clothes to get to the green fog. Colors rushed her, creating a familiar electrical surge, but none of the energy she attracted belonged to Rolf.

She slumped into the chair at her vanity table, cradling her head in her hands. There was no way Rolf's energy could materialize in her bedroom in Cleveland. Was there? Of course not. Not unless his body was nearby. That fueled a line of questioning. Perhaps the government was hiding him in Cleveland? But she and Rolf would also have to be linked, and they were not. She could not control the shiver racing through her body, making her scalp tingle. Unless he had turned.

Her doorbell rang, shaking her from her thoughts. She checked the time on her cell phone. Six a.m. A little early for someone to be calling.

Geneva closed her eyes, placing herself in the zone. Familiar rays of violet light, dotted with red and gray, exploded on the psychic plane. *Julia*. A distressed Julia, if she wasn't mistaken. Geneva rushed to open the door. Julia fell into her arms, sobbing.

"What's the matter?"

"We're in danger. The man told me. The man in my dreams."

Geneva placed an arm around her friend's shoulders. "Julia, it's okay. Everything's fine. I promise I won't let anything happen to you. Come inside."

Geneva tugged Julia through the doorway and led her to the couch, where she pulled her friend into her arms to stop the shaking. "Shhh. You'll be okay. Let it go. It's a dream. Your dreams are one possible outcome. You know as well as

I the future's uncertain. Not even a dream man can predict with one hundred percent accuracy."

"Yes, but this—this is different. The man, I know him. He's been appearing in my dreams since I was a child. Several times his warnings have saved me. He's usually right. This time he, he, he...told me..." Julia's chest heaved.

"Shh, it's okay. You're safe. I promise. Get a hold of yourself. Take your time."

Julia swallowed, her sobs subsiding. "He said my life's in jeopardy."

"That doesn't mean you're fated to die."

"Yes, but the man knows things. He warned me of Percy's death. Told me he was connected with the crystals. Now he tells me my life is threatened. Only one thing can save me. But that's not the worst of it."

Geneva gazed at her friend, watching the play of color cross her aura. She'd never seen this mix of violet with spikes of dull red. Julia was close to a nervous breakdown. Geneva rubbed her back, removing some of the negative energy waves, and schooled her voice to an even tone. "There's worse?"

Julia nodded. "Yes. Yes, there is." Her brown eyes were wide in her face. Tears leaked from the corners. "He told me —he said whoever has Rolf would use him to kill me."

A cold spike of energy passed through Geneva's heart. "No. The dream man is wrong. Rolf would never agree to hurt you, his sister."

"I know it. I do. But the dream man never lies. He warned me my life is in danger from Rolf."

"But he told you something can save you. What?"

Julia gazed at her, eyes wide, uncertain. "You. He said you're the one who might prevent my death."

Geneva sighed and squeezed Julia's hands. "That settles it. You'll stay with me. I'll keep you safe. I promise. On that, I agree with your dream man."

She thought that might make Julia smile, but her expression remained scared and serious. Geneva studied her aura. Gray flecks mixed with violet. She grasped Julia's chin and lifted. "What aren't you telling me?"

Julia sniffed. "Damn that talent of yours. It's...well, you may also be killed in the process. He says you will make a choice. And there's no telling whether you'll make the right one."

"What choice?"

"I don't know. I asked him. He said he was forbidden to say. You have free will, and he cannot influence your decision."

Geneva snorted. "Sorry, but that's convenient. If it's a choice between saving your life or mine, you have nothing to worry about. I'll choose yours. What now?"

"I'm worried for Rolf. Do you really think the government is forcing him to use dark energy?"

Geneva sighed. She couldn't lie. "I don't know. One thing I do know is Rolf's strong and stubborn. He'd never let anyone tell him what to do. But who knows what his captors are capable of doing to him? The government has all sorts of ways to coerce a patient to accomplish a task. We need to find him."

"Rolf, where are you?" Geneva called to him for at least the hundredth time. And for the hundredth time, she didn't get a response.

Where was Rolf, and why wasn't Peter doing more to find him? Come to think of it, Peter hadn't spoken to her about Rolf since she'd arrived back in town. That was out of character. Could it be Peter knew where Rolf was being held but was unable to tell her? Or maybe—an ache twisted in her stomach. The truth ripped through her mind, a lightning flash obliterating every other question in its path.

Peter believed Rolf had turned rogue.

30

PLAN

"So you're saying Rolf's a sociopath?"

Geneva stood facing Peter in the downtown Cleveland headquarters of the CMU. She'd barged into his office first thing this morning, ignoring his refusal to see her due to some trumped-up emergency in New York. He should know better than to dissemble. Even with the blocks the government put in place, gray bled through his arctic blue aura. He kept secrets.

"It's likely, yes."

"I don't believe it. Not..."Geneva's voice shook, and she took a moment to disperse the energy waves coiling in front of her hands. "Not that I don't understand what they say about dark energy. It may be hard for Rolf to love another. But I know Rolf. He's an honorable man. He's not a killer."

She leaned her hands against the hard desk to stop them from trembling. Heat rushed up her spine and out through her fingertips. A clap of thunder sounded overhead, and the lights flickered.

"Remain calm." The sternness in Peter's voice cut through her anger.

He raised his iPad. A long crack ran across the center of the glass. He gestured for her to sit.

Geneva forced a breath, sucking the air deep into her lungs. "I'm sorry. I'll buy you a new one." She breathed out, drew her energy inward, pulled the chair out across from him, and sat. "Do you know where Rolf is being held? Don't lie to me. I'll know it."

"No." He leaned back in his chair and rubbed a hand across the back of his neck. "Not yet, anyway. Your brothers have been searching."

"Where?"

"Arizona."

"And?"

"He's not there."

"How do they know?"

"Danny hacked Grimshaw the day before his death. He spent five minutes in the doctor's mind—enough to know Grimshaw sent Rolf somewhere in the Midwest."

"Was the doctor suicidal?"

"Negative. There were no suicidal thoughts. Dr. Grimshaw believed his cause was just. He experimented on you in the name of science. Used a special serum to immobilize you and make your mind susceptible to suggestion. We believe he shared the serum with a silent partner who provided the synthetic crystals."

"Someone higher up in the government?"

Peter shook his head. "We were wrong about the government being involved. They don't have him."

Her heart beat a furious rhythm. She gritted her teeth. "A CMU agent is kidnapped from a government-run facility, and you're telling me the government has no idea where he's being held or who has him? You must have some intelligence."

Geneva watched Peter for any sign of deception. He met her gaze head-on. "Nate also managed to do some hacking. The more conventional sort. He broke into the CMU's database and made a copy of Rolf's classified file. According to the file, the government doesn't know where Rolf's being held. No one does. What's more, Grimshaw's death was made to look like a suicide. The government believes, as do I, that whoever has Rolf killed Grimshaw."

"Anything else?"

"According to the classified file, before Grimshaw was murdered, he made a statement. He indicated the person who collected Rolf was a CMU agent with the proper paperwork."

"Who?"

Peter's grim gaze fastened on Geneva's. "I have no record of any other CMU agent near Dr. Grimshaw except you, Julia, and Percy. Percy is dead. I believe you and Julia are innocent. If the CMU doesn't know who the mysterious agent is, then we must assume it's a private citizen."

Geneva leaned forward. "Of course. It's this Gemcatcher, like Julia and I both told you. You have no other leads on where he might be holding Rolf?"

Peter sighed. "No, I don't."

She flung her hands toward him. Her eyes blazed, fast and furious. The room took on a scarlet haze. "Dammit, how could you keep all this from me? You know I'm the best tracker the department has. Why wouldn't you bring me in?"

Pens and pencils rattled in the canister on Peter's desk. A gush of wind swept the pile of papers he had been working on, scattering them in every direction. Peter stood, clutching the few papers he'd managed to grab to his chest. "Get a hold of yourself. Now!"

Geneva didn't waste time apologizing. She couldn't afford the time it would take. She closed her eyes and focused on the tangled mass of energy flooding the space in front of her. She sucked in a breath and another and blew it out, working to calm her racing heart and eliminate the psychic bomb about to detonate in Peter's office.

"This is precisely why I didn't involve you," Peter said minutes later, after Geneva had the situation under control. "You're far too close to Rolf. It's like lighting a match and firing a heat-seeking missile. You're liable to get yourself and the rest of the crew killed."

Geneva hunched in her chair, fighting to calm her raging temper. She had to help Rolf. She would go crazy otherwise. But how to convince Peter she wasn't a liability? "Peter, you need me. Please. I want to help."

"It's not that simple."

"What do you mean? It's simple. You assign me to the case. I join my brothers, find Rolf, and put this nightmare to rest."

"I'm afraid I can't let you."

"Why the hell not? And don't give me some bullshit about Rolf trying to kill me."

Peter let out a sigh and ran his hand through his hair that seemed whiter since the last time she'd seen him. At any other time, she might have retreated, not wanting to add to his stress. But right now, she could strangle him.

"Your latest tests indicate your talent has grown. Maybe out of your control. Explains the incidents you've been having when you get lost in the colors around Rolf. I've been ordered to have you watched."

"What are you saying?"

"I can't involve you in this case for your own protection. If you were to lose control and cause someone's death, I'd have a hard time convincing the government of your innocence. They'd lock you away for a long time. Forever."

Geneva kept her gaze trained on Peter's. "The man at Grimshaw's funeral. I didn't recognize him, but he was from the CMU. You had me tailed, didn't you?"

Peter hunched his shoulders and added the papers he'd collected during her temper tantrum to the piles on his desk. "For your own good. If anyone else dies, I'll need proof it wasn't because you lost control of your ability."

Geneva sat on her hands to stop them from fisting. "Do you expect me to do nothing while Rolf's turned into something he's not? I'm sorry. I can't do it. I will find him."

Peter shook his head. "It's too dangerous. We suspect his captors are forcing him to manipulate dark energy. A dark master who uses his energy without reprieve will let it overtake him. If he cannot control his energy, he will turn on anyone he has a strong connection to. He will kill you and Julia and show no remorse. You will be the target of all his hate and rage. He will show no mercy."

"I'm not afraid of Rolf."

"You should be."

She stood, crossing her arms. "Peter, I'm helping my brothers find Rolf whether you assign me to the task or not."

"I had a feeling you would say that."

The office door opened wide and in walked Nate and Danny as though they'd been summoned. Geneva looked at Peter, suspicion edging her voice. "I'm not budging."

"I told you it was pointless to argue with her," Nate said to Peter.

"Yes, you did," Peter said, coming from around his desk to stand in front of Geneva. "I will allow you to join your brothers."

"Wonderful, I..."

Peter held out a hand, cutting her off. "On one condition."

"What?"

"If Rolf Jorgensen has turned into a killer, my orders to you and your brothers are to shoot first and ask questions later."

"He's not a killer."

"That remains to be seen. You wanna help track Rolf and protect Julia? You *will* agree to this condition."

"And if I don't?"

Peter nodded at her brothers. "That's why your brothers are here. And if I have to pull your father out of retirement, I'll do that too. This is for your own protection. We can't let a dark master destroy you and everyone else around you."

Geneva looked from Nate to Danny. They watched her, eyes unblinking. Her brothers could be a fierce combination working together. They would never harm her, she knew. But they were also not above forcing her cooperation if they thought it would protect her.

"So, what's it to be?" Peter asked. "Will you agree to my condition."

"Yes," she said and winced when a painting fell from the wall, the glass splintering.

"Good." Peter did not look at the wall. Instead, he gave her a small smile, straightened and returned to his seat behind his desk. "Now, here's what we're going to do."

31

CONTACT

R olf shouldn't have been so hard on the woman. She'd been trying to comfort him. But he'd turned on her like a lunatic. It was too easy to read her thoughts. She never bothered to disguise them. She didn't want him remembering Geneva. She was jealous. Still, she should not have wished Geneva dead.

He made his way to her section of the room. Amazing how his eyes had grown accustomed to the dark. How many days had he been trapped in this cave? Time lost any meaning when the sun never rose or set.

He sat on the edge of her cot and reached a hand to touch the woman, who lay curled in a ball in the center of her bed, rocking back and forth. She let out a small kittenish sound.

"I'm sorry." He found he meant it. "I didn't mean to turn on you. Being in the dark messes with me. Makes me irritable."

The woman found his hand. "It's okay. I didn't mean to think what I did. About her. Don't hate me."

He clasped her hand. "I don't. But you need to under-stand. Geneva is important to me. She keeps me sane."

"Do you love her?"

The woman's words hung in the darkness between them, like stars glimmering in the night, forever out of reach. *Love.* Was that what this was? This craving, raw, protective feeling whenever he was around Geneva for more than a second? Like he needed to be better—deserving of all her desire and admiration. Like he would do anything to have her atten-tion. Like they were meant to be together forever? Was this love?

And when they were apart for any length of time, his temper grew short and mood sour.

He shook his head before he remembered the woman couldn't see him. Geneva made him long for something greater than himself. To be the kind and generous and honorable man she thought he was, instead of the dark, cold, dangerous man he was fated to be. Why would he argue with Mother Nature? He would never be good enough to deserve Geneva. He wouldn't attach her to a monster.

"I don't know."

"Well, in that case, maybe I can provide some distrac-tion." She ran a hand up his arm, stopping at his biceps. "You've been in my mind, haven't you? You know I have feel-ings for you."

"Yes."

Her hand stroked his arm until it reached his shoulder. He placed his palm on hers, stopping the movement.

"There's something I need you to do for me."

GENEVA FOLLOWED her brothers out of the downtown Cleveland headquarters. They each had their marching orders. Peter had demanded she return to her apartment. She needed to fill Julia in, and they were to continue with their normal routine. Geneva hated the plan. But Peter had been insistent it was the best thing they could do to find Rolf.

"You're a target," he had told her. "Julia, as well. You know too much, and Gemcatcher is aware of it. He can't afford to keep you alive."

"So, our sister and Julia will be bait?" Danny had asked. "I don't like it. What if he kills them?"

"You two won't let that happen, will you?" Peter had left the question hanging in the air.

Her brothers' pride in their abilities prevented an argument.

Geneva drove to her apartment and used the remote to open the garage door.

"Everything feel normal?" She could hear the question in Nate's words, who had followed her in his car. One of her brothers would be watching the apartment all night. Nate had this evening's duty, Danny would take over during the day, and then Nate would be back for the next night's watch.

Geneva gazed at the ebb and flow of colors in the garage —normal yellows. *"Yes. Everything's fine."*

"Good. Make sure you tell me if anything seems suspicious when you get inside."

"Aye, aye, Captain." She hated taking orders from her protective big brothers. Of course, she would tell them if someone was inside.

She opened the door.

"What took you so long?" Julia called from the kitchen. "I'm a nervous wreck."

Geneva set her purse on the table. "Oh, you know.

Family obligations." She sniffed the air. "Smells good in here. Whatcha making?"

Julia turned from the stove, where she stirred something in a pot. "Tomato soup. Your dad called from Florida. He's worried about you. Wants you to stay close to your brothers until he gets back next week—said they're in town."

"He's right. Peter assigned them to the search for Rolf, and he didn't invite us to the party."

Julia dropped the ladle she held. Tomato soup went everywhere. Her face turned white.

"What's wrong? Are you okay?" Geneva rushed to Julia's side. She grabbed the ladle and placed it in the sink, careful to step over the mess of soup on the floor.

"I'm sorry. I know this is silly. But the man in my dream told me your brothers joined the search. I had forgotten until now."

"It's not silly. But also not hard to imagine. They're a good team. The best ones to find Rolf." Geneva studied her friend's muted red aura. "Tell you what, you sit, I'll clean this mess and serve." She forced a smile. "Nothing like a bowl of soup to put it all in perspective."

Geneva grabbed the dishrag and wiped the soup off the floor. She filled two bowls. She'd take a third out to Nate later, along with a sandwich. She didn't like that her brothers had agreed with Peter to put her on house arrest, but she wouldn't see them go hungry.

"Why didn't Peter involve us in the search?" Julia's emotions must have settled, and her mind now worked on the problem. "Is everything okay?"

Geneva took a spoonful of soup. Her stomach rumbled in response. It seemed ages since she'd had a decent meal. "Our emotions are involved. We're liable to slip and cause bigger problems." She sighed. "He compared me to a heat-seeking missile ready to detonate."

Julia giggled. "Sorry. I can see how he might say it, though. You pretend to be cool and off-limits, but you like my brother. I've known it forever. You act as if you hate him, but I can always see it in your eyes whenever you talk about him. I see it now. There's no way you'll ever stop searching." She released her spoon, the smile on her face dying a slow death. "It's me who's falling apart."

"You're not falling apart. You're worried about Rolf. I am, too. I know what you're feeling. I can't stop thinking about who has him and what they might be doing to him."

"Have you tried again to reach him?"

Geneva wiped her face with the napkin. "Not today. Today, I was told to act normal. You, too. This is about as normal as it gets for me."

Julia grinned. "Me, too." She stood and placed her bowl in the sink. "I think you should keep trying to reach Rolf. If he would find a way to communicate with anyone, it would be you."

Geneva watched the spoon in her dish rattle on its own. "Settle." She touched the vibrating object to silence it.

Julia joined her at the table. "What's got you so annoyed?"

Geneva sighed, wiped her sticky fingers on her napkin, and took a drink of her coffee. "Something Peter said."

Julia's eyes widened. Geneva read concern, fear, and a host of other emotions.

"About Rolf?"

Geneva nodded, swallowed. "Yes."

Julia didn't say anything, but Geneva knew she waited. Waited for the horrifying truth. Who was she to withhold it? She was not a fan of subterfuge. There was power in knowledge. "Peter thinks Rolf has turned. That he's being forced to use dark energy on a regular basis."

Julia covered her mouth. "Oh God, no."

"That's what I told him. I don't believe it. Rolf's an honorable man. The only way he'd turn is if whoever's holding him has a way to coerce him."

"The dream man warned me Rolf would try and kill me."

"I know, but remember your dreams aren't always accurate. Many times, they're symbolic. You have to remind yourself of that."

"You said you joined your brothers on this assignment. What does Peter want you to do?"

Julia had always been perceptive. Geneva searched the colors in her aura for any sign of a nervous breakdown. Violet dominated the landscape.

"He wants to use us as bait. He believes Gemcatcher wants me dead. I know too much."

"He suggested you return home and wait for Gemcatcher to attack?"

"That's about it. When he does, my brothers will be here. Together, we'll prevent him from succeeding."

"But that's awful. What if he kills you before we can stop it?"

"If it helps us find Rolf, it's a risk I'm willing to take. I would hope my talent would offer us some protection."

Geneva's phone buzzed, and she glanced at the incoming call. A jolt of fear surged through her system. Her hand shook so hard, the phone fell to the tiled floor before she could answer. The kitchen lights flickered, but she didn't pay any attention. She dropped to the ground, scrambling for her phone.

"Geneva, what is it? What's wrong?"

"It's...It's...him. It's Rolf." Geneva's hands shook as she slid her finger across the screen. Julia hovered over her. "Hello? Hello, Rolf? Where are you? Are you okay?"

"It's about time you answered. Listen, I don't have much time."

Rolf's deep, familiar voice sent a wave of aching relief through her stomach. He was alive. He was not dead, and he didn't sound like a hardened killer, or that he'd been missing for days. He sounded like he had the last time she'd talked to him. "Where have you been? What have they done to you?"

"I don't know. I've been kept somewhere dark. Some kind of room. Listen, I don't have much time. I need you to pay attention."

"Okay."

"Where are you?"

"I'm home. In my apartment."

"Are you alone?"

"Julia's here."

There was a short pause, and Rolf spoke again. "You and Julia need to leave your place immediately. Go to the coffee shop around the corner—Coffersations. Don't tell anyone where you're going. No one. If you do, they'll kill me. Do you understand?"

"Yes, but Rolf..."

"They're coming. I have to go. Remember, tell no one. I'll meet you there."

"Rolf, wait."

The call ended. How had Rolf managed to make a phone call? Why hadn't he answered all the countless messages she had left since he'd been gone?

32

MISTAKE

"We should alert your brother. It's probably a trap," Julia said. Vivid red sparks flickered within her aura.

"What if it's not? What if Rolf's found a way to escape and needs our help? If we take Nate along, he'll kill Rolf. Peter has told him Rolf is rogue or close to turning. He'll shoot him before he'll listen to what he has to say."

"My dream man told me Rolf would try to kill me, remember? We'd be foolish not to tell Nate."

Geneva sighed and ran a hand through her hair. Much as she didn't want to believe Julia's dream, she'd be foolish to ignore the warning. "Okay, I'm sure you're right. But I swear, if Nate shoots Rolf, I'll never forgive him. Let's go then."

Julia turned toward the door, but Geneva laid a hand on her arm. "No, wait. Someone could be watching the house. Let me get his attention first."

She opened her mind. "Rolf's alive."

Almost immediately, Nate answered. "Stay inside. I'll be right there."

Twenty seconds later, Nate appeared at the door, and Julia let him inside.

"He's been in touch?" Nate's eyes glittered, and his aura was tinged with lime green, indicating his excitement.

Geneva nodded. "He called a few minutes ago—said he was being held somewhere in the dark, but he'll meet Julia and me at Coffersations. We're to come alone. He said they'd kill him if we didn't."

"Who's they?"

"I don't know. He hung up before I could find out."

"I don't like this. Does Peter know?"

She shook her head. "There hasn't been time to contact him."

Nate pulled out his phone and called Peter. "Rolf contacted Geneva. Yeah, says he's at the coffee shop around the corner. He wants Geneva and Julia to meet him there alone. Claims whoever has him will kill him if they don't."

There was a pause while Nate listened to whatever Peter had to tell him. "No, he didn't tell her...you're kidding. All right. All right. I'll tell her."

Nate ended the call and turned toward Geneva, his expression a thin line.

"What is it?"

"Peter wants us to meet Rolf at the coffee shop."

"And?"

"There's a good chance Rolf has gone rogue. Peter's contacting Danny and others for help. We're to shoot at the first sign of danger. Got it?"

Geneva wasn't sure she could pull the trigger. The mere thought had her stomach turning over. But she nodded because she was anxious to get moving.

"You two go first." Nate motioned toward the front door.

"I'll follow close behind. But try and make him think it's just the two of you."

Geneva opened the door and started the short walk to Coffersations. She didn't hear Nate leave, but when she looked back a few seconds in, he was gone. She pointed toward the street corner. "It's that brown building up ahead." Her pulse quickened at the thought of seeing Rolf again. God, how she'd missed him.

They reached the corner, and she held out an arm to keep Julia from crossing the street, so she could do a quick scan of the building up ahead. She searched for Rolf's familiar green energy waves. Nothing. "Let's go." She motioned Julia to cross the street.

When they reached the other side, she took a breath and opened the door, jingling the bell. "You look left, I'll look right," she said to Julia, whose face had grown pale the minute they stepped inside. "What's wrong?"

Geneva's gaze moved to where Julia stared. Rolf sat in a corner booth. He looked how she remembered him the last time they'd been together. Tight T-shirt, blue jeans, and a smile that could charm the devil himself. Except where did the green in his aura go?

Geneva's gaze rested on Rolf's eyes, which seemed to grow larger in his face. That's when fear grabbed a tendril of her heart and unwound it, bit by bit. The look in Rolf's eyes was frigid—like the icy cold waters of Lake Erie in the dead of winter. Not a hint of recognition sparked from their frozen depths.

Geneva grabbed Julia's hand and stepped backward. Rolf's eyes pulled her in and held her captive so she couldn't look away. He tilted his head. Dark energy blasted forth in a steady stream. "Get down," Geneva ordered.

Her friend remained motionless, her skin chalky white.

In seconds, she would be swallowed by the dark energy. Panic ripped through Geneva's system. Time slowed to a crawl until it seemed to stop altogether. In the split-second Geneva had to consider, she noticed many details at once. Patrons, oblivious to the psychic storm about to erupt, chattered and ordered drinks. Energy shimmered in the air. Nate's energy, who had entered behind them. She pulled it inside as the dark reached for Julia with deadly hands. Tears trickled down Geneva's cheeks, and the swollen bubble inside her chest popped.

Energy blasted from her body with all the focus of a spewing volcano. A sound screeched through the shop, like a train derailing and plowing into the building. The foundation shook.

"Earthquake," someone yelled.

People ran in every direction, plowing into her in the process.

"Get down." Nate pushed her and Julia out of the way, missing the black tendrils stretching toward them by mere inches. The dark energy swallowed the tables and chairs in its way, creating a clear path in front of Rolf. Debris flew through the air, striking her cheek.

"Julia!" Nate yelled, crouching over Julia's body. She lay on the floor, unmoving. He had his hands on hers. Nate was working to bring her to consciousness.

Rolf stood and moved toward them.

Oh God. Geneva blinked. A shadowy figure stood beyond Rolf and moved toward the back of the shop. Her eyes couldn't pick out features, but her heightened senses revealed a bright yellow. A familiar yellow. Where had she seen it? Was the mysterious person controlling Rolf?

"Rolf, no." Geneva pleaded, hoping for a sign of the old Rolf. Hoping for compassion. "Don't do it!"

He didn't stop moving. His eyes weren't eyes at all, but two black pits inside his skull. He grinned, and the horrifying sight sent Geneva's heartbeat ricocheting in her chest.

"He's turned." Nate looked up at her, his eyes reflecting the panic she felt. "Kill him."

Her heart was being ripped from her chest and stepped on, splintering into hundreds of tiny fragments. She must kill or be killed.

"Hurry. Do it. Now." Nate sent her round balls of teal energy.

She sucked the energy inside, careful to avoid the dark waves. She closed her eyes, not wanting to watch Rolf's destruction. She crossed her fingers and let the gigantic ball of energy she'd gathered flow through and out of her.

TEARS LEAKED from Geneva's eyes. She and Nate traveled back to her apartment in his flashy black Mustang. She could see her brother's anger in the red pulsing from his aura, but there was mauve in the mix, too. He knew her sorrow. He was giving her time to grieve. And grieve she did.

Geneva cried for unrequited love and empty promises. She cried for Julia, who lay in a coma in the hospital, fighting for her life. She cried for the man she loved, who had turned from her fiercest protector into a soulless demon she didn't recognize.

Nate's phone buzzed, and he answered. "Hello."

Geneva half-listened. She stared out the window at the scenery flashing by her window, not bothering to wipe the tears that continued to roll down her cheeks.

"She's fine. I don't agree. Why the hell would you do that?"

Geneva watched her brother's reflection in the glass. He glanced her way. Dark red energy spread across his form, blotting out his normal teal aura.

"All right. Okay. I got it. I'll call you later."

She turned toward him. "What's the matter?"

Nate's lips thinned. "It's not good news."

"What do you mean?"

"The CMU has listed you a threat. They're stripping your badge."

"I'm not a threat."

Nate pulled the Mustang into her apartment complex. "Peter doesn't think so, but he has no choice. You caused a 4.0 magnitude earthquake back there, injured Julia and dozens of others, and you didn't kill the bad guy. He's having a really hard time explaining that."

"What will happen to Rolf?" She clasped her fingers together to keep them from shaking or latching onto the energy shimmering in front of her, waiting for her to exercise her talent.

"What do you mean, what will happen to him? You were there. Jorgensen's snapped and on the loose. You're clearly his target. I've got to stop him."

Shivers racked her body, and she wrapped her hands around her body. Why couldn't she stop shivering?

"I'm sorry, Sis. I know this is hard for you to accept. You're too young to remember the last time a dark master snapped and went on a rampage. But I was ten. I remember it well. It was right before our mom died."

A shudder struck her. "What...what happened?"

"The guy attacked a summer camp of children. Killed almost a hundred kids and injured a hundred others. It took Dad and a dozen hackers from many countries to band together to bring him to justice."

"Where is he now?"

"Dead. He died in prison after serving multiple terms."

The engine sputtered and stalled. A muscle ticked in Nate's jaw. "Get a hold of yourself."

Geneva folded her hands together in her lap and dug her nails into her palms. Then she filled her lungs and emptied them. She'd kill the sons of bitches who had done this to Rolf. The man she knew would never harm his sister, let alone try to kill her. And he'd protect Geneva with his last dying breath. If it was the last thing she did in this world, she'd find who had made him do this terrible thing, and she'd kill them.

She wouldn't think beyond that. Couldn't think beyond that. Without Rolf, nothing else seemed to matter.

33

ESCAPE

"*Rolf, no, please no. Don't do it!*"

The words screamed in his head, but he remained in the dark room, the madwoman nearby. Or was it he who was mad?

"*Geneva? Are you hurt?*"

Silence greeted his frantic thought. He couldn't sit still, knowing Geneva needed him. He rose and walked toward the woman. Geneva's fear vibrated over the dark psychic channel that allowed him to share in her distress. Anger, hot and white, stabbed into his brain. He grasped the sides of his head as if doing so could take away her agony.

The doorknob turned. Although he'd lost track of time in his prison, their only visitor since he'd arrived had been Cynthia. Cynthia, who drained him of energy on a regular basis with her cold and merciless talent. Today, she'd handcuffed him when she left.

Dark energy erupted, incited by his fury. Cynthia was smart to cuff him. He couldn't stand one more second in this godforsaken place. He would escape.

"It's time." He motioned to the woman who moved

toward him, although there was no way she could see his arm movement. Funny, his plans all hinged on her cooperation.

With his cuffed hands, he pushed her toward his cot. She ripped off his shirt, and her lips somehow found his. The door opened, and lights flooded the place, blinding them.

"What the hell?"

The scene distracted Cynthia, giving him a few precious seconds to attack. He shoved the woman out of the way. Dark energy exploded from his chest and arms like he'd lit a can of gasoline. He didn't wait for Cynthia to recover enough to disperse the dark energy, but exploded past her in a rush, using the energy to dissolve his handcuffs and yanking them apart to grab the door from her startled grasp. He tore through the hallway, the woman close on his heels. "Follow me," he yelled at the woman who scrambled after him.

More footsteps sounded close behind. He didn't waste time looking to see who followed. He kept running, running, running, his eyes closing in on the exit door ahead. Five more seconds until he reached it. Four, three, two. He burst through the solid wood door. Thank God it wasn't locked.

A set of stairs led to the next level. What was this place? Some sort of underground bunker from the looks of things.

"Stop, or I'll shoot."

The man's voice called after them, but Rolf ignored it. He plunged toward the steps, the woman close behind him. He could feel her warm breath on his back. Hear her gasps for breath. A gunshot rang out, the sound amplified by the open stairwell, then two more.

Up, up, up they went, a mad dash for freedom.

He reached the top, blinking at the dimness of the second level. More gunshots. This time a bullet grazed his neck. He flinched and yelled, stumbling and running. A stinging pain numbed his skin, and a gush of blood smeared his neck. His hand found the spot and rubbed and came away wet. But there was the doorway to the outside. Three seconds more to freedom.

He grabbed the woman's hand and lunged toward the exit.

"If you leave, you're a dead man." Cynthia's voice came from the bottom of the stairs. "The CMU has a warrant for your arrest. They'll find you and kill you."

He didn't bother to respond but rushed through the door, the woman on his heels. An empty parking lot greeted them. He paused a moment to catch his breath, glancing back once at the building. Moonlight shined on what appeared to be an abandoned factory. Nothing moved. No one followed. He grabbed the woman's hands and fled into the night.

They ran and ran and ran until they could run no more.

"Please."

He stopped and glanced back at her. For the first time, he got a closer look at his companion. Blonde curly hair, wild eyes, a thin, narrow white face. She looked giddy and frightened at the same time. Her clothes hung on her thin frame.

She gasped and bent over to catch her breath. "Please."

He stilled. She looked familiar. A dim memory of someone he knew. A familiar ache started at his left temple, and he winced. The pain struck sharp and deep. He doubled over, clutching his skull.

"Rolf, what's wrong?"

The woman had crouched next to him. He caught a breath. The pain eased.

He raised his head. "I remembered your name."

"My name?"

"Yes. You were the sister of the rogue hacker on one of my last big jobs. Your name is Kaitlyn Girard. You're an illusion talent."

Now it was her turn to wince and moan, holding her head in her hands. He watched her recover, helpless to take away her pain.

He wiped his sweating palms on his jeans. "We should— we should keep moving."

"Where?"

"I don't know."

But he did know. The dark energy knew. It craved the light. With his psychic senses on full throttle, his feet moved forward. "Follow me."

Large hills appeared to the side of the road they traveled. What were they? The glow of a streetlight ahead helped him get acclimated to their surroundings. They were in the Flats in Cleveland. The hills were large piles of iron ore. They kept walking until they came out of the Flats onto Euclid Avenue. They had no money, but he managed to flag a cab that happened to be passing.

"Take me to Lakewood. Summit Street."

The cabbie nodded, and off they went.

"Where are we going?"

The woman would not like his answer. But he told her anyway. *"Geneva's apartment."*

"She won't want me."

"Don't worry about Geneva."

"Here's Summit Street." The cabbie interrupted their

secret conversation. "Where do you want me to drop you off?"

"This is good."

The cabbie pulled over. They opened the doors and got out. The total on the meter read thirty-two dollars.

"What is your name?"

"Adolpho."

"Give me your business card, Adolpho. I'll mail you the payment." He injected a pulse of energy with each word. Dark energy filled his chest, eager to break through and devour every scrap of living tissue in its path. Sweat dripped from his forehead. He gritted his teeth until they hurt.

The cabbie's eyes widened. "Yes, okay." He handed Rolf his card.

Rolf punched the door shut and watched the taillights as the cabbie pulled away from the curb. The dark in him had taken control. Thank God the cab driver had been cooperative.

Fear dislodged another memory he'd forgotten until now. He winced and gasped as the pain came, and he doubled over. He'd been twelve, walking home from school, when he'd run into the neighborhood bully. The kid had made fun of his beloved Nonna, telling some fantastic tale about how she could pull a person's soul back into a body at the moment of death. Before he could stop it, dark energy shot from his hands and covered the bully. He hadn't injured him, though. Nonna had been horrified when he'd recounted the story to her.

"Sticks and stones. There've been far worse things said about me." She'd gotten down on one knee, and looked him in the eyes, a fierce expression on her lined face. "You mustn't ever use dark energy unless your life is in danger. Understand me?"

Funny that. Hackers were always in danger.

The pain had lessened now. He straightened and thought more about that day—the day his lessons began. That was the day Nonna began training him to master the darkness. And she'd succeeded, too. But he'd always known there would be a day of reckoning. Nonna had known it, too. That's why he'd been sworn to secrecy. Until now. *I'm sorry, Nonna.*

Thinking of his grandmother made him wonder if she'd recovered, and if his father cared for her at her home, as he'd promised. He turned to the woman, who stood watching him. "Are you coming or not?"

She nodded. "I'm staying with you."

He walked toward Geneva's apartment. He didn't wait to see if the woman followed. But his feet slowed when they were four houses away, and the woman bumped into him.

"Sorry. I need a second."

He studied the house. Light shone from the windows. The curtains were drawn. But something was wrong. He closed his eyes and allowed his mind to wander.

"Danny and Dad are on their way over here."

Nate paced her apartment, walking back and forth from the fireplace to the couch to the windows and back again. "I hope to God Julia survives."

"I know. Me too." Tears rolled down her cheeks. She sat on the couch and clutched a throw pillow to stop the shakes. "I never believed Rolf would try to kill his sister. He loves her. I'm sure of it. The man in Coffersations...he...it couldn't have been Rolf."

"What do you mean?" Nate stopped pacing midway to

the windows and turned to face her, concern etched on his face.

"I mean the man I saw looked like Rolf and sounded like him, but his eyes were dead. Like someone controlled him."

"That's what they say about someone who has turned. They can't express emotion. The dark energy rules their nature. That's what you observed."

"Yes, that's what I thought, too, when he took aim at Julia. I thought he had turned. But..."

"What?"

When she didn't answer, Nate walked to the couch and sat next to her. He took the throw pillow from her hands and set it aside. Then he wrapped a long arm around her shoulders and gave her a squeeze. "Geneva, what happened in there? You could have killed him. I know you could have. You let him escape, didn't you?"

She nodded. "Oh God." A fresh deluge of tears spilled from her eyes. Nate handed her a box of tissues, his aura going from teal to mauve. *Pity.* She took a couple tissues and held onto the box. No doubt she'd need them.

"Why'd you do it? Why'd you let him go?"

"Because I saw a figure behind him. Someone else was there in the shop. Someone was manipulating him—making him do it."

"Are you sure? I didn't see anyone.

"Positive. There was someone else there."

"Who was it? Anyone you recognized even vaguely?"

"No, it was too dark. But..." She blew her nose into the tissue.

"But what?"

His answer was interrupted by the chime of the doorbell.

"Hold your thought. I'll be right back."

Nate went to answer the door. Geneva spent the time reviewing the decision she'd made. In the split second she'd had to decide Rolf's and Julia's fate, she had faced a life-altering choice in the truest sense of the word. A choice to allow Rolf to live or die. A choice to give him a chance to redeem himself and keep Julia safe from harm.

She rubbed her hands across her face. She'd chosen life —or so she thought. She'd directed the energy ball to the right of Rolf so he wouldn't receive its full impact. It should have been enough to stun him until the authorities arrived. But in the aftermath, her attention had been diverted to Julia, who had been knocked unconscious when a piece of the crumbling building struck her in the head. When Geneva turned back, Rolf had disappeared.

She heard raised voices, announcing her dad's and Danny's presence before she saw them enter the family room. That and the force of the trio's energy. The familiar colors in their combined auras leaped across the room at her. Bright cornflower, royal blue, and vibrant teal.

"Dad." She surged to her feet, swiping at her eyes.

Her father took two giant steps and enveloped her in a massive bear hug, pressing her face into his red-checkered, flannel-clad chest. "I'm here now, Geneva, my girl. It's going to be okay."

Her dad smelled like the great outdoors—all campfires, apples, and fresh air. That and the familiar endearment caused a rush of tears to roll down her cheeks, wetting the front of his shirt.

"It's going to be okay." He smoothed a calloused palm across her hair as if she were five and had awakened from a bad dream. He would take her pain away if he could.

But he could not. This was real and not a dream. Plus, she was no longer five and afraid of the dark.

"Thanks, Dad." She pulled her head from the comfort of his burly chest to get a better look at his larger-than-life presence. Her father could be Santa Claus's twin. He always wore red, and he sported a full head of blond hair and a matching beard. He had the heart of Santa, too, always willing to help or lend a hand.

"Sit down now and tell us what happened." He gestured to the couch. "Don't you worry. We'll figure this out."

She complied, and he sat next to her. Nate took the over-stuffed leather chair across from them, and Danny occupied the loveseat.

"They know the basics already," Nate said. "But you'd been about to talk about the figure you saw in the shop. Who was it? Do you know?"

She frowned. "I couldn't tell. It was much too dark to see anything."

"What did you observe with your psychic senses?" her dad asked, stroking his beard.

She glanced at her dad, then Nate and Danny. They studied her with three pairs of bright gray eyes. Blue light in various shades bounced from their hands toward her.

She took a deep breath. Her family was much too obser-vant and caring for her to keep secrets. "The energy, it was an odd shade of yellow. I'm certain I've seen it before. If I could only remember where."

"You're going to need to remember everything you can if we are to get you away from the Corvey Institution," Danny said.

Geneva's eyes widened. "What do you mean?"

"Peter's been ordered to have you removed from the CMU. He wants you under evaluation at the Institution until he can decide what to do. You're classified as a poten-tial threat."

Adrenaline ripped through her system. She curled her hands at her sides. "I'm not a threat to anyone. I was trying to protect Julia from Rolf."

"We know. Peter does, too," her dad said.

"But the fact remains, you didn't take him out," Nate said. "And if Rolf's on the loose killing people, you and Julia will be first on his list. When dark masters turn rogue, they go after the ones they care about the most. The theory is they want to blot out their past feelings. Frankly, the safest place for you both is the Corvey Institution. Grimshaw is gone. There's a new head doctor in place, and he's got a great reputation from all accounts. You'll be in good hands until we can find Jorgensen."

"Why, so you can kill him?" She stood and faced her family. "He needs help, not a death sentence. I can find Rolf. You said yourself he wants to kill me. What better way to draw him out in the open? Let's find a way to take him peacefully."

Her brothers looked at each other. "You aren't thinking," Danny said.

Nate stood and resumed his pacing. "Danny's right. You're talking about finding a peaceful way to terminate a cold, hard killer capable of blotting out our existence with a single shot of dark energy. It's too dangerous. If Rolf were in his right mind, he would be the first to tell you he would not want to live as a sociopath. He'd be begging you to kill him so he wouldn't kill you."

"No." She swiped tears from her eyes and rubbed her aching head. "No. I don't believe this."

"It's true," Nate said. He placed a solid arm across her shoulder. "Geneva, I promise you. If there's a way to take Rolf alive, we'll do it. Please don't make this difficult for us. We cannot allow Rolf to harm you or Julia or anyone else.

Let us escort you to the Institution where you'll be safe. We can have Julia moved there, too, so you can watch over her —keep her from harm."

Geneva gazed at Nate's calm demeanor. Her brothers were hardened members of the CMU, but they'd never outright lied to her, and the turquoise color coming from their tall forms meant they told the truth. Her gaze moved to her dad. He nodded, letting her know he agreed with her brothers.

She stood and moved to the windows, parting the curtains and looking toward the empty street. Rolf was somewhere out there. Right now. On the loose. Capable of killing multitudes. She thought again of his dark, soulless blue eyes and of Julia, lying on the hard coffee shop floor, pale as a corpse. She couldn't stop the shiver that traveled down her spine. *My fault. No one else's.*

She turned to face them. "All right."

34

HE SPEAKS

Geneva left her apartment, suitcase in hand. Rolf and the woman watched from the bushes across the street. Rolf grimaced and grabbed the side of the house, as if it would keep him standing. When he had lain in his bed in his prison, fighting the dark energy sweeping through his system, he'd imagined seeing Geneva again. But the sweet image paled into insignificance next to the real thing. Her soft face glowed in the moonlight, striking next to her long blonde hair.

God, he'd missed her. An incredible urge to launch himself across the yard, pull her into his arms, and kiss the hell out of her swept over him. He took one step forward, then two. Nate appeared, followed by Danny, triggering Rolf's internal alarm system. He stepped back into his hiding spot. Where were they headed? And why were they carrying suitcases?

They put their luggage in the trunk and piled into Geneva's car. She gave the keys to Nate.

Rolf frowned. Why wasn't she driving? For that matter, why wasn't she more aware of her surroundings? If she had been, he and the woman wouldn't have been able to hide this close without being detected. She would have spotted the shift in his energy that accelerated upon seeing her.

He clenched his fists, his mind racing with possibilities. He found a crack in her defenses, then latched onto a thought and another and another.

Rolf...killer...Coffersations...Corvey Institution...Julia...coma... my fault...airport.

Julia, my God, how had he forgotten her? His sister. But why was Geneva imagining Julia in a coma and himself a killer? What had happened, for Christ's sake? What had Cynthia and her partner made him do?

The slam of the car door snapped him to the present. He would have answers. He moved from his hiding place. But it was too late. He watched as Geneva's Honda Civic sped south, toward what he suspected was the Cleveland airport.

He turned to the woman. "We need to figure out where they're taking her."

"You do realize this could be disastrous for us." Gemcatcher kept his voice cool, although he was anything but. "I warned you your infatuation with Rolf would cause us trouble. You should have heeded my warning."

After Rolf's escape from the abandoned glass factory they used for their experiments, Cynthia had followed him to his Cleveland condo, out of breath and full of apologies. Now she sat at the kitchen counter, gazing at him with wide eyes.

"I didn't think he was interested in Kaitlyn Girard. Why would I? He seemed indifferent to her. I did tell you, if you'll recall, that he'd remembered Geneva. I assumed she was the one he wanted."

Gemcatcher rubbed his chin and regarded Cynthia with what he hoped was a calm expression. He needed to make sure she was following the right plan—his—and understood the severity of the situation. "And you assumed right. He's using Kaitlyn. A man would never endure the kind of pain he endured to remember a woman he didn't care about."

He didn't wait for Cynthia to respond but moved to the liquor cabinet, poured himself a shot of Maker's Mark, tilted his head, and downed it in one swallow. He set the glass in the sink and turned to face Cynthia, who opened her mouth to argue. He held up a hand. "I'm not sure you comprehend the consequences of your actions. I promised our buyers two hundred and fifty charged crystals. We're only able to deliver fifty."

She made a so-what face and shrugged a shoulder. "Still fifty million dollars. Not bad."

Blood rushed to his head. A vein pulsed at his temple. His left eye started its damnable twitching. "Not compared to two hundred and fifty million, it's not."

The words came out on a hiss and hung in the air, but Cynthia didn't seem to notice. She rose and stretched. "What do you expect me to do? I can't very well chase after Rolf, can I?"

If she hoped to stump him, it didn't work. He had an answer. "Why not? You know where he'll go, don't you? Don't look at me like you don't know what the hell I'm talking about. He'll go after Geneva, of course. I understand from Ortiz she's staying at the Corvey Institution. I'd suggest you hightail it out there on the fastest flight."

"Alone? What about you?"

"What about me? I can't be seen at the Corvey Institution. Someone will recognize me. It's too dangerous. You, however, are a roving reporter. Isn't it interesting your latest assignment involves interviewing a few of the patients at the renowned Institution?"

Cynthia stared at him a moment, a blank look in her pale green eyes. He waited for her brain to catch up. "You want me to travel to the Corvey Institution on the pretense of interviewing Geneva? Whatever for?"

He gave a short bark of laughter, although his thoughts were far from funny. "Brilliant deduction, Watson."

"She'll never agree to talk to me."

"Ah, but then, you're not really going to interview her, are you? You only need to use your position as a member of the media to get access to the Institution. Once you're in, you'll corner Geneva in her room when no one else is there. Threaten her life and allow her to alert Rolf. If he's there, Jorgensen will show, I promise."

"You make it sound easy."

Gemcatcher tightened his jaw. "All you have to do is zap Jorgensen and make him charge the rest of those crystals. Got it? We'll be able to collect the full two hundred fifty million. Get moving and call me when you get into Chicago."

Cynthia frowned and found her purse and keys. She moved to the door slowly and grasped the handle, turning at the last moment to fling a final question his way. "And how do you expect me to zap him? He'll be on the lookout for me. He won't get close."

"Simple. Make him believe you've harmed Geneva Ericksen. He'll get close if he thinks it's necessary to save her."

"I assume you'll make sure I'm cleared with security?"

"Of course. But be ready with that talent of yours. Jorgensen's probably turned rogue. You won't have more than a second to react."

GENEVA PRESSED her fingers against her temples and counted. *One-thousand one, one-thousand-two, one-thousand-three.* Maybe if she applied pressure, it would keep the nasty headache from turning into a migraine.

She sat next to Julia's hospital bed at the Corvey Institution and studied the still, silent figure. Julia's father and her own had stopped by earlier but left to get some sleep at a nearby hotel. Her brothers had left her alone for a moment so they could consult with the doctor and nurses.

The blood caking Julia's forehead had been wiped, her head bandaged. An IV ran from her hand to a tube, pumping water and nutrients into her system.

Geneva should never have allowed Julia to go with her to Coffersations today. Her friend had warned her about what was in store, and Geneva had downplayed her concerns. Why hadn't she listened? If she had, they'd both still be hanging out in her apartment instead of this damn Institution. And Julia would not be in a coma.

A nurse entered and checked Julia's vitals. She must have been satisfied because she left. Silent tears slid from Geneva's eyes. She did nothing to wipe them. Her thoughts raced in every direction. *Oh, dear Rolf. Why would you do this thing? I can't believe it. I can't believe you're a cold, hard killer. That person in Coffersations was not the man I know. It wasn't you. It couldn't have been. What have they done to you to make you want to harm your sister?*

"*You're right. It wasn't me. I don't remember any of it. I didn't do what you're thinking.*"

She straightened and looked around the room. "*Rolf? Rolf? Is that you? Where are you?*"

"*I'm nearby. What's happened to Julia?*"

But of course, he was nearby. They weren't linked. He couldn't speak to her in her mind unless he was close. But what if this was a trap? "*Why'd you do it? Hurt your sister. Try to kill me. Do you hate us that much?*"

"*Never, Geneva. I would never try to kill you or Julia. I didn't hurt her. It wasn't me. Believe me.*"

"*I saw and talked to you. You told us to meet you in Coffersations. When we got there, you tried to kill us with dark energy. I stopped you, but Julia got hurt. She's in a coma.*"

"*I'll kill them.*" Rage and frustration and panic vibrated over their psychic link before Rolf swept it inward. "*I didn't do it. I swear. I wasn't in Coffersations. I didn't call you.*"

"*You were there, Rolf. I saw you. Did—did someone make you do it? Who? Tell me.*"

"*No. I mean, I don't remember doing anything. I wasn't anywhere near Coffersations. I would have had to be to attempt to kill her. And I would never kill my sister. I swear it.*"

Voices sounded in the hall. "*My brothers. They're coming for me. I can't talk now.*"

"*Wait. Don't go. Why are you there?*"

"*Ortiz's orders. He believes I'm a problem because I didn't kill you when I had the chance and allowed Julia to be...to be injured.*"

Her brothers entered along with a nurse. Their stoic expressions gave nothing away, but the various shades of red enveloping their bodies recorded their deep anxiety. "Okay, Geneva. Time to go. They're putting you in the quiet ward so you can get some rest. You'll be safe there." Nate gathered her suitcase and gestured toward the doorway.

Rolf spoke in her mind. *"I can't believe they would place you back with Grimshaw."*

"Rolf, Dr. Grimshaw is dead."

Danny slung an arm around her shoulder. "We've got you checked in. It's been a long day. Let's get you to your room. Diane, here"—he gestured toward the nurse—"will take care of Julia and let you know if there's been any change."

Geneva followed her brothers across the hall and around the corner to the elevators. Nate pressed the button, and when the doors opened, ushered her inside. Danny followed.

Rolf was somewhere close, otherwise he would not have been able to exchange thoughts with her. She shivered. Nate, of course, noticed.

"What's wrong?"

"Nothing. I'm fine."

"Cold?"

"Yes." Her brothers wouldn't be happy to learn she and Rolf had spoken.

Nate's gaze sliced into her brain. Energy slammed into her mind before she could stop it. She sucked in a breath and blew it out in a rush and fought off his entry. She snarled. "Stay out of my head."

"You've been talking to him, haven't you?"

She wouldn't answer. It wasn't a lie if she didn't answer.

"I know you care about Rolf. But the Rolf you care about is gone. You can't trust the new Rolf. He's not the same person. Don't believe anything he tells you."

"What if he didn't do it? What if someone made him do it?"

Nate blew out a breath, crimson fog spewing into the air around him. The elevator doors opened, and they got out on the third floor. "That kind of thinking will get you killed."

Soft lights and plush carpet gave a homey atmosphere to this portion of the Institution. For now, she was being treated as a guest and not a patient. Her family's doing, Geneva suspected.

She trailed Nate through the hall with Danny close behind, as if they feared Rolf would snatch her from under their noses. When they arrived in front of room 406, he stopped. This wing of the Institution was designed to include small efficiency-style apartments. Nate swiped a keycard in the lock and opened her door.

The small room contained a bed with a purple bedspread, a flat-screened TV, a maple dresser, nightstand, bathroom, and a small kitchenette. Nate set her suitcase by the bed, and Danny drew the gray shades on either side of the large window. The Corvey Institution was set on ten acres in a beautiful resort atmosphere. Elm trees outlined a grassy landscape. The evening sun sank against a backdrop of a purplish skyline.

"Rolf, are you still here?" Silence. To calm herself, she spoke. "When's your return flight to Cleveland?"

Her brothers glanced at each other. Nate answered. "We're sticking around. If Rolf's talking to you, he's close."

Geneva looked from Nate to Danny and back to Nate. "You're planning to kill him, aren't you?" She didn't wait for an answer but rushed on, her voice deep and raspy and hardly recognizable even to her own ears. "What if you're wrong about Rolf? What if he hasn't turned? How will you feel if you kill an innocent man?"

Nate sighed. "I've been thinking about that. I have. I hope to God Jorgensen hasn't turned, and he'll come out of this whole thing unscathed. We know you care about him. Contrary to what you believe, we don't want to hurt him. But our job is to keep you safe. We'll do what we have to do."

"I don't need or want two babysitters."

"You have no choice," Danny said. "Peter's ordered us to stay close. Besides, Dad's worried. He's not leaving. He wants to try and get you released into his care. In the meantime, we promised to look out for you. And we're all concerned about Julia."

She grimaced. Her brothers' ideas of looking out for someone and her own ideas weren't the same. "You can't stay here."

Nate raised one eyebrow. A small frown marred his features. "We've rented hotel rooms down the road. One of us will be here every day. That's final. Now get some sleep. You won't see the doctor until tomorrow morning, and we've been assured no one will disturb you until then."

She drew in air to argue, and he raised a hand to silence her. He gestured to Danny. "Let's go."

They walked to the door, but Nate paused and turned. "Listen, Geneva. If Jorgensen contacts you again, we need to know. Understood?"

She sighed and sat on the bed as weariness took over. What good would it do to argue? She rolled her head in a slight motion, which she supposed Nate interpreted as agreement because he didn't press her.

"Try not to worry about Julia. Get some rest, and Danny will be over first thing in the morning to check on both of you. You'll be safe here—the door will lock behind me. It's a special door, impervious to the use of your talent, so don't try to force it. We don't want anyone going out or in."

She opened her mouth to protest and shut it again. The click of the lock reverberated in the small space.

35

PUZZLE PIECES

My God, her brothers had locked her in this room like a prisoner. Could she blame them? They believed she had lost her reason and would open the door for Rolf if he managed to get by the staff. And perhaps they were right. She didn't quite know what she would do.

"*Rolf, are you there?*" Geneva wasted little time attempting to contact Rolf. Where had he gone after their brief discussion?

She waited, her stomach twisting. Silence. Maybe he'd been re-captured by whoever held him. Maybe she'd imagined his familiar, cool voice in her head. Maybe it had all been wishful thinking or a trap.

She put on her PJs, removed her makeup, brushed her teeth, turned off the light, and slipped into bed. The normal routine calmed her fears. But even with her eyes closed, she couldn't erase the image of Rolf as she'd last seen him in Coffersations. His soulless eyes tore her heart from her chest and ripped it in two. What if Rolf tricked her? What if he lied to earn her trust, so he could kill both his girlfriend and his sister in one swoop?

Geneva rolled over and punched her pillow before falling into a fitful sleep. A few hours later, she woke to—what? She opened her eyes, got up, and turned on the bedside lamp. Something disturbed her psychic senses, interrupting her dreams. She turned toward the corner, her gaze sweeping the room—the door, the dresser, the night-stand. Her eyes returned to the corner to the right of the window before moving on. Nothing. Her imagination. She sunk onto the bed.

A glimmer caught her eye. A green light in the shape of a man materialized and stepped through the wall, shimmering in the corner. Adrenaline tunneled through her body, and she backed against the headboard. Who the hell was it? *Gemcatcher?* But no. The hologram shifted, hardened, and took solid form. A man stood in front of her in his full physical form, gazing at her with a devil-may-care smile she'd recognize anywhere. *"Holy shit! Rolf, is it really you?"*

She scampered off the bed. He raised two fingers in a cocky salute and grinned.

Geneva expected to feel his anger or fear or madness, but calm reflected from the dark figure still giving off sparks of green energy.

"Yes. Sorry to startle you." This wasn't a disembodied voice in her mind but the real thing. He needed a haircut, a shave, and probably a shower, but otherwise—dear God, he looked good. She couldn't remove her eyes from him. A warm wave of relief washed over her, followed by a rush of cold fear. Earlier today, Rolf had tried to kill her.

She would have stepped back, but the bed was behind her so instead, she sidled sideways toward the door. Rolf made no move to stop her but spoke out loud, his deep voice sending chills through her body.

"Don't be afraid."

"How are you doing this?"

He took a step toward her. "I'm not sure. It's never happened before. At least, not that I recall. It's the effect of the dark energy I've been forced to channel. Nonna told me this was possible. I didn't believe her at the time."

"Where did you come from?"

"Beneath your window."

Geneva walked to the window, making a wide arc around Rolf and looked at the ground below. A tall figure shifted and lifted a face toward the window. Clouds parted, and the moon shone on a mane of golden hair. A woman. She gazed at Geneva, giving nothing away in her expression. Harsh yellow-green light drifted around her body. The color seemed familiar.

"Who is she?" Geneva whispered, putting a hand to her chest, as if the pressure could stop the jealous pang hitting her heart. Colors flew to her from every corner of the room. She wanted to absorb their energy and fling them at the woman beneath her window. *Irrational.* The woman wasn't a threat.

Before she could do anything stupid, Geneva closed the window shade. She breathed in, using the meditation techniques she'd mastered years ago to slow her breathing and heartbeat. When she was convinced she had herself under control, she turned back to study Rolf, who lingered in the corner.

So what if Rolf traveled with a beautiful woman and was capable of transporting himself through walls? He lived. That's what mattered. Except the CMU believed he'd turned from a good guy into a serial killer. Maybe his appearance in her room was an illusion meant to trick her. She crossed her arms. "What are you doing here?"

His aura shifted from green to mauve. Her words had caused him pain.

She shook her head. "I'm sorry. I'm relieved to see you alive. You know I am. But why did you never tell me about your dark power?"

"I tried to tell you, remember? When we were in Flagstaff. Before then, I swore to keep it a secret. I never meant to use it."

"How can I trust you? How do I know you're not here to kill me?"

He sighed in response, and the sound carried such a wealth of weariness and heartache Geneva wanted to touch him. Instead, she took a step backward.

"I would never hurt you. You're the only thing that kept me alive when I was trapped in the dark."

"You were held against your will? How did you escape?"

"I distracted my jailer and took off."

She filled her lungs and stared at the window. An odd choice of words, distracted. And his aura had shifted to a steel gray. Rolf didn't want her to know the details of his escape. Why? She shifted her gaze back to Rolf. "How's the bump on the back of your head?"

Rolf winced. "Bump? He touched the back of his head as if he remembered it for the first time. "It's fine."

"Who's the lady with you?"

"Kaitlyn Girard."

"Kaitlyn Girard? Isn't she dead?"

He must have sensed her disbelief because his glowing figure drew closer. His voice softened, causing her to strain to hear him. "She was a prisoner like me. We depended on each other to escape. If not for her, I'd still be there, trapped in the dark."

She cocked her head at the green in his aura, examining it for any hint of color revealing a lie.

He took another step toward her. His voice deepened. Flecks of purple light twinkled and disappeared. "What kept me from going stark raving mad was you."

"Really?" She sucked in another deep breath. Sweat dampened her brow. Why was it so hot in here?

Although she'd seen Rolf this morning in Coffersations, he had been an illusion. They hadn't spoken. Not like now. All she wanted was to fling herself into his warm energy and rejoice at his presence and these sweet, sweet words. But what if he had turned? Could she be certain he told the truth? Auras didn't lie, she reminded herself. Still, Geneva sat on the side of the bed and clutched the mattress so she didn't do something stupid. Like reach for him.

The green figure sat next to her. Sparks of energy surrounded her. Rolf raised a hand to turn her face toward his. His touch vibrated against her skin like the gentle hum of a low-powered electrical wire.

"Yes, really. You help me contain the dark."

Geneva turned her face to the side.

"What's the matter? Please don't be afraid. I'd never hurt you. Ever."

"I want to believe you." Geneva turned toward him, alert to any change in his energy. "What happened in Coffersations last night? Who held you prisoner? And why?"

Rolf made a sound—a low rumble. "You aren't going to like it."

Geneva's heartbeat accelerated; her muscles tightened. "Try me."

He sighed but didn't lower his eyes from hers. "Cynthia Torra."

Geneva straightened and frowned, rising from the bed and moving toward the door. "Now that's unbelievable. I mean of all the incredible events to transpire. Why would your ex-girlfriend hold you captive? Quit playing me. What the hell is going on, Rolf?"

Rolf followed, stopping when he reached her. "She's not my ex-girlfriend. There's only one woman for me. Ever. You, Geneva. I'm telling the truth."

Why should she believe him? It all sounded so fantastical. The glass shook in the window behind her. "What would Cynthia hope to gain? Kidnapping is a serious offense."

He grumbled. "Money. Power. I don't know. She's not acting alone."

Geneva glanced his way and injected sarcasm into her voice. "Is that how she was able to kidnap you? A helper? Who was it? A hacker? Someone with extraordinary abilities who could knock you out?"

His hand fell away from her. "Please believe me. I need you on my side. I don't have all the answers. But I'll tell you what I do know. Cynthia's working with a man. I don't know who. I heard the man yelling when I broke free. He had a gun and fired at me. Have you ever been shot at?"

She frowned.

"No? Well, let me tell you, I didn't wait around to figure out his identity. I sorta figured running away with a bullet in my side would make escape harder."

"Rolf, you're a dark master. How could anyone kidnap you?" Geneva watched Rolf's aura for any change in color. It remained a steady, loyal green.

"I was drugged. Whatever was in it made it impossible to remember anything. Even my own name."

"Did it prevent you from using your talent? Is that what happened?"

Rolf shook his head. "No. I kept my talent. They needed me to have it, you see, so it could be channeled into crystals they've fabricated. They're selling the crystals to other countries for profit, as we suspected."

Storing dark energy in crystals and selling them? Geneva's legs shook. She returned to her bed and sat. Rolf followed her.

"Why couldn't you stop them? Jesus Christ, it's Cynthia Torra we're talking about. She couldn't hurt a fly."

"She's one of us."

"She's—what? What do you mean?"

"She's got talent. Loads of it. She's a beacon. One touch from her, and I was useless."

"You mean to tell me she has the ability to stun you?"

Rolf gave a short nod.

Geneva stood tall. Fear froze her insides for an instant before her blood flowed, cutting a chugging iceberg toward her heart. The too-bright yellow light in the coffee shop. She knew it seemed familiar. Cynthia Torra's aura, of course. Cynthia forced Rolf to use his talent against her and Julia. He'd tried to kill her. But he didn't remember or know what he'd done. Maybe that's what this late-night visit was all about? Cynthia was manipulating him now. Or maybe it was the woman below her window. What a fool she'd been.

Shivers erupted, shaking her small frame. A rushing sound formed in her ears. Her heart lunged forward and beat a rapid rhythm, urging her to take action. A crack of sound split the air. A giant fissure appeared in the mirror. She pointed to the window. "Get out of my room."

Rolf held a hand toward her. "You have nothing to fear from me. I wasn't in the coffee shop. I swear it."

"You're under Cynthia's control, Rolf. You just don't know it."

Rolf approached her.

She held her hands out. "Don't come any closer. Don't make me hurt you."

Rolf stopped. "I left Cynthia back in the Cleveland Flats in an abandoned factory. I've been on the run ever since. She's not controlling me. If she were, I would've never escaped."

"Maybe she let you escape. If she's controlling you, she knows your thoughts. She would know what you planned. She would know you are here, in my room, wouldn't she?"

She swiped one hand across her cheeks to stamp out the tears flooding her hot eyes. Peter had warned her Rolf was dangerous. Her family, too. She hadn't wanted to believe them. *Foolish, foolish, foolish girl.* Now she'd be forced to stop him with the only means she had at her disposal.

She held up a hand. "Rolf, I love you. But if you don't get the hell out of my room right now, I'll be forced to make you leave. Don't make me do it."

Rolf remained immobile, but the color in his aura flared into a brilliant display of lime, yellow, and red. *Joy, knowledge, worry.* He tipped his head back and laughed. But it was not a happy laugh. This laugh sounded surprised and anxious and angry.

"Dammit, they're good. Geneva, my love, I wasn't at Coffersations. They didn't need me—they had the crystals."

36

TRUST

"I'll kill them for attacking you and Julia." Rolf's form rose large in her room, dominating the open space. He paced from side to side, his figure in the lamplight casting bits of shadow on the wall. "If Julia dies, I'll find Cynthia and her partner and kill them with my bare hands."

"Rolf, stop. You're scaring me." A solid wave of darkness infiltrated Rolf's aura, dominating the green. His eyes, however, were still his. They didn't have the black, soulless look she'd seen in Coffersations.

He turned to her, his soft tone in direct opposition to the tension in his aura. "You have nothing to fear from me, Geneva. You never have."

He held one arm out as if she were a butterfly about to take flight. "You don't understand what you mean to me. And what they've done. They've used the crystals they've been making to create a believable illusion—the illusion I was there in Coffersations, trying to kill you. And they activated another crystal containing dark energy to make it real." His voice vibrated with sincerity. "Make no mistake, if you had not attacked the illusion, you and Julia would both be dead. Your error was in trying to save me. Why didn't you listen to Peter and aim to kill?"

"Because I couldn't. I knew it wasn't you. Someone was there with you, making you act. I couldn't bear the thought of attacking you. I didn't think at the time it was an illusion." She frowned. "Wait, where did Cynthia get a hold of illusion energy? The only one I've known capable of producing illusion energy is, oh my God, Rolf. The woman. The one you're traveling with. I remember now. She's an illusion talent."

Rolf put a hand to his forehead. "Yes, I remembered earlier tonight."

"You mean you didn't know before then?"

Rolf nodded, his hair flopping in his eyes. He sat on the bed, looking dear and familiar and tired.

"It's the drug they gave me. It makes it challenging to recall certain memories without pain. But it came to me earlier. Kyle Williard's sister was imprisoned after his capture. You'll recall they were twins but went by different last names, to disguise their connection. The woman told me they killed her brother. I had no idea at the time who she was talking about."

Geneva sat on the bed next to him and gripped his hands.

"Kaitlyn Girard. The kidnappers must have been holding her for months, making crystals capable of creating illusions."

"It appears so." Rolf gripped her hand, and a reassuring warmth filled her. Not dark at all.

"That explains how they were able to create the elk and make me believe Julia was being attacked by a security guard. I wonder how many other illusions they've created?" Geneva placed a hand on his shoulder. His muscles and bones were the real thing. "I shouldn't have doubted you."

"Understandable under the circumstances." He tipped her head up to his. His intense blue eyes flashed a mix of contrary emotions—frustration, tenderness, fear, desire. "Did you mean what you said? Do you really love me?"

She couldn't look away from him. "Yes."

His eyes flamed with purple light. "You don't know how many years I've longed to hear you say that. I didn't think I had the right."

Before she could respond, he bent his head so their lips touched. His spirit filled her as sure as his tongue filled her mouth. She lost herself in a tide of emotion. His, hers, and everything in between. Where did he end and she begin? She didn't know.

"Mine."

"Yes." But a dark suspicion reared its ugly head and hissed in her mind. *Remember the dark masters. They cannot love.*

His mind locked on hers, a question in his thoughts. Every molecule in her seemed to scream at her to establish a portal between them, an instantaneous gateway between their minds allowing them to link whenever and wherever they desired. It was the link of lovers. It could only be established when the deepest trust existed between two people.

Dark masters cannot love.

"You doubt me." He pulled away without establishing a portal. Strange how she missed his lips on hers and warm breath on her cheeks.

"No, Rolf, it's..."

"You forget I was in your mind, privy to your thoughts and desires."

"God, Rolf, I want to connect with you like that. I don't know why I can't. It's what they say, about dark masters, they aren't capable of loving another."

"Yes. Believe me, I know what they say." His deep voice sent a tingle through her body. "But I'm not like that. I have you."

"But you walk through walls. What am I supposed to think? The legends say dark masters can't be held. Once they turn. Don't look at me like that."

"Like what?" The tone of his voice was a whip, lashing her from all sides. He dropped her hands and rose from the bed. "Like I'm disappointed? Like I don't understand why you doubt me? Why you don't feel what I feel for you? You want honesty between us? Let me be honest."

His eyes glittered and shimmered, until he turned from her to look at some distant place, as if he was still in his prison and not here in her bedroom. His voice bit into her heart, taking a chunk with him. "I have never been so close to turning as I have over the past few days, lying in the dark, waiting and wondering if and when I might escape. Plotting my revenge. The dark has a power all its own, Geneva. Make no mistake, it's a seductive mistress. It tempts and taunts and teases me without end. It tells me I can have everything I desire, including you. If I wanted, I could unleash a darkness so great it would cover this entire building."

She stood and opened her mouth to protest, but he turned his back to her, fists clenched at his sides. Flames of darkness ripped through his aura, burning everything in its path. She stilled, watching his struggle to control the dark energy yearning for release. His aura shifted green, and his fists unclenched. He turned and walked toward her, first one step and another, until they stood face to face. She looked into his eyes—twin flames of torment flickered in their shadowy depths. He grasped both her hands in his. Her skin tingled.

"It's okay, Geneva. I won't turn. I can't. Ever. You see, I don't want to destroy. I want to love. You."

He sighed—a breath deep and swollen with understanding. "I can see why you might believe the legends over me. We've all been warned since we were children. I tried to protect you from myself. Do you remember that day right after you graduated from high school when you went to a bar?"

"Yes, how could I forget? You told me to go home and play with my Barbie dolls. I cried all the way home."

With the pad of his thumb, he wiped away a single tear that rolled down her cheek. "Believe me, it hurt me to say that to you as much as it hurt your feelings. I'm sorry. I never meant the horrible things I said. They were all lies. But the lies were meant to keep you safe."

He raised their joined hands and kissed her knuckles, the touch sending tiny vibrations throughout her body and causing an ache in her heart. "Without trust between us, we have nothing. But whether you believe me or not, this is real. I haven't turned, and you're the reason why. You stand between me and the dark, Geneva, with a light so bright I cannot turn away from it. I will not let the dark take me if there's a chance in hell you can love me as I am, filled with darkness but also love for you. Please tell me that's the case."

In the end, it all came down to trust. Did she trust him with her life? Did she trust him with her heart?

"Yes." She wrapped her arms around him. "It is, Rolf. I swear it. I need more time to establish a portal. To see for myself your love is real and not some figment I've dreamed about because it's what I want to be true."

He smiled and placed two fingers over her mouth. "Shh, it's okay. We have time. As long as I know you're on my side, there's hope for us. I promise, I'll handle the dark energy and anything more they throw at me."

"But what will you do now? The CMU believes you've turned into a serial killer. They have the whole department on the lookout with orders to shoot on sight. Come to think of it, how did you manage to get here from Cleveland after you escaped?"

Rolf grinned. "We hitchhiked. I persuaded the driver to pick us up, and Kaitlyn created the illusion we were two sweet old ladies. Worked like a charm."

"You're not safe here, Rolf. You need to hide."

He tucked a loose hair behind her ear. "Keep my visit here a secret. I don't want you to suffer any more than you already have. I'll find a way to expose Cynthia. Do you have any clue who her silent partner might be?"

"I call him Gemcatcher—your cousin Percy's name for him."

"Fitting."

Rolf turned and approached the corner of the wall, where she had first spied his glowing figure. Was it only minutes earlier?

"Where are you going?"

He stopped and glanced back with a quick grin. "To see Julia, of course. I believe I can help her."

Faster than she could blink, he was in front of her again, his lips on hers, soft and full, leaving her breathless with need and desire and wanting so much more.

"Don't go anywhere. I'll return soon."

"Rolf, wait. Don't leave. Not yet."

He had released her again, not stopping as he headed toward the corner.

She spoke quickly. "It's too dangerous. My brothers are

expecting you. They'll find you. And when they do, they won't ask questions. They'll kill you."

"Geneva." He paused and glanced back, her name a prayer on his lips and his eyes swallowing her whole. "I must." He turned to the wall, his form going from a solid, physical shape to glowing green in an instant. He pushed his right leg through the surface as if it were water and vanished.

"Rolf, no." She raced to the window and pulled the shades, expecting to see him and his companion. But neither of them appeared beneath her window.

37

JEOPARDY

After Rolf disappeared, Geneva forced herself into bed but left the light on in case Rolf returned. It seemed she slept for hours, but upon opening her eyes and checking her phone, mere minutes had passed. The door creaked, and she lifted her head.

"Rolf, is it you?" Funny Rolf would use the door when he could walk through walls. And hadn't Nate told her talent wouldn't open it?

"Has Rolf been here to see you?" A female voice spoke, causing Geneva to jerk her head toward the door."

She blinked, not trusting her eyes. Buttercup yellow floated around the figure inside the doorway. She gasped. For the second time tonight, the impossible was happening in her bedroom. "How did you get in here? The door's locked."

Cynthia Torra smiled a smile that could melt ice. Everything about her was fake. Too bright, too shiny, and much too slim. From her fancy hairdo, to the veneers on her teeth, to the over-bright halo surrounding her head. The woman reeked of privilege and trickery. She sat on the side of the bed, trapping Geneva under the covers, and pointed a loaded revolver in her face. She also didn't bother to answer the question.

"Now, that's interesting. It really is. Rolf is fast, that man. Last I heard he was on the run, the government on his tail. Now you talk as if you expected him. Has he been in this room?" She shook her head when Geneva didn't answer. "You do know he's a suspected criminal? A hardened serial killer, incapable of human love or compassion. I've been sent to investigate and given special access to the lone witness—seeing the only other witness may not survive. I pity the woman who falls in love with Rolf, don't you?"

Despite the gun, or maybe because of it, adrenaline flooded Geneva's body, opening her to energy waves in every shape and color. She drew the colors to her, arming her mind for what she suspected would be a battle. "What are you doing in my bedroom? What do you want?" She kept her voice low and even, no hint of panic.

"Nothing, really." Cynthia still pointed the gun, but now she used her other hand to tap Geneva's forehead, scattering the massive energy cloud in an instant. She laughed, a tiny chirp. God, even her laugh was fake.

"Oh, please now, honey. And I thought we were friends? Don't go trying anything stupid. I do know how to shoot this thing. My daddy taught me when I was a little girl. And at such close quarters, well, I don't want to make a big mess. I don't have time. Settle back now, and don't try any tricks."

Rolf wasn't lying when he'd told her Cynthia was capable of zapping energy. Her touch had drained Geneva dry. She fell back on her pillow. Unbelievable.

"Rolf, uh, sorry to bother you, but if you're still here I could use your help."

She worked hard to keep her emotions from her face

and called to Rolf. With her energy so low, only Rolf, with his ability to use dark energy, might hear her. God, would this day never end?

Cynthia's lips moved. "You're not that pretty. Not like I expected."

Keep her talking. That's what they did in the movies. "What did you expect?"

"Oh, I don't know. A face with a bit more substance, I suppose. Something to attract and hold the attention of Rolf. If he hasn't turned yet, he will, you know. He won't be able to help himself. It's the fate of all known dark masters."

"Rolf isn't like other men." Pride bloomed in her chest.

"I know. Rolf and I have a bit of a history, you understand."

There went the annoying chirp again. Geneva shouldn't antagonize Cynthia, but she couldn't help herself. "Any history you have with Rolf is ancient history."

"I beg to differ. I'd say our history isn't over. In fact..." This time the laugh was louder, her excitement spilling into the room. "I'd say it's just beginning."

"What do you want with me?"

"Oh, I'm not interested in you. God, no." Cynthia gave an exaggerated shiver, and her gaze flitted toward the door, which Geneva now noticed was propped open, and back to Geneva. "You're a means to an end. When Rolf arrives, we can get this little show on the road. You did call to him, did you not?" She tipped her face in a question. By her smile, it was clear she knew the answer.

Fear plunged a cold stake through Geneva's heart. How could she have been such an idiot? Cynthia had set a trap for Rolf using Geneva as a lure. *Rolf, ignore my earlier panic. I had a nightmare. But everything's fine. I'm safe. Don't worry about me.*

Too late.

Rolf stepped through the doorway, his deep voice filling the room almost pleasantly. The door clicked shut behind him. "Hello, Cynthia. Why am I not surprised to see you here? It's me you want, isn't it? Let her go."

Cynthia let out a peal of laughter as if Rolf's words were the funniest thing she'd heard in some time. "Brilliant. I suspected you would appear. I left the door open for you. You know your girlfriend means nothing to me. It's you and your wonderful dark energy I need. That's why I brought along this."

Cynthia kept the gun pointed at Geneva with one hand and with the other, she drew out a small bag of glittering crystals from her pocket. She spilled the crystals on the bed in front of Rolf. "Fill these with dark energy, and you'll both be free to go. I won't kill her."

"Leave Geneva out of this."

"Sure, hot stuff." Cynthia pressed the gun to Geneva's temple. "Get busy, or I'll blow your girlfriend's brains out."

"Rolf, don't do it. It will turn you into a monster."

"If she hurts you, I may not be able to control myself anyway. I'm not letting her kill you."

"Oh, I almost forgot." Cynthia separated one of the crystals from the rest of the pack, the one glowing a brighter yellow, and plucked it from the covers to hold in her palm. "I'll give you thirty more seconds, and I'll activate this crystal. It's beautiful, isn't it? It's called a moon crystal. Its maker is long since dead. There's no other stone quite like it. I don't know how it got its silly name, but the energy trapped inside is capable of transporting us all back to our little underground lab."

She closed her fist around the gem. "Now, are we ready?"

"No, Rolf!"

"Yes."

"Wonderful. I knew you'd see it my way." She lined the crystals a few inches apart on the bed. "Get busy, or you can kiss your girlfriend goodbye."

Rolf's aura mutated from its customary green to darkness. His eyes changed color. Grew cold and hard as granite and black as coal. This wasn't happening. She couldn't sit by and watch Rolf lose all compassion and humanity.

Cynthia's attention landed on Rolf and stayed there. Dark energy streamed from his chest, pouring into the synthetic crystals.

Geneva's nerve endings tingled. Colors returned. She opened her psychic senses, searching, searching, searching until she spied a familiar color. Danny in the parking lot of the Institution. Cynthia underestimated Geneva's talent. Although not strong enough to interrupt the scene in front of her, she had plenty of energy to alert her brothers.

"Danny, come quick."

"Geneva? What is it?"

"Hurry. You have to stop Cynthia Torra. She's in my room. She's forcing Rolf to use dark energy."

"Hang tight. I'm on my way."

A stinging slap hit her cheek, forcing tears from the corners of her eyes. Cynthia stood in front of her, palm raised, eyes flashing fire. Gone was perfection. In her place was a steely-eyed witch. She jammed the revolver in Geneva's chest. "What the hell do you think you're doing? This gun is loaded, you know. Don't make me use it."

Geneva's fingers ached to touch her sore cheek, but she didn't dare move. *"Stall her,"* Danny said. *"Don't let her leave."*

"What do you mean?"

"Don't play dumb with me, you little bitch. You've

contacted someone, haven't you? I can tell by that vacant look on your face. Who is it?"

"No one. Who would I contact?"

"Liar." Her lip curled at the corner. "It doesn't matter anyway." She pointed to Rolf, who had collapsed on the floor. "He's done. I don't believe you'll recognize him when he awakens. No dark master can channel that amount of energy without losing himself to the darkness. Your Rolf will be a bad, bad boy." She smiled, triumphant. "I wonder how much you'll like him then."

Cynthia swept the glittering crystals from the bedcovers and moved toward the door. "I'd love to stick around and see how this plays out, but I have to finish producing my story. I'm delivering a special report on the hacker gone mad. It will be all over the news soon. I can't let the competition beat me to the punch, now can I?"

She kept the revolver pointed at Geneva and hustled to the door, passed a card over the lock, and kicked it open. "By the way, no one knows I'm in your room. If I were you, I'd keep quiet. It'll be your word against mine. And you'll have no proof. Everyone knows you're not in your right mind. Making up fantasies."

There went her annoying laugh.

"I wonder who they'll believe?"

38

PORTAL

Energy buzzed in the atmosphere, hitting Geneva's psychic senses. *The moonstone.* Cynthia's solid form flashed a blinding yellow for a brief moment. She moved through the exit and disappeared. The door slammed behind her. Minutes later, Danny came tearing into the room, two orderlies with him. He took one look at the scene in front of him and was on Geneva in an instant, grabbing both arms and yanking her toward the door.

"We need to get you the hell away from here before he wakes."

"No, I'm not leaving him like this." She tore herself from Danny's clasp and flung her body on Rolf's prone one. Heat radiated from his flesh. "He's feverish. We need to do something for him, Danny. Don't stand there. Get a cold washcloth, for Christ's sake." Tears leaked from the corners of her eyes. When had she become such a crybaby?

Danny shook his head. "He's too far gone, Geneva. The change is on him. The heat is his body's way of dealing with it. You have to let him go. We can't save him. And if we stick around, he'll kill us both."

"No, I don't believe it. I can reach him. I know I can. You have to let me try."

Danny moved toward her. "I can't allow it. I'm sorry. I've called for backup. Let's get you out of here."

"Don't touch me!" Energy, white and hot, vibrated the air around her. The chair next to the desk toppled over, missing Danny by inches. "I won't leave him."

Rolf moaned, as if his unconscious self sensed the combustible energy in the atmosphere.

Danny stared, eyes hard. "You'll risk both our lives for his? Don't you understand what he'll do to you?"

"I love him, Danny. I always have." She took a breath and expelled the air in a rush, swiping at the tears continuing to flow. "I have to help him."

The door creaked. Rolf groaned and stirred. One hand went to his head.

She pointed toward where Nate stood with a bevy of armed officers in the open doorway. "Get out of here. Go. Leave us alone. He's waking up."

"Don't be crazy. You can't save him. Let us do our job, Geneva," Nate said. He took two steps forward.

Those were the last words she heard. One second she was aware of Danny, Nate, the officers, the room, her heart-beat pounding in her ear. The next moment, Rolf's eyelids fluttered and opened, and she was lost. She stared into crystal blue eyes—glassy, hard, and glittery.

"Too late." Icy tentacles pressed on her temple. Sharp pain ricocheted through her skull.

"*No.*"

His mind gripped hers and wouldn't let go, forcing entrance. A sob erupted, and her throat constricted. She couldn't breathe. Rolf controlled her body's autonomic functions. Oh God. He was going to kill her. Like the legends claimed. Coldly, cruelly. Cutting off her air supply by controlling her mind, forcing her heartbeat to cease. But she couldn't go out this way. Not without a fight.

"Rolf, please, no, not this way. Not in this awful Institution."

Spots appeared in front of her eyes, blinding her. She had maybe seconds. Fitting her last thought would be of him.

"I love you, Rolf. I always have."

A strange hum seized her brain. The room dimmed, fell away. *"I always will."*

Energy pounded her mind, dark and dangerous. Heat flooded her body. Burning, burning, burning. Dragging her down, down, down into deep and darkest black.

Fire. He was on fire.

Sweat drenched Rolf's body, but it did nothing to cool the fever ravaging his system. Darkness rushed in, coating his mind in anger, emptying his soul of all goodness. Rage pounded the surface of his brain. He would make them pay —all of them. Every last blessed one who'd ever crossed him or made him suffer. He would find them all and eliminate them, one by one, until there was no one left. The darkness must have its say. There was no room for mercy in his heart.

Cool hands touched his chest, absorbing a small amount of the dark heat. He groaned, opening his eyes. A spark of light surfaced, a lone candle flame amid a sea of blackness. *Mine*. A memory. His cells reached for her. Reached for the light.

Energy vibrated. Anger. Their anger. His anger. Voices at the door. Familiar voices brushed his consciousness. They would take her from him. The one bright spark in a sea of madness. All would be lost. "No," he said. Or did he think it?

His mind reached for hers and clipped the barriers she'd erected as easily as clipping a hedge. His reach extended farther, farther until he occupied her brain. Controlled her body and soul. Sweet, sweet sunshine. He would have her. They could not take her from him. Ever.

"Rolf, please, no, not like this. Not in this awful Institution."

Her voice tugged at his black heart, warmed it. A portal formed between their minds. Safe harbor from the darkness. He squeezed the life from her, and she offered herself to him without protest. Offered the mind link. Freely. Completely.

"I love you, Rolf. I always have."

He snagged the portal she'd created, cemented it in his mind and held on tight.

"I always will."

He forced her to breathe, her heart to beat. Dark filled him, and he welcomed it but kept it from her small form. He pushed it toward those who would capture them. They would either clear out or risk death. He smiled. Or grimaced; he wasn't certain.

The men backed away. Smart move. Nate raised his gun and fired, hitting him in the chest. Dark filled in where there once was flesh and blood.

A growl tore from his throat at the impact—more monster than man. He rose in one smooth move, Geneva in his arms. The wall shimmered in front of him. Time to get them both the hell out of this place before he did something he'd regret to her brothers or the others. With their minds locked together, he could perform the mental maneuvers needed to take her with him. More shouts trailed behind them. The voices faded. He focused his mind on the wall, turning the solid surface into liquid particles. He slipped through the wall, which carried them outside and to the ground and then sprang back into place, a solid structure once again.

Geneva remained unconscious, her head slumped against his. He cupped the back of her head to avoid jarring her and continued moving forward. He half-ran with her in his arms until he stepped through the barbed wire fence surrounding the complex.

He reached the main road. Kaitlyn had parked their rental car nearby as they planned. He glanced once in the driver's seat. Although he knew it was Kaitlyn, he almost didn't recognize her. While he'd visited Julia and fought with Cynthia, Kaitlyn had picked up disguises for them all and tucked her long hair under a short black wig.

Rolf placed Geneva in the back seat and climbed in with her, cradling her head on his shoulder. "Drive. Hurry. But not too fast. We can't afford to attract attention."

Kaitlyn floored it. In moments, they entered the highway. "Are you okay?" She handed him a brown paper bag.

"I am now. Will we make it before the helicopter departs for Cleveland?"

"Yes. We should have plenty of time."

"Good."

They were quiet. He could sense the buzz of Kaitlyn's thoughts circling for a safe place to land. Her eyes caught his in the mirror. "Will she be okay?"

"Yes." He wouldn't allow any other outcome. If he had to function as her heart and lungs forever, he would do it.

Rolf's mind remained lodged in Geneva's. She had resumed breathing on her own, but he kept watch, sensitive to any change. With one hand, he dug through the brown paper bag and pulled out a pair of wigs—a straight, brown one for him and a long, curly red one for Geneva. He reached in again and pulled out a mustache, fake eyelashes, and a new cell phone. Gemcatcher had stolen his old one.

Geneva moved her head. Her heartbeat had slowed to a steady, even beat. *Thank God.*

He reached into the bag a final time, pulled out a baseball cap and a hoodie, and put them on. He glanced at his reflection in the rearview mirror. Amazing how a few simple props worked miracles. Guilt gnawed a hole in his heart. Feelings flooded through, emptying into his mind, breaking through the iron control he maintained. Feelings he could no longer deny.

Fear, anger, awe—love. Yes, that was the feeling overriding all the others. What an amazing woman he held. Brave and foolish beyond measure. One part of him wanted to hug her close, wrap her in bubble wrap, and never let go. The other could strangle her for offering herself to him. He had nearly killed her. A moment more and perhaps he would have. Only the portal she'd erected between their minds had saved them both. Her light to his darkness—the perfect combination.

Geneva stirred in his arms. Her breath warmed the spot where her lips touched his cheek. He smoothed a hand over her golden hair.

"Hmm." *"Is this heaven?"*

He smiled. *"For me, it is."* He breathed in her roses and vanilla scent.

"Where are we going?"

"Home." But that was a lie because he was already home.

"Okay."

She snuggled into his chest. Her trust disarmed him, shook him to his core. His hand trembled against her scalp.

"What's wrong?"

"I might have killed you."

"I know. But you didn't. Why are you sad?"

"Because." He leaned toward her and brushed a kiss on the top of her golden head. He breathed her in, wanting so much more than scent. *"I love you. You have to know how much I love you. But you deserve better. I never wanted to tie you to me. I knew I would cause you pain."*

"Rolf." She said his name with such tenderness he nearly choked. *"I always knew you were the one for me. That hasn't changed. We're meant to be together."*

He placed a kiss on her forehead. *"I'm not arguing. Not anymore. What's the matter?"* But he understood. Her thoughts were his. His thoughts were hers.

"I'm afraid for you. My brothers will search, find, and kill you. They're tracking us. I can sense them."

"I know. But you have nothing to fear, my love. I won't let anyone take you from me. As long as I have you, I can handle anything that comes our way."

"What will we do? Where will we go? The CMU won't rest until they find us. We'll have to hide from them. It will never end."

"That's why we won't hide. I don't want you to live a life of fear."

"What are you saying? You will give yourself to the government? I won't let you."

"No, I'm saying we will let them come."

"We've arrived," Kaitlyn said from the front seat. "Will she be well enough to fly?"

"Yes," Geneva said before Rolf could answer for her. "I am. What airline?"

"None." Rolf held her close. "My cousin and your former partner, David Jenkins's, private helicopter. I've called in a favor." He held up the red wig. "He supplied us with these disguises, too."

"What do you mean we won't hide, Rolf? You're not thinking of confronting them, are you? That would be foolish."

He took a moment to slow her racing heart, ignoring Kaitlyn's frowning face. She tossed her head in irritation and got out of the car.

Rolf grabbed the wig and fitted it on Geneva's head. "Yes, but with proof. We're going after Cynthia. I suspect she's hiding in Cleveland, and she's the key that will lead to Gemcatcher. We cannot let them sell the crystals to other countries. Once the CMU is aware of her talent, and whoever her silent partner is, they'll understand how they could have held me captive. Plus, we'll have the crystals as proof."

She applied the fake eyelashes to her beautiful blue eyes, first right, then left. The long lashes made her look angelic. All she needed was a halo and the picture would be complete. He would never tire of looking at her face. He would never tire of her.

"She'll be expecting us, won't she? She'll learn the CMU didn't kill you. That you've kidnapped me and are on the run."

"She'll believe I've killed you. That's what your brothers believe. I caught their horror before we fled the Institution. That's the statement the police will make to the news media."

"Let's go." Rolf took her arm and guided her from the car.

Kaitlyn pulled a black suitcase from the trunk.

Rolf nodded at the suitcase. "David also supplied a change of clothing and personal items for all of us."

Kaitlyn glanced at Geneva, and their eyes met before

Kaitlyn looked away, her expression remaining stiff and remote. She didn't like Geneva—viewed her as competition for his attention. She didn't like Geneva—viewed her as competition for Rolf's attention.

He massaged Geneva's neck. *"It's okay, G. Trust me. You're proof enough I didn't kill you."*

"But if everyone thinks you've killed me, they'll be out for blood. Yours. My God, I'm surprised we've made it as far as we have."

"If Cynthia believes I've killed you, she'll have no idea I have an ace in my back pocket. You. She'll be in hiding. But you, my love"—Rolf placed an arm around her shoulders and led her toward the waiting helicopter— *"will be able to find her."*

39

AT LAST

"We'll need an alias." Rolf wrapped an arm around her and pulled her close.

"Mr. and Mrs. Smith?"

They'd arrived in Cleveland without incident and were on their way in a rental car to the hotel they selected for its proximity to the Cleveland Flats. Rolf had Kaitlyn drive, insisting he needed to ride in the back with Geneva to keep an eye on her.

Now he grinned, threading his free hand through hers and kissing her on the lips, his embrace firm and warm and possessive. Energy sparked in the air around them, tingling her nerve endings and causing her heart to pound.

"I can't wait to make you mine."

Although she knew he spoke privately in her mind, she found herself blushing and looking toward the front. Kaitlyn's cool green gaze caught and held hers in the rearview mirror. Dark red mixed with brown and black rolled off her shape in large quantities, mixing with the odd yellow-green of her aura. Anger, distrust, bitterness, frustration. She didn't bother to disguise her dislike. Her aura oozed hate.

"How about Mary and Bill Williams?" Rolf's question brought her attention back to him.

"I like it," Kaitlyn responded, looking at Rolf through the rearview mirror, her voice soft and sickly sweet and seductive.

Geneva bit her lip and tried desperately to stem the tide of insecurity and jealousy rising in her. The suddenness and intensity of the emotion surprised her. Why did Kaitlyn Girard believe she had a chance with Rolf? Of course, they'd been alone together, in the dark, day after day, while Rolf had been forced to channel his energy into crystals. Had something happened between them?

"No, nothing."

Rolf's thought echoed in her head, but with it came a barrier in his mind. He hid a truth from her. Something he didn't want her to know. The secret increased her anxiety. Energy morphed in weird patterns and colors around her.

"I've always wanted to be named Gretel," Kailyn said. Her aura flickered from yellow-green to brown, and through Rolf, Geneva caught her unvoiced thought. *Kyle would have been Hansel.*

She breathed out slowly and carefully. Still, Geneva couldn't stop a shiver.

"Cold?"

She shook her head and forced a smile. If he wanted to keep secrets, so would she.

He reached into his pocket and held a fist out to her. When she gave him a puzzled look, he opened it to reveal an ornate platinum wedding band. "Mr. and Mrs. Williams it is."

"Where did you get this?" She eyed the vintage ring. "Is it real?"

From the front, Kaitlyn's aura morphed into blackness.

Rolf appeared oblivious to her hate, smiling and brushing a strand of wayward hair behind Geneva's ear.

"It was Nonna's. She gave it to me the last time I saw her. Claimed I would need it soon. Looks like she was right." He reached for the ring finger on her left hand. "Put it on."

Geneva complied. Then he kissed her, a full-on frontal assault in front of Kaitlyn's wide-eyed gaze. His lips consumed her like he was parched and she was a glass of cold water. Heat tingled her lips and spread through the rest of her body until she was on fire. *"You're the only woman I have ever wanted. Kaitlyn means nothing to me."*

When he lifted his head from hers, he smiled with such tenderness, she thought her heart might shatter into a thousand pieces. But then her gaze met Kaitlyn's horrified one in the mirror. Daggers of hate shot from the woman's eyes. Blackness flooded the area surrounding her. If Kaitlyn could kill with a thought, Geneva would be dead before she could take her next breath. The woman may mean nothing to Rolf, but clearly, he meant everything to her.

Next to her, Rolf leaned forward. The dark energy in Kaitlyn's aura must have caught his attention. He automatically drew some of it toward himself, and Geneva cringed and pulled away. She didn't want to be infected by Kaitlyn's hatred. But Rolf was used to the dark energy and didn't flinch. What did it mean that he could absorb that much hatred?

She didn't have more time to contemplate because they'd reached their destination and the next few minutes were occupied making sure her disguise was firmly in place and fetching the bag Kaitlyn had stored in the trunk. Minutes later, they'd checked in using their aliases, and Geneva and Rolf were alone in their hotel bedroom.

Rolf strolled to the window and drew the curtains. Then

he turned to face her where she stood in the doorway. "What is it?"

She frowned and shook her head, stepping inside and pulling the door closed behind her.

He stayed still and silent, studying her. The expression on his face gave nothing away. He took a step toward her as if she were a bird he didn't want to frighten. When he reached her side, he stopped, but he made no move to touch her. Geneva wished he would—then she wouldn't have to deal with the doubts racing through her head. What secret did Rolf keep? Could dark masters love another? Did Rolf truly love her? What if all of this was an illusion created by Kaitlyn Girard?

"I don't want to hurt you." Now he reached a finger and tilted her face so he could see into her eyes. The turquoise light coming from his aura nearly blinded her. He wanted her to know he spoke the truth.

She did not flinch from his gaze. "Then don't keep things from me."

The time for secrets between them had passed. He either trusted her or not. He either loved her or not. Something of her thoughts must have transferred to Rolf because he held out his hand, asking her without words to trust him. She placed her hand in his, and he led her to the bed, where he pulled her down next to him.

He cuddled her into his chest and rested his head on top of hers. For a long moment they stayed that way, silent, absorbing one another's energy. Then he spoke, his deep voice rumbling through her body. "The dark was endless. Each day I grew closer to snapping, to letting it control me."

"Why didn't you?"

He stroked her hair, his touch soothing and exciting at the same time. "One thing. I had retrieved a memory of you.

It's all I had, but it was enough. Enough to know that you were out there. Somewhere. That I needed to make my way back to you—make sure you were okay."

He kissed the top of her head. She felt warm and safe and loved. But was it an illusion? "How did you escape?"

He sighed, and the sound lay like a heavy burden on his shoulders. "I made Cynthia believe Kaitlyn and me had the hots for one another."

She stiffened. A picture rose in her mind—a memory. Rolf and Kaitlyn together, kissing, his hands on her body. A sick feeling filled her and then flooded outward, bursting into vibrating energy molecules. The air around them warmed and the closet door rattled. Neither of them bothered to look toward the noise.

"You kissed her—made out with her. No wonder she believes you want her."

"I had to. It was the only way to distract Cynthia long enough to use my talent. I needed to be convincing."

The lightbulb in the lamp on the nightstand burst. Static electricity snapped and crackled in the air above their heads. She pushed at his chest. "Kaitlyn loves you, you know." She stood, taking deep breaths to calm her racing heart. She couldn't do this. Be with Rolf. Her body had taken on so much of the energy in the atmosphere she was liable to blast him the moment he touched her.

He frowned but did not move. "She thinks she does. I can't help that. It doesn't change my feelings for you. G, I need you."

"She hates me. She'll hurt me if she can find a way."

He shook his head. "I won't let her."

She walked toward the window, one step, then another. "I don't want you to kill her. That will only make the dark in you stronger. Besides, you may not be able to stop her. She's powerful, and she's been held captive for much longer than you, which has turned her into a lunatic."

"That's not what you're worried about."

She stalled for time. "What do you mean?"

Although she hadn't heard him move, she turned to find him by her side. His eyes glittered with turquoise energy. She couldn't look away.

"You're worried you'll hurt me. Being around me makes your talent stronger. Your feelings for me will override your self-control if we're intimate. You'll cause an explosion, and I'll die."

She didn't answer. She didn't have to. He was inside her mind—understood her deepest fears.

He placed his hands on her shoulders, drawing her toward him. "I won't keep any more secrets from you." His breath warmed her cheek, his aura morphing into deep purple. "We'll take it slow—stop if things get out of control. Will you trust me?"

It all came down to this. This moment. He already held her heart, but did she trust him enough to give her body, too? Did she trust herself enough not to harm him?

He waited, patient, not forcing her decision but letting her make up her own mind. This was a man who not only understood her struggle but lived it on a daily basis. If he was capable of overcoming his dark nature for her, surely she could conquer hers enough to keep from harming him. She leaned forward and placed her lips on his. Sparks of green and rose and purple energy flared around them, brightening the corner of the room where they stood.

Rolf crushed her to his chest. Geneva touched his pounding heart through his T-shirt. She raised her hands and ran them through his thick hair. Over and over, like she'd wanted to do countless times over the years.

A flame lit between them, and they tumbled onto the bed, his hands and mouth everywhere at once. He chanted a string of endearments, flooding her mind. *"Gorgeous. Sexy. God, you smell so good, like vanilla. I'm not letting you out of my sight."*

Her energy fed his, so that their combined auras sparked, signaling their deep excitement. *Whoa, girl.*

"Don't be afraid. You won't hurt me."

Rolf stripped her first with his eyes and then with his hands, tossing her shirt, bra, and jeans, one by one, onto the floor. *"You are breathtaking. Beautiful. I've dreamt of this moment since we were teenagers."*

He had? He'd despised her then.

"Never. I've wanted you for as long as I can remember." He bit a sensitive part of her ear. She gasped. He seemed to be everywhere at once, raining kisses on her face and neck, running his hands down her chest, seizing her arms in an iron grip, pinning her to the bed. *"I'm never letting you out of my sight."*

Her thoughts slowed. Her body reacted to his warm hands, stroking her chest and sides. He took his time perusing her body, worshiping her with his mind. Geneva tried to stem the tide of energy, but it arced between them, rising like a Fourth of July fireworks display in a ray of color. Lavenders and violets entwined with deep greens and rose. Their energy met, clashed, and melded. Their thoughts became a singular word. *Mine.*

His mouth found her breasts, and she shivered, enjoying the duel sensations of his wet mouth and hard, contoured body. Because he had parked himself in her mind and wouldn't budge, he caught the essence of her every thought, satisfied her unspoken desires.

Energy waves shimmered, sparked, burst forth, and a

dam let loose inside of her. *"Rolf. Rolf, please."* She begged, writhing on the bed, fighting the rising tide of energy threatening to overwhelm her.

His voice was gruff with passion. "Let yourself go. I'll keep you safe. Trust me?"

She gasped. "Of course."

"Good." He sounded satisfied. "Now's the time to prove it, honey."

The pull of his warm, wet mouth and the heated sensations pushed her close to the edge. Tension coiled, threatening release. Geneva struggled to rein in the cloud of energy and the rising storm around them. *Too late.* The balloon inside her popped, sending waves of pleasure through her body. The feel of Rolf hot and hard inside her had her hurtling over the edge of the precipice she'd been riding. She panted and moaned, her limbs tingling, watching a giant mushroom cloud burst outward from their chests, as if it happened to someone else. An explosion of every color in the rainbow filled the bedroom. Rolf's eyes took on a strange glow above her. He cried out, but whether his cries were from pain or pleasure, she did not know. Geneva closed her eyes. She couldn't watch.

"Dear God. What have I done?"

40

BEACON

Geneva opened her eyes and blinked. A naked Rolf sprawled across her, unmoving. "Rolf, are you okay?"

Silence. "Rolf, open your eyes and look at me, please."

More silence. *Oh dear God.* She shook his solid shoulders, her fear pulling tiny pulses of energy from his body. "Rolf Henry Jorgensen, you wake up right now."

Rolf groaned and stirred beside her.

She sucked in air. "What's the matter?"

"I've died and gone to heaven." He rolled to his side, pulling Geneva with him.

"I, wow, I didn't hurt you?"

"Of course not. It was incredible. You're incredible."

Rolf's words released something inside. Soft tears slipped past her cheeks out of control.

"Hey, hey, that's a good thing. Don't cry." He stroked her hair, fingers gentle, smoothing the stray strands away from her eyes.

"I'm sorry. I worried I'd hurt you. And..." Geneva gulped

and tried to stem the flow of tears. "And then I got carried away."

He lifted her chin so he could see into her eyes. "Sweetheart, you could never hurt me. I've told you before. Now will you believe me?"

"Yes, yes, I do. I'm relieved and happy, I guess."

"You never have to be afraid with me. I want you to be yourself. Think you can manage that?"

She nodded.

"Good." He settled her on his chest. She could hear the reassuring beat of his heart.

She stilled. "What's wrong?"

He sighed, stroking her hair. "I don't want to put you in any more danger. I still don't want you using your tracking ability."

"Oh, I totally forgot to tell you—I only seem to have that little problem when we're together. Your energy makes mine stronger. But now we're linked, I should be perfectly fine. What is it?"

"Cynthia."

"You sense her with your dark talent, don't you?"

"Yes."

"Where?"

"That's the trouble. I'm not sure. She could be in Cleveland or it may be another state altogether. But I think tomorrow morning we ought to start our search by exploring the abandoned factory where Kaitlyn and I were held. We can try and pick up her energy and track her location."

She smoothed a hand across his chest. "It's okay. If she's there, I'll know it."

"That's all you'll do. Once you pick up her trail, I'll go after her. Now that I have you, I won't risk losing you."

IN THE MORNING, Geneva rode with Rolf and Kaitlyn to the Cleveland Flats and the building where Rolf and Kaitlyn had been held. Once again, Kaitlyn drove, and Rolf sat in the back with Geneva.

They parked, and Geneva studied the abandoned factory that had functioned as Rolf and Kaitlyn's prison. She opened her senses to the energy in the atmosphere. No hint of Cynthia's buttercup-yellow aura appeared on the premises. "She's not here."

"Dammit." Rolf reached for her hand. "I was certain she'd be holed away here. This place is massive. There would be plenty of places to hide. Are you certain?"

Not a speck of energy came from the derelict structure. "Yes."

"Time to regroup."

Geneva shivered, a someone-walked-over-her-grave kind of shiver.

"You okay?" Rolf put an arm around her shoulder.

Geneva eyed Kaitlyn in the driver's seat, their gazes meeting in the rearview mirror before she could look away. "No."

"What?"

"Nothing."

Rolf turned her chin until she looked at him. "Never lie to me. I'll know it."

"She's insane."

Rolf looked toward Kaitlyn. *"Yes."*

"She's infatuated with you."

"I know."

"She hates me."

Rolf frowned. *"I know."*

"You're repeating yourself."

"I owe her. She helped keep me sane when we were trapped in the dark." She sensed his bitter laughter in her mind. *"Ironic, isn't it? An insane woman keeping me sane."*

"Rolf, what are we going to do with her? We can't allow her to go free, can we? She's liable to hurt someone."

He sighed and rubbed a hand across the shadows on his face. He probably hadn't had a good night's sleep in days. How did he do it? Remain steady and keep the dark energy trapped inside? How long could he keep at it knowing they were hunted?

"I don't know. I'll arrange something, though. In the meantime, we need to find Cynthia—and fast. What's wrong?" He pulled her into his hard chest.

"Nothing." She breathed in his scent. He smelled of sunshine and rain. *"Only a thought. I didn't mean to worry you."*

He rubbed his hand through her hair. *"What an ass I am. Julia's fine. I've been meaning to tell you. In all the craziness, I forgot. I'm sorry, G. I brought her to consciousness before you called to me. I called Nonna, too. She's at home and doing well. I'm sure she's probably fussing over Julia right about now."*

"Does Julia know you were there? That you saved her?"

"No. If she remembers me, she believes it was one of her dreams. That's for the best, though. I'm sure the CMU will question her. I hope she doesn't believe their lies."

"She won't. Julia has faith in you." She entwined her fingers with his. *"Like I do."* Geneva gave him a smile. It trembled at the corners. *"It's such a relief to know she's okay."*

He lifted a brow and shot her a look both hot and gentle. Her skin tingled. *"Yes, I know."*

She laughed out loud, the sound surprising her. Despite all the craziness, he could make her laugh. He lifted her chin, his fingers warm and sure. His lips descended on hers, soft and firm, claiming her as he claimed her mind for his own.

She closed her eyes. A rainbow of colors flirted behind her lids. Energy moved through her body, dark and delicious. Her toes curled. How could a kiss be felt in her toes?

He pulled away, a devilish smile on his face. She would need to get used to the mind link. There would be no secrets between them.

He placed a palm on either side of her cheeks. *"I'm sorry I didn't think to tell you about Julia until now. I've been a little preoccupied."*

Rolf's aura flamed passion purple, and his lips found hers again, as if he couldn't help himself. He took every opportunity to remind her of their link. He shared her thoughts, understood her emotions. She sensed the fear nagging at his mind like a persistent toothache.

He lifted his head. His eyes met hers. The link between them would only grow stronger over time.

She squeezed his hand. *"If Cynthia's in Cleveland, we'll find her. I'll trace her. We need to get close to where she's hiding. Her energy is unique, which makes it easier for me to track. She won't stay hidden for long."*

He entwined his fingers with hers. Once again, Geneva caught Kaitlyn watching them from the driver's seat—eyes unblinking, expression blank. The yellow-green-brown colors surrounding her set off an internal alarm inside Geneva. *Madness. Unbalance. Hidden Secrets.* The colors screamed for help. Bile rose in her throat, but she swallowed it. Geneva noted how Kaitlyn's energy surrounded Rolf. Flecks of black bled through the customary green in his aura.

She dug her nails into her palms and counted to ten.

The woman was stark-raving mad, and she wanted Rolf. Rolf could read Kaitlyn's mind if she let him. But he couldn't "see" the extent of the woman's madness. Not like Geneva could. Kaitlyn Girard's energy was a fast-moving cancer, infecting everyone she came in contact with. Infecting Rolf.

"Where to now?" Kaitlyn asked.

Rolf glanced in the back seat. He frowned, a question in his mind. "*You up for a neighborhood search? I don't want you using your talent if it makes you ill.*"

He was gentler and kinder with Geneva than he was to Kaitlyn. He had to know the potency of the woman's unbalanced nature. If Geneva opened herself to the colors, she would make herself vulnerable to Kaitlyn's sick energy. But what was the alternative? If she did not, the CMU would find and kill Rolf. Her brothers would be first in line. She would not let Rolf be hunted and killed like an animal."

Geneva filled her lungs and exhaled, pushing her damp hair from her face and the sick blend of colors from her body. "*Yes. It's okay. Let me try to track her.*"

She closed her eyes. Rolf's dark energy surrounded her, its familiarity comforting. She brought it inside herself. Two portals appeared. Pain lanced her forehead, robbing her of air. An electrical charge raced through her body. Beads of sweat formed on her back and neck. An unfamiliar mind launched at hers like a spear, breaching her protections. Someone else was in her head. Another person in addition to Rolf—an intruder.

She drew in oxygen, but not enough to do any good. *The mind link!* She broke the gateway from her mind to Rolf's before the hacker could use it to enter Rolf's head and kill him.

She opened her eyes.

What the hell?

She was no longer in the car. She stood on the side of a cliff on the opposite side of the abandoned factory.

"Reestablish the portal to Rolf."

Geneva gasped and turned. A man stood not five inches from her. His lips curled in a frosted smile. *Senator Torra?*

Cynthia's father looked much like he did on television. He hadn't bothered to disguise himself. A cold shock of fear froze the marrow in her bones. He planned to kill her, no doubt. This was Cynthia's silent partner. Her father. And he was a hacker? If he was a hacker, he should have been able to freeze the portal. But she'd been able to remove it.

Pain sliced through her skull. Cold chills shivered along Geneva's spine, settling in her stomach. She swayed and would have toppled over the cliff wall if Senator Torra hadn't dropped a manicured hand on her shoulder.

"What do you want? How did I get here?"

"You know what I want. Recreate the link to Rolf's mind." His deep voice rang out, echoing over the cliff wall. His cold, dark eyes froze hers.

She frowned. "Why?"

"What a foolish woman. I could almost feel sorry for you. Except you've become a nasty thorn in my side."

Geneva yearned to pull energy to her from the hillside, but the scenery was fake, of course—a mental image of what the hacker wanted her to see. Her talent was useless in the landscape of her own mind.

Senator Torra gave her a shiny-toothed grin. "Exactly. The only thing you can do is call your lover. I'm sure he'll come running. Either that, or I'll see to it you die a slow and painful death. You'll lie in a coma for weeks on end, wasting away. And Rolf? Well, dark ones aren't known for their patience. He'll succumb to his darker nature. And when he does, he'll snuff the life from you and toss you away like a few bones to a dog."

"You're him, aren't you?" she managed to ask between another bout of needle-numbing pain. "You're Gemcatcher. A hacker."

"Yes." The senator puffed out his chest. "I do have a knack for finding ancient crystals. In some circles, I'm considered an expert on rare stones. But you're wrong about the hacking."

"What do you mean?" Despite the horror of her situation, Geneva found herself both repelled and fascinated. If Senator Torra wasn't a hacker, how had he gotten into her mind? How did he control her?

The senator smiled, but it wasn't a happy smile. No, it spoke of deep-seated anger and frustration. "I never did inherit the talent. It skipped a generation."

"So—" she swallowed— "how did you get to me?"

"Oh, I can't reveal all my secrets. We've talked long enough. Call your boyfriend."

She gasped and doubled over. The sting of a phantom knife blade cut into her skull. She wasn't sure how long she could resist the hacker's demands, but for Rolf's sake, she would try. "Why? So you can kill him?"

Senator Torra snagged a fist through Geneva's hair and yanked her to her feet. The pain forced tears from the corners of her eyes. "Listen, you little bitch. You do know what happens to the rare dark master who links with a partner only to lose them, right?"

She couldn't think through the pain to respond, but it didn't matter. The senator kept talking.

"Let me spell it out for you. Right about now, Rolf's frantic with worry. He's no longer linked to you since you closed the portal in your mind. He knows you're missing but doesn't know where to find you. Can you imagine the panic that will ensue? The dark in him will know where to find you. He will let it fill him, so he grows more sensitive to the light. He'll come after you, but it will be too late. He'll be a dark monster. He'll kill you. Is that the last thing you want to remember of this life? Being killed by your lover?"

Geneva stared into Gemcatcher's frightening eyes and shook her head from side to side. *No.* She wouldn't believe it. Rolf had conquered his dark nature once for her. Surely, he'd be strong enough to do it again? But as much as she wanted to deny the horrifying picture Gemcatcher sketched, she dared not. She had sensed Rolf's desperation through their mental bond. Every day he wrestled the darkness within himself and conquered. He admitted it was her light that kept the dark at bay. What if in her absence he could no longer contain the beast within?

"Do what I say. Call him now or let the dark overcome him. You know I speak the truth. Call to him. Open the portal. Reestablish the link. Let's see if your boyfriend can resist his dark nature."

Burning agony tore through her head as if she were being scalped. Her teeth clamped hard on her tongue. She tasted the saltiness of her own blood. Her eyes rolled back in her head. She gasped and scraped for air. Spots appeared in front of her eyes. The cliff spun away, and she was falling to her knees to keep from going over. Her lungs loosened, and she drew in a single, aching raspy breath. She could not control the scream that followed.

She called to Rolf.

THE SECOND GENEVA closed her eyes, Rolf knew something was wrong. Her mind shifted from his; the portal diminished and winked out of existence. Panic pounded his tenuous self-control. Dark energy rushed through his system, sweeping all reason aside. "Geneva, Geneva, what's happened?"

He tore open the door and launched himself into the back seat. Her body lay lifeless against the brown, cloth interior. He cupped her head and attempted to reach her. Silence. Kaitlyn opened and closed the driver door, but he paid little attention.

Darkness seized his body, controlled his mind. He craved. Craved the light. Dark to light. One canceled out the other. Get out. He'd get out of the car, or the dark would swallow Geneva's body whole.

He tumbled from the car, landing on the ground on all fours. Fire. He was on fire. Dark energy poured from his body. The grass under his hands and feet faded and disappeared.

He stood and wrapped his arms around his middle as if the motion could keep the dark energy contained. *"Where are you?"* he roared. *"Answer me!"*

He could not let the dark rule. It had no mind, no feelings. It craved light. Hers. It could find Geneva, but it could not save her from him. Only he could do that. *"Answer me. By God, Geneva, answer me now."*

Jesus, he'd never been so helpless in his life. In his mind, a tunnel formed, disappeared, reappeared. A woman screamed.

"Rolf, Rolf!"

Rolf hovered at the edge of the portal, sensing the cloying presence of the hacker like a poison in Geneva's mind. He almost lost it. Her pain. His pain. He couldn't tell them apart. On and on and on Geneva screamed in his head, calling to him, an endless cry for help.

The dark side of his nature demanded he answer the call. Commanded him to enter and destroy. But it's what his enemy wanted, wasn't it? To let the dark consume him? To enter her mind and stamp out every bit of light?

This was what they all believed of him. His comrades in the CMU, Peter, Cynthia, Gemcatcher. That the dark would overpower his control. That he was or would soon become a hardened psychopath. Why disappoint them?

He gritted his teeth. Because Geneva believed in him. Not a speck of fear constrained her love and admiration. She believed in his goodness. Believed he would rescue her. Believed in his strength to contain the dark forces that drove him. She loved him without condition. He would not fail her now.

For her, he could do it. He would do it. He'd conquer the dark. He'd find a way to save her and himself.

He filled his lungs with air. He managed a logical thought. How had the hacker broken into Geneva's mind without Rolf knowing?

The truth exploded in Rolf's consciousness with all the force of a nuclear weapon, dazzling in its audacity. God, the hacker had tricked them both by using dark energy—his. Because the hacker was Gemcatcher. That had to be it. He had access to the crystals and the knowledge of how to use them.

Rolf straightened, the darkness once again contained. If Gemcatcher was the hacker, why had he not tunneled through the portal and into Rolf's mind before Geneva eliminated the mind link? Any normal hacker would have used the portal to seize control. But Gemcatcher hadn't. *Why?*

Unless—Rolf frowned. Unless Gemcatcher wasn't an

experienced mind hacker? Maybe he wasn't a mind hacker at all. He wouldn't need to be one. He had the crystals filled with dark energy. But how had he activated them?

Another thought struck, a second atomic bomb, leaving destruction in its wake. *Kaitlyn.* She had done it. She was a trainer. She'd assisted Gemcatcher. Why hadn't he put it together before now? Gemcatcher hadn't believed Rolf was capable of controlling the dark energy long enough to figure it out. *Hell, not surprising.* Rolf hadn't trusted himself.

Kaitlyn had hated Geneva the moment she understood Rolf's need of her. Was insanely jealous, especially after she learned Rolf and Geneva would share a hotel room. Kaitlyn must have contacted Gemcatcher and made a bargain with Rolf as the prize.

So Kaitlyn gave Gemcatcher safe passage into Geneva's mind. Of course, she did. That's why Gemcatcher didn't need to be nearby. With a trainer establishing a portal and his energy in the crystals, Gemcatcher could be any number of places. That also explained why Geneva hadn't sensed psychic energy coming from the factory.

Now Gemcatcher had seized control of Geneva's mind. He used her as bait to lure Rolf into a trap. Once Gemcatcher had both of them under his control, he'd kill them. He'd probably told Kaitlyn he'd hand Rolf over to become her little plaything, ensuring her cooperation. Except Gemcatcher had no intention of handing him over to anyone. No, there was no way Gemcatcher planned to keep either Geneva or Rolf alive. He wanted them dead. If they remained alive, Gemcatcher's identity could be discovered, and both he and Cynthia could be captured and imprisoned.

Rolf opened his eyes and looked toward the driver's seat. He was careful to avoid glancing toward the back lest the sight of Geneva excite the darkness. Where had Kaitlyn disappeared to? Had she gone into hiding? She'd be somewhere close. She'd have to be for Gemcatcher to control Geneva.

He cracked the windows, grabbed his flashlight in case he needed it, and locked the car, searching the open landscape for Kaitlyn. His gaze settled on a spot in the distance, where a figure disappeared into the abandoned factory. He didn't waste more time thinking. Who knew how much time he had before Gemcatcher decided to cut his losses and kill Geneva? Terror filled his belly, stirring the cauldron of darkness.

He ran after Kaitlyn.

41

ILLUSION

Rolf had ample time to study the red brick building as he ran toward its entrance. Most of the windows were missing. A lone shutter hung in one opening. Trees grew out of the roof, bushes surrounded the building, and ivy grew on its sides. The entrance he and Kaitlyn had fled through a few short weeks ago looked as dark and ominous as he remembered, like a yawning mouth wanting to swallow him whole. What had the factory produced once upon a time? Bricks, bullets, steel? The rotting exterior gave no clue.

The wail of police sirens sounded in the distance. Rolf didn't hesitate but ducked through the dark opening and eyed the steps to the lower level. Something scurried in the darkness. A rat? Was this another trap designed to lure him back to the dark room where he'd been held prisoner? Would Cynthia be near, ready to zap his energy?

Geneva had failed to detect Cynthia's presence, he reminded himself. Even so, he turned left instead of heading to the basement lab. Rolf imagined even a lunatic would avoid the prison where they'd been trapped.

He rounded a corner. His intuition paid off. Footsteps sounded in the distance. With Geneva in danger, he wouldn't chance using dark energy to walk through walls. Instead, he listened, moving at a rapid pace. When the footsteps continued, he pushed with his mind. *"Come to me."*

The footsteps stopped and started again.

He waited a beat. *"I need you. Don't hide from me."*

He moved toward the noise. *"Why do you run? Don't you want to be together?"*

Rolf stopped, straining his ears for any sound leading to her presence. *"They will kill me, you know. They can't afford to allow me to live. I know too much and can't be trusted not to turn them into the authorities. Is that what you want? My death?"*

"No! No, never." The footsteps stopped again.

"Come out from wherever you are hiding."

"I...I can't. They told me not to."

"Since when do you listen to what they tell you? I thought you and I were friends."

"We are! Yes, we are, Rolf. More than friends. You're mine. They promised."

"You can't trust their promises, Kaitlyn. They plan to kill me. More than likely, they'll kill you, too. Don't hide from me. Let's talk like we did back when it was the two of us locked in the basement. You do remember how we used to talk, don't you?"

A rustle came from his left side. He turned, shining the flashlight in her wild eyes. He had her now.

"Oh, Rolf." She twisted herself into his side. "You're mine. Forget about the girl. Forget her. You don't want her. She doesn't understand the dark. She doesn't appreciate the man you are."

She entwined her hand in his, rubbing herself against him. "Not like I do."

He squeezed her hand until she gasped. "You think I

care about that? You allowed Gemcatcher entrance into her mind, dammit. Wake her. Now, before it's too late."

"I can't, Rolf. The angry one has her. He'll kill me."

He growled deep in his throat. Dark energy leaked from his pores. He wrestled with the beast and won, pulling his energy back inside in the nick of time.

Kaitlyn twisted in his arms, entwining her hands around his shoulders. "They said you would do it. You'd go to her. They said you would try to rescue her and fail. You would be mine. Why didn't you do what they said? Why aren't you mine?"

He pushed at her mind again. "Because they're liars. They thought I'd allow the dark to rule. But I don't. They planned to kill me. They would have never handed me over to you. Aren't you angry they lied? As they lied about harming your brother, Kyle."

She moaned, the sound echoing through the long hallway. "They took my brother from me. He went mad."

"Yes, I know. That's why you should stop them. Make them pay for what they've done. You and I will punish them together. Allow me entrance into Geneva's mind without Gemcatcher knowing."

"But I can't."

He grabbed her hands from around his shoulders and squeezed. "Yes, Kaitlyn. You can. You're an illusionist, aren't you? Create an illusion he'll believe."

———

KAITLYN GIRARD WAS one heck of a trainer, Geneva thought, in the brief moment of clarity before the senator inflicted another bout of torture. She breathed in and did her best to calm her racing heart. To conserve her energy.

Trainers were anesthesiologists administering a potent drug. They had to channel the exact amount of energy needed to hack into a mind. Too much and the target would be aware and eject the hacker, possibly killing them in the process. Too little and the hacker would be trapped in a mind forever until their physical body wasted away. In these cases, it was not uncommon for the trainer to be sucked inside the target's mind, too.

Kaitlyn managed to eject the proper amount of energy into the mix to allow Senator Torra entrance into Geneva's head. Geneva recognized Kaitlyn's energy the minute the senator hacked into her mind. And he wasn't budging, no matter how much Geneva tried to make him leave. All she got for her efforts were a splitting headache and less oxygen. Seemed the senator's favorite form of torture was cutting off her air supply. When Rolf failed to enter her mind using dark energy, the senator made sure she suffered for it.

Geneva lost track of how long or often she screamed for Rolf to come. In real time, perhaps a few minutes. But it could have been hours. No matter how long or often she screamed his name, he never answered her call. The senator paced.

"Where is he? He should be here by now."

"He'll come." Geneva wasn't at all sure that was true. But she needed to sound convincing, or the senator might decide to cut his losses and wipe her mind. If that happened, she'd end up in a coma, unlikely to recover.

"I underestimated him. He's not as enthralled with you as I thought."

"He loves me. He'll come. I know he will."

The senator stopped walking. "No. I don't believe it. He would be here by now. Makes for an interesting dilemma."

"No, please. Give him another minute."

The senator moved toward her, his face tight with tension. "Time's up." His hands reached for her neck. Of course, Geneva knew he didn't reach for her. Her mind created pictures so her brain could process what was taking place inside her physical body. The senator cut off the part of her brain controlling her air supply. This was it. This was how she would go out.

Odd, now the moment of her death was upon her, all Geneva could feel was calm. She'd fight. Of course, she'd fight. She twisted her head from side to side and placed her hands over his to loosen his grasp. His hands didn't budge. Her windpipe constricted and closed. White spots appeared in front of her eyes. Her vision narrowed and shrank. That's why she didn't see the dark shape next to her until the last second.

The senator released her neck, and she gasped for air through her bruised throat. "Rolf, look out," she croaked. She doubted whether Rolf could hear her.

Too late. The senator pointed a wicked looking shotgun toward Rolf. His eyes were twin mirrors of evil, calculating his next move. "I knew it was a matter of time before you'd appear, Dark Master."

Rolf glanced her way. His eyes appeared cold and blank. He'd looked at her like this once before, she recalled, in the coffee shop. Of course, it had been an illusion. She let out a gasp, reining the thought in before it could expand and alert the senator. He was so focused on Rolf, he failed to notice her agitation.

The senator fired his gun. The sound bounced off the surrounding hills. A giant red spot appeared on Rolf's chest. He toppled to the ground.

Oh God. It looked real. Not an illusion at all. A piercing scream echoed over the cliff. Her scream.

The senator stood over Rolf, the shotgun near his dark head. Before he fired, he flicked a glance Geneva's way to make sure she watched, a look of glee on his face. He returned his attention to his victim. "Goodbye, Rolf Jorgensen. I can't say I'll miss you."

"Good, since you won't have to."

The voice. The voice didn't come from the fallen man on the ground, who faded and disappeared. No, the voice came from behind the senator, calm and in control, no speck of dark energy present.

Rolf thrust a powerful arm around the senator's neck. The senator let out a gurgle. That was all he could manage.

Rolf was speaking, spitting out words like bullets. "The great Senator Torra. I should have guessed you were the mysterious Gemcatcher. How does it feel not to be able to breathe, you coward?"

The senator's eyes widened, his face a mottled red.

"Not good? I didn't think so."

Rolf turned to Geneva, his gaze raking over her body. Looking for signs of damage? He lifted his gaze to her face. "Do you think he's trying to tell us something?"

Geneva didn't know if Rolf expected an answer. But she gave him a thumbs-up sign because it was all she could manage. In response, Rolf let up on the senator's windpipe.

"Please, please."

"Please, what? Please don't kill you? Show you mercy you wouldn't have shown to either one of us?" Black light encircled Rolf's broad form.

Oh God. Rolf wouldn't make it. After all this time, the dark would win—was winning.

Rolf turned to her, his face a grim mask of anger, revenge, murder? He raised a brow. "What? He deserves to die for what he did to you, doesn't he?"

"Yes." She kept her tone steady. "But you'd be like him then, wouldn't you?" Her voice cracked. She could no longer control the tremor in it. She found herself doing something she never thought she would. Begging to save an evil man's life. Not for the sake of the evil man, no. But for the sake of Rolf, who would not survive the killing whole. His soul would be crushed in the process. "Please, Rolf. Don't do it. Don't let the dark win."

Rolf stared, his eyes devoid of emotion. Her heart sprang a leak, drowning her hopes for a bright future.

She'd lost, hadn't she? Rolf would kill the senator. The dark side of his nature demanded it. He'd kill and be killed. Nothing she could do. Unless—she straightened—unless she ejected him and the senator from her mind. She could do it, couldn't she? The senator no longer had control. He couldn't stop her. Rolf was so intent on killing the senator, he'd not yet assumed control. But Rolf and the senator would be killed when she ejected them. Unless she projected the proper amount of energy—enough to close the portal but not enough to inflict damage as they transitioned back to their physical bodies.

Rolf had focused his attention on the senator. She had a few seconds. She'd run out of time. Deep breath in, a snap as the portal disconnected, a shout, and total darkness.

42

RESCUE

Her brothers found her first. Geneva opened her eyes to see relief and something else in theirs. Fear? She lay stretched across the back seat of the rental car. Rolf and Kaitlyn were nowhere in sight.

"Where is he? Where's Rolf?" Nate asked.

"I'm not sure." Her voice came out in a whisper.

"Was he here? Did he do this to you?" Danny asked.

She attempted to rise. Why was she so weak? "Not Rolf. I will find him. Please, let me go."

"You're going nowhere." Nate pushed her back against the seat, his expression grim. "You're in no condition. We need to get you to a hospital. Then we need to find the son of a bitch and strangle him."

Geneva managed to raise her head. The tiny movement radiated pain through her skull. "Not Rolf. Gemcatcher. Senator Torra. Dead. Make sure."

"What are you saying? We'll find Jorgensen. I promise. The son of a bitch is a dark master. He deserves to die for how he's mistreated you."

"No." She gasped, a thousand arrows splitting her skull.

She flattened her hands against her ears as if it might stop the ringing. "You—you don't understand. Gemcatcher, it's Senator Torra. He's stealing our energy. Stores it in synthetic crystals to sell. He stole Rolf's energy. Used it to hack—" a wretched dry cough interrupted her speech— "into my mind. He almost killed me. Rolf saved me."

The brothers exchanged glances. Streaks of navy bounced between them.

"We can see what he did," Danny said. "It's going to be okay. We'll find him. Don't worry."

Geneva gazed into Danny's gray eyes, so much like her own. "You don't believe me. You think Rolf—" Another spasm of coughing interrupted her words.

"That's enough. You've suffered a shock," Nate said. "The ambulance is here. They're going to take you to the Cleveland Clinic."

Beyond Nate's head, Geneva could see flashing lights from the ambulance parked nearby. The driver had turned off the siren.

Nate tried to pull out of the car to let the crew inside, but she grabbed a hold of his shirt with what remained of her strength and twisted.

"Listen, listen to me."

"Geneva..."

"Please. Rolf could be hurt or worse. He's a good man. He rescued me from Senator Torra. Stood between me and death. He hasn't turned. He won't as long as I'm alive. Give him a chance. Go after Senator Torra." Tears glistened in her eyes, but she refused to let them fall. "Promise me. Promise me you'll save him."

"Yes." Nate nodded, or was it a medic? Something stung her arm. Nate didn't know how to give shots, did he? "Let's get you to a hospital."

"Wait." Had someone siphoned the oxygen in the car? She could still feel hands around her neck where Senator Torra strangled her. She had to warn them. "Cynthia Torra. Beware. A beacon. She's a...a..." What did she need to warn them of? Senator Torra. Senator Torra came for her. He would not rest until he'd squeezed the life from her.

"It's okay. You're gonna be okay. Sleep now. Easy does it. Go to sleep."

THE MOMENT GENEVA rejected the portal, and he returned to his body, Rolf braced himself for injury. Every hacker heard the stories over the years. Careless hackers sent back to their bodies who got caught in the cross waves of the brain's magnetic field and absorbed into the target's mind. Those who survived told horrible tales of missing body parts and endless agony.

Despite their descriptions, even he couldn't fathom the jarring impact of his return until it was upon him. Pain radiated from the top of his forehead to his toes. He forced himself to wiggle them to make sure they were still connected to his body. They moved, so he had to believe they were.

Rolf lay on the dark factory floor and contemplated death. Death was better than this relentless pain. It pummeled his body like ocean waves in a storm. Cold, piercing, endless. It stripped his mind of every thought save one: Geneva. Had she survived? Why had she condemned him to endless waves of torment?

The illusion had worked. He'd taken Senator Torra by surprise. He'd been about to teach the bastard a lesson he'd never forget. But he'd made the mistake of looking at

Geneva. He'd not bothered to mask his feelings. She needed to know who he was—a man capable of exacting revenge on any who would dare threaten the woman he loved.

She'd seen him, and she'd rejected him. She'd chosen to push him from her mind, knowing the torment he'd suffer. She'd chosen to condemn him to endless hours of agony, writhing on the floor where rats scurried back and forth in the darkness. She'd chosen to prevent him from murdering the son of a bitch who would have snapped her windpipe if Rolf hadn't intervened.

Even as he cursed her actions, he loved her. Loved the light of her goodness that refused to allow the monster inside him to surface. Loved how she protected him, despite knowing she'd also suffer and risk losing her own life. He loved her, but he'd strangle her the next time he saw her for putting them both through this agony. If they survived, he'd strangle her for not trusting him enough to control the dark side of his nature. He'd strangle her, and he'd love her for the rest of their lives together.

His breathing slowed. His heartbeat steadied. His hands clenched and unclenched against the hard floor, then relaxed. Crippling pain coursed through his body, retreated and disappeared. His mind cleared and reached for Geneva. Nothing. Had Cynthia found her? Worry nagged at his self-control. Darkness stirred on the psychic plane. Someone was in the building. More than one person. And they were coming closer. He sat and rose in a single motion. He needed to beat a quick exit. Now was the time to walk through walls. His foot hit against a solid object. *Shit.*

He crouched, his hands landing on his cell phone and a hard shape—a body. He used the flashlight on the phone to take a closer look, but he knew who it would be. *Kaitlyn Girard.* Dead. He knew it but went through the motions of checking, feeling for a pulse in her neck, where there was none. *Shit, shit, shit.* Kaitlyn had gotten caught in the cross waves during his sudden exit. There hadn't been time to warn her. *His fault.* But he hadn't anticipated Geneva would break their connection.

He had to get out of here. The CMU would never believe her death had been an accident. And who could blame them? He rose and connected with a hard metal object. Stars exploded behind his eyelids.

———————————

ROLF REGAINED consciousness to find himself in a bed in what he suspected was a dark hospital room. His throat was dryer than a desert. He raised a hand to scratch his nose. Or at least he tried to raise a hand. He couldn't lift a finger. Neither could he move any other part of his body. Last thing he remembered, he'd connected with a hard object. Did the Ericksen brothers find him? Had he injured his spinal cord?

A voice spoke. "Don't bother struggling. You won't be able to move until I let you. You'll need your strength."

Rolf couldn't turn his head to see who spoke, so he stared at the dark ceiling. He'd be damned if he'd answer any questions to some disembodied voice while he lay paralyzed and strapped to a lousy hospital bed. He cleared his throat and licked his lips with what little moisture remained in his mouth. God, if he wasn't so angry, he'd beg for water. "You have me at a disadvantage. Who are you?"

The voice came closer, the tone smooth and melodic. "My apologies. My name is Caleb Stone. I'm employed by the CMU. I handle the dark ones. Let me give you a piece of advice. This will go much easier for you if you cooperate."

"If you're from the CMU, why haven't you killed me? The

CMU's mode of operation is not to question hackers they think have gone rogue."

"Ah, you get right to the heart of the matter. I like that. And apparently, your brain's still working, which is more than I can say for the rest of you. This may take a while. Let me pull up a chair."

There was a scrape of metal against the hard floor, and a bedside light flicked on, and Rolf stared into dark-blue eyes as frigid as an iceberg. Fear raced along Rolf's nerve endings, screaming for him to distance himself, screaming danger. He'd never been one to shy away from a threat, though.

Caleb Stone's face was blunt like an ax, and his nose as sharp as it was long. His lip curled in an Elvis Presley semi-smile. In an instant, Rolf knew Caleb Stone enjoyed his job, whatever the hell he did to handle dark masters. Rolf wasn't aware there were all that many running around for Caleb Stone to have much work to do.

Caleb Stone smiled, or did he sneer? Rolf wasn't certain.

"Let me be clear with you. Geneva Erickson claims you rescued her from Senator Torra, who hacked into her mind and attempted to kill her. There's evidence of strangulation to indicate someone did harm Ms. Ericksen. However, the perpetrator's a mystery. Senator Torra was thousands of miles away during the attempted murder. And he's not a hacker. You, however, are a hacker, not to mention a dark master, and made off with Ms. Ericksen from a government-run high-security facility. Tell me, Mr. Jorgensen, how is it both women traveling with you, two powerful trainers, were harmed. One dead."

Anxiety loosened Rolf's iron self-control. Not worry for himself. No. His voice shook before he could steady it. "Geneva? Is she—how is she?"

There was a long pause. Rolf didn't think Caleb Stone would answer. Until he did.

"Alive, barely, but she'll survive. Her brothers guard her day and night. Geneva Ericksen was lucky. Kaitlyn Girard, not so fortunate. What did you do to her?"

"I didn't kill her."

"Don't bullshit me. You are this close—" Caleb Stone held two fingers in front of Rolf's face. Heat traveled from those two fingers straight into Rolf's brain— *"to being wiped from existence."*

Rolf stared at Caleb's fingers a moment, trying to slow the adrenaline rush in his veins inciting the dark energy. Now wasn't the time to lose control. Rolf didn't think Caleb Stone would take it well. He had extraordinary abilities if he could hack into Rolf's mind.

"Yes, Mr. Jorgensen. I'm a rare breed. You have no idea. Capable of feats you can only dream about."

He let out a short laugh as if he'd told a joke, but Rolf found nothing about Caleb Stone amusing.

"I've been sent to wipe your mind, you know. Render you harmless, which in a hacker of your caliber involves death. Fortunately for you, I don't always follow orders. Unfortunately, I'm impatient and bored enough to take action. Now tell me what happened. Much easier to have you tell me than having to root around in your head for memories. No lies. I'll know it."

Rolf spoke rapidly. "Geneva was hacked by Senator Torra and Kaitlyn Girard. The senator used dark energy— my energy—to complete the hack. He and his daughter, Cynthia, forced me to release it into fabricated crystals capable of storing psychic energy. Geneva believed the energy was mine and because she trusted me, made herself vulnerable to it. You haven't killed me."

Caleb Stone sighed. "Not yet."

"Why not?"

"Because your sister believes in your innocence. I have a soft spot for your sister."

"Julia? You know her?"

Caleb Stone smiled. "We go way back."

"Last I saw her, she had come out of a coma. Is she fully recovered?"

"Recovered enough to plead for your life. I don't care to disappoint her."

"If you're not planning to kill me, why am I immobile? Why did you hack into my mind?"

"Precautionary. You see, despite Julia's assertions, I wasn't sure what you'd become."

"I haven't turned."

"You're close."

"I won't turn. Will you grant me my freedom? You're in my head. You can see I speak the truth."

"I'm afraid it's not that easy. The CMU believes you're a threat. They want hard evidence that what you say is true. Your memories don't count. Whoever held you captive could have tampered with them. Geneva isn't a credible witness. She loves you. Her brothers have gone on record stating you hacked into their sister's mind and would have killed her if she hadn't ejected you in self-defense. They believe you've gone rogue. That you've brainwashed Geneva into thinking you care for her. That you are using your dark energy to keep her enthralled, manipulating her for your own selfish motives."

"But that's ridiculous."

"Is it, Mr. Jorgensen? Did you not hack into her mind?"

"Yes, but I had to. The senator would have killed her otherwise. I had to save her."

"I can see you believe what you say. But why did she eject you?" He raised one eyebrow, those strange blue eyes peering into Rolf's as if they magnified all his fears and insecurities. Which they did. "Ah, there's the rub. The one who loves you most doubts your ability to control the dark side of your nature."

Caleb Stone rose from his chair and walked across the room. Rolf heard the sound of running water. He returned some moments later with a cup, propped Rolf's head forward and brought the cold liquid to his lips. "Drink. I'm not a cruel man, despite what you believe."

Rolf didn't hesitate. He drank, greedy for every last drop. He finished, and Caleb Stone moved away. Rolf heard the rattle of a dish, so assumed Caleb returned the cup to wherever he'd gotten it. A moment later and he was once again leaning over Rolf's bedside.

"We need evidence, Mr. Jorgensen. We need the crystals you say the senator and his daughter made. We need to find them, wherever they're hidden, and present them to the CMU. Only then will we be able to convince the CMU of your innocence."

"That's easy enough. Hack into the senator's mind. You'll find all the evidence you need." He frowned, and would have rubbed his chin if he wasn't paralyzed.

The ax-faced Caleb Stone broke into his smile-sneer. "That's impossible."

"What do you mean?"

"The senator is dead. Found in his Washington D.C. apartment an hour ago by his assistant. The official autopsy report is death by massive aneurysm."

Of course. Some of the senator's energy had gotten caught in the cross waves and absorbed into Geneva's mind. He hadn't made it back in one piece. "That leaves..."

"Cynthia Torra."

"Yes. She'll know where the crystals are."

"I told you I'm a specialist. There's a reason for that. I can go after hackers and only in a dream state. I pursue dark rogue monsters like yourself."

"I told you, I haven't gone rogue. If you can't hack Cynthia, assign someone else the job."

"Who? The Ericksen brothers? They're convinced of your guilt like everyone else in the CMU. I'm afraid the only one who can save you is—you."

"How am I supposed to save myself tied to this damn hospital bed?" Did the man think he had superpowers?

For the first time since he'd introduced himself, Caleb Stone smiled, a genuine smile. "Oh, I can remedy that." For a moment, Rolf was taken aback. With his dark hair and glint in his navy-blue eyes, his interrogator almost looked kind. "However, you need to know something. If I let you go, and you turn to the dark side of your nature, I will hunt you down, and I will kill you, despite your sister's protests. Do you understand?"

Rolf nodded. "Of course. I won't turn."

Caleb Stone frowned. "If I had a dollar for every time I've heard that I'd be rich. They all turn sooner or later, Mr. Jorgensen. Dark ones are incapable of finding true happiness with another. They cannot love. It is their destiny."

"No. Not mine. I do love another. I always have."

Caleb Stone reacted so fast, Rolf did not see his movements. But he couldn't avoid looking into those searing blue eyes that saw everything when the man leaned over his face. "Do you, Rolf Jorgensen? Do you love her?"

Rolf tried not to blink. "Yes."

Caleb Stone reared, his expression triumphant. "Good. Prove it. You're going to need Geneva's talent to outsmart

Cynthia Torra. But as the saying goes, 'There is no greater love than to lay down one's life for one's friends.' Remember that, Mr. Jorgensen. Now, let's see if we can get you moving."

A glint of silver caught Rolf's eye, and his heart lurched in his chest. Caleb Stone wielded a wicked-looking sword. He raised it above his head and slashed downward in a movement so fast Rolf forgot to breathe. The sword lanced his skull, sending a white-hot stabbing pain through him, and he was once again falling into blackness.

He opened his eyes. What the hell? Where was Caleb Stone and the hospitable room? Rolf lay sprawled over Kaitlyn's lifeless body. He'd struck his head on some metal object hanging from the ceiling and hallucinated Caleb Stone. That had to be it. But what a hallucination it had been. He could still feel the slash of the blade where it had sliced into his head.

Voices came from the darkness. Geneva's brothers. He had just enough time to launch himself into the wall.

43

THE SCARLET HEART

Running had never been Rolf's favorite form of exercise. He preferred more adventurous outdoor activities—rock climbing, mountain biking, skiing. But he'd never run for his life before, dashing through factory walls with the mad Ericksen brothers in hot pursuit. It brought a whole new level of meaning to the words "extreme sports."

He lost the brothers somewhere close to Tower City Center, when he managed to slip through the walls of the building and lose himself in a crowd of shoppers. The entire time, he couldn't stop thinking about the dream man, Caleb Stone. What had he meant with his cryptic comments? Could any of it be real? His sister was the dream talent, not Rolf. So what had prompted such an intense dream?

One thing Caleb Stone was wrong about. He wouldn't use Geneva's talents to outsmart Cynthia. He refused to let Geneva anywhere close to Cynthia Torra again. Not if he could help it. He wanted her safe. He'd find another way to locate the missing crystals.

"DANNY, WHERE'S ROLF?" Geneva asked the moment she opened bleary eyes to spy Danny, dressed in a black T-shirt and sweatpants, sitting next to her bed. She fingered her blue hospital gown. It appeared she had returned to a hospital. "You look worse than I feel. Where am I?"

"Take it easy. You're at the Cleveland Clinic. You've had a rough go. You're lucky to be alive."

She lifted her head, or at least she tried to, but her body wouldn't cooperate. She put a hand to her forehead. The effort zapped her strength. "No one's harmed him, have they?"

Danny sighed. "Leave it to you to come back from the dead, and the first thing you do is ask about Rolf."

"Danny Ericksen, if you don't tell me what I want to know right now, I swear I'll, well, I don't know what I'll do, but it won't be pleasant.

"All right, all right. Don't get excited. He's still alive as far as I know."

"What do you mean?"

Danny settled back in the chair. "After we found you, we tracked him to where he hid out in an old factory, but he leaped through the wall. We lost him after that."

"Thank God. Do you believe what I told you?"

"Sure."

Geneva blinked. Gray and brown energy waves issued forth with his words. "Don't lie to me. I may be sick, but I still see colors. You don't believe a word of what I told you. So let me repeat myself. Rolf's a good man. He's not a threat. We are—were—linked. We will be linked again. He saved my life from Senator Torra, who tried to kill me. What?"

"You need to rest."

She propped herself on her elbows. "Dammit, what aren't you telling me?"

Danny's lips tilted down, his aura shifting from gray to his customary royal blue.

"Senator Torra is dead."

Geneva didn't blink. "Yes, I told you he was. I killed him. Self-defense—the man's evil. He hacked into my mind. I closed the portal he used, ejecting him. I did my best to make sure he got caught in the cross waves."

Danny's gaze shifted away from her. He shook his head, his energy drawing inward, but a bit of dark navy escaped. He didn't believe her. "The CMU investigated Senator Torra. He isn't a hacker. He doesn't have talent. It would have been impossible for him to hack into your mind. Cynthia Torra has disappeared. Her publicist issued a statement. She denies there are any crystals and fears for her life. She claims you and Rolf stalked and killed her father and are now after her. She's gone into hiding until Rolf is found and you're both arrested for murder."

Geneva grimaced and lay back on the pillow, the small amount of exertion exhausting. "It's the other way around. Senator Torra tried to *kill me*. He used Rolf's energy—the energy he's been storing in crystals—and Kaitlyn Girard, who's a known trainer, to hack into my mind. I thought it was Rolf and let him in. The crystals exist. Cynthia knows where they are. That's why she's hiding."

Danny patted her hand, a mixture of worry and pity in his eyes. "Geneva, we all saw Rolf turn. He hacked into your mind. Then took off running like a madman through the Institution wall with you in his arms as a human shield. Rolf's gone rogue. It's more likely he let the senator into your mind in some deadly game he's playing. And he's more dangerous than you can imagine. He killed Kaitlyn. He doesn't love you. He can't. He's a dark master."

A bubble grew in the back of Geneva's throat. She couldn't seem to swallow it. "Kaitlyn is dead?"

Danny sat on the side of the bed and clasped Geneva's hand. "I'm sorry."

She pulled her hand from his and jabbed a finger at his chest. "Rolf didn't do it."

"Don't be naive. He was the only one with her. Who else could it have been?"

She glared. "Me. I'm the killer. Kaitlyn got caught in the cross waves. I didn't mean for that to happen. But you know it's a risk trainers take every time they magnify energy waves."

"It doesn't change the fact Rolf's a dark master. The guy's a hardened sociopath."

"Stop calling him that—he's not a sociopath! The legends are wrong about dark masters, Danny. Rolf can love —he loves me. He has himself under control. You have to help me find him. He hasn't gone rogue. I would know it if he has."

Danny let out a huff and stood. "Even if I thought Rolf innocent, and I don't, we'd need hard evidence to convince the CMU he's not a killer. Peter's orders are to bring him in dead or alive. He's considered unstable. If he hasn't turned, as you say, the likelihood of him doing so is high. Until we have proof, he's a threat to society and the CMU."

He strolled toward the window, stopped, and turned. Royal blue laced with streaks of muted red leaked from his aura, revealing more to Geneva than words conveyed. Her brother worried for her.

"Honestly, Geneva, I'm more concerned about you right

now. The government is investigating Cynthia's allegations. If they find evidence, anything at all, you colluded with Rolf to take her father's life, who knows what the full consequences will be. Are you sure there's nothing more you want to tell me?"

She sighed. "I already told you. I ejected Senator Torra from my mind because he tried to strangle me. He died in the cross waves. Rolf had nothing to do with it, other than he distracted the senator enough I could eject them from my mind. I don't care what the government ordered. You mustn't kill him. I promise you, evidence exists. Cynthia Torra knows where the crystals are hidden. We can find them, Danny. Once the CMU sees the crystals for themselves, they'll know I'm telling the truth. I'm sure we can convince them to take a closer look at Rolf. He hasn't turned. He's promised me he won't. I believe him."

Danny flung a hand through his dark-blond hair, causing it to stick up in three different directions. His wrinkled shirt and whiskers indicated he hadn't slept, or at least, not well. Red warred with bright blue in his aura. Blue won. Geneva released the air in her lungs.

"I'll tell you what. I'll take a look around, talk to a few people and see if I can discover any info on Cynthia and the crystals. But you will stay here in this hospital room and give your body time to recover. Promise?"

"Even if I wanted to, I don't have the strength to chase after you."

"I'll take that as a promise." Danny moved toward the door.

"Danny, wait." Adrenaline pounded in her veins.

Danny half-turned around, a question on his face. "What is it?

"Cynthia's dangerous. She can wipe your talent. Don't confront her."

Danny gave an exaggerated eye-roll. "Still giving orders? Don't worry. I'll be discreet. You worry about getting better." His gaze held hers a moment. "If Rolf contacts you, I need to know. I'm risking a lot for you. My career could be on the line."

Geneva didn't flinch from his gaze. "Agreed. But he won't contact me. He'll want to protect me. He'll go after Cynthia. Find her, and you might get a lead on Rolf."

44

SPA DAY

Cynthia Torra pounded the pavement with her cowboy boots as she walked down Euclid Avenue, dodging a businessman in a suit and tie. It was a Wednesday, and the lunchtime crowd sought out the popular Cleveland restaurants on East 4th Street, creating a buzzing beehive of activity on the downtown city streets. Cynthia watched for anyone suspicious following her. She paused at a crosswalk, waiting for the light to change to green, giving her plenty of time to think.

Was it yesterday morning her father's assistant discovered his body? Gina had grown worried when he didn't appear for his weekly staff meeting. She'd found his crumpled form on the floor of his D.C. office and called the police, who in turn called Cynthia. She'd been taping a show in New York. As Daddy had anticipated, if anything went wrong with his attack on Geneva and Rolf, they would point incriminating fingers at Cynthia. Being in New York would give Cynthia an airtight alibi.

She crossed the street and continued toward her destination: a tiny store housed in The Arcade, a grand Victorian-era structure and one of the oldest indoor shopping malls in America. The building contained five stories with gold balconies on four levels, fancy staircases on either end, and what she guessed was a three-hundred-foot glass skylight. A hotel occupied the top levels. Shops and restaurants lined the lower floors.

A flash of hot pink in a nearby store window caught Cynthia's eye, and she took a moment to admire the glittering dress on the mannequin posed there, as well as her own reflection. A stranger with curly auburn hair under a cream cowboy hat stared back at her. Cynthia smiled and blew herself a kiss. Even a wig and hat couldn't alter the striking lines of her face. She'd downplayed her natural good looks by not wearing any makeup and dressing in this ridiculous cowgirl outfit, boots and all. *Yuck*. The only thing missing were chaps and spurs.

She grimaced, promising herself a visit to a spa when all this was over. Hard to believe her clever father was dead. Aneurysm, according to the police. A massive brain hemorrhage with no hope of recovery. Estimated time of death— six p.m. the prior evening. Only Cynthia and that scumbag, Rolf Jorgensen, knew the truth. Her father had been murdered by Geneva Ericksen.

Cynthia still had trouble believing Daddy died hacking into the freak's mind. Daddy said the crystals would work. Cynthia had no reason to doubt him. For Christ's sake, her father was a senator, who'd planned a bid for president. He had a degree from Harvard. He was the smartest person Cynthia knew, and now he was dead. What a waste.

She turned from the store window and continued toward her destination. Her father's death would not be in vain. No way. Not if she had anything to say about it. And she had plenty to say. She'd made sure her publicist issued a statement implicating Geneva in her father's death. The CMU would have no choice but to investigate. And of course, they'd do everything in their power to keep the public unaware of their existence, which meant Geneva could kiss her freedom goodbye. And Rolf, too.

Now Cynthia could continue with the original plan. Sell the crystals to the buyers her father had made a deal with and live as a multi-millionaire. Except she wouldn't sell *all* the crystals. No, she'd already planted a few synthetic crystals in Geneva's apartment for the CMU to discover. Geneva would have a job on her guilty hands explaining those away.

Cynthia opened the pair of walnut doors leading into The Arcade and headed to the marble steps and toward the opposite side of the building. She stopped in front of a small window display in the far corner and studied the closed sign —Gem Alley, the store Daddy opened more than twenty years ago.

Once she sold the crystals, there would be no evidence to tarnish his sterling reputation. She had plenty of buyers in line for the crystals. All she had to do was coordinate their transfer and make damn sure Geneva paid for her crimes.

She used the keypad to unlock the door and went inside to pull the crystals from the hidden safe where her father kept them. Her heart lurched, as it always did when she opened the safe door and spied the two velvet bags—one green and one black. The black bag held the synthetic crystals, but the green bag was her father's pride and joy. It held the only charged crystal remaining from the lot he'd stolen from Lucinda Ericksen years ago.

She pulled both bags from the safe, setting the black aside and opening the green to take a closer look. An icy pink crystal glittered against the plush velvet. *The Scarlet*

Heart. Cynthia hardly dared breathe lest she activate the energy stored in its rosy depths. Her father always said his acquisition of the Scarlet Heart was his crowning achievement. Its pink prettiness drew the eye, but Cynthia knew the power it contained could stop a heart from beating. She would use the Scarlet Heart to kill Geneva Ericksen.

Then Cynthia would have her spa day somewhere far away from Cleveland and the long arm of the CMU.

45

PREMONITION

The rambling dirt lane leading to the white farmhouse was lined with evergreen trees. Driving through them always seemed a bit magical to Julia, like fairies and gnomes were hidden in their branches. Of course, her childhood home had always been a magical fortress. Nonna made it so.

A haziness hung in the air. Julia made her way across the wide front porch and raised a hand to knock on the solid wood door that opened before her fist made contact. Nonna stood there, looking healthy and vivacious, and not like a few weeks ago when she'd been in the hospital. *A dream. It must be.*

Nonna's black hair was streaked with a smattering of white and pulled into a tight bun on the back of her head. The smell of gingerbread wafted through the opening, and she carried a cup of tea in her hand. "Come in. Come in. How are you feeling? Heard you've been through a bit of a trauma. But you'll be okay now, won't you? Thanks to Rolf and your nice young man."

"What young man, Nonna?"

"Oh, you know." Nonna gave her a secretive smile and nudged her with an elbow.

"No, I don't know."

"The handsome one who comes to you in your dreams."

Julia blushed. "How do you know about him?"

"Oh, I have my ways. I may be old, but I'm not senile yet. Now sit and tell me why you've come to visit."

Nonna pulled out a wooden chair from the old oak table where Julia and Rolf had done their homework as children. Julia set her purse and car keys on the kitchen counter and sat. Nonna bustled around the kitchen, filling a cup with tea from the kettle and setting it and a couple of homemade gingerbread cookies in front of Julia. She pulled out the chair opposite. "What is it you want to know?"

Julia fiddled with her teacup. She and Rolf never talked about Nonna's mysterious talent. They'd never wanted to make her feel uncomfortable. "I'm concerned for Rolf. He's in serious trouble. The CMU's issued orders to bring him in dead or alive. Everyone believes he's dangerous."

"That poor boy." Nonna shook her head. "He's in for a rough time."

"What do you mean, Nonna? What's going to happen to Rolf?"

Nonna peered into her teacup. "It's hard to say. His destiny is linked with Geneva's. One cannot live without the other. He loves her. He always has. But he needs to prove it, or no one will ever believe him, even Geneva herself."

"How can he prove it?"

Nonna no longer read the tea leaves. Instead, she gazed through Julia as if she saw the wall beyond and farther, much farther. She sighed—a big, hearty, drawn-out affair. "It looks like your brother is going to need my special gift."

"No." Julia shook her head, rising from her chair so

abruptly it fell behind her with a bang. "No, Nonna, it can't be so."

"Yes, I'm afraid it is." Nonna patted Julia's arm. "There's nothing we can do about it. Don't be afraid. All is well, my dear. I may be old, but my talent hasn't failed me yet. I'll be there for Rolf when the time comes. See to it, okay?"

Julia sat up in bed, her heart beating double-time. Sweat covered her body, although the window was open and early morning light filtered in along with a cool breeze. A rooster crowed from the backyard where Nonna kept her girls, as she called them. Goose bumps covered Julia's body.

She got out of bed and put on her jeans and T-shirt from the day before, shaking like she'd seen a ghost. Of course, with a dream like she'd had—a premonition of what was to come—it was like seeing a ghost. She didn't want to believe the vision, but she'd be a fool to ignore its warning.

A shiver erupted at the top of her head and made its way to the base of her spine. Julia had spent the last few weeks at the family farm with Nonna and her dad, pretending everything was normal. But of course, she'd known all along their life was far from normal. How could she not be anxious knowing Rolf was hunted by the CMU and Geneva was in the hospital?

Now it appeared her worst fears were about to come true. Rolf would die. Unless she and Nonna could find Rolf and alter fate. And for that, they'd need Geneva.

Julia hurried to Nonna's room, but Nonna wasn't in her bed. She had her suitcase packed and sat in an armchair next to the bed.

"Nonna? How did you..."

"Pshaw." Nonna cut her off with a wave of her hand. "You don't think you're the only one entitled to have strange dreams, do you?"

"You mean, you dreamt I'd come for you?"

Nonna pursed her lips. "Yes. Such a handsome gentleman I dreamed about. He claimed it's my job to keep you and Rolf out of trouble. As if I ever could."

Julia's stomach sank like a rock to the bottom of the ocean. "You dreamt of a man? Did he tell you his name?"

"Sure he did. Said it was Caleb. Anyone you know?"

Julia's legs wobbled until she collapsed on the side of the bed. "God, I—all these years—I never thought him real. Thought I'd made him up to make myself feel better. But there's no way the same man could appear in both our dreams unless he exists. He's a hacker of some sort. He, Caleb, comes to me in my dreams. He warns me of danger. What else did he tell you?"

Nonna grasped Julia's cold hands in a warm clasp. Her one blue eye was clear as ever. The brown one wandered as it always did, searching out a truth of its own, Julia supposed.

"He said it wouldn't be easy. If we want to save Rolf, we have to work together." Nonna's brown eye focused, and her hands tightened around Julia's. "I figured that meant you and I were going on a scouting mission."

"Yes, we will find Rolf. I'm sure he's staying away to protect us. I think the best chance we have of finding him is Geneva."

Julia's cell phone buzzed, and she glanced at the incoming text message from Nate Ericksen. What she saw pummeled her heart until it pounded in her chest.

Geneva is in deep shit with the CMU. Cynthia Torra implicated my sister in her father's murder.

"Sorry, Nonna. It's Nate Ericksen. Geneva's in trouble. Give me a minute to find out what's going on."

Nonna nodded. Julia texted back. *Why would CMU believe Cynthia?*

Found synthetic crystals in G's apartment. Crystals analyzed in lab. Doesn't look good. Ortiz ordered G locked up for life. Any word from Rolf?

No, nothing.

Julia didn't figure a dream message counted. The Ericksen brothers had made it known they didn't trust Rolf. They'd haul him away before they believed in his innocence. She continued typing. *What do you plan to do? Take her to the Institution?*

Hell no. If she goes there, the CMU will never let her return. Doing digging. Sorry, your brother's dangerous. But Cynthia is not innocent. Word on the street is she's got something a number of countries want. We need to find her and the crystals. Any dreams?

Yes

Spill

Geneva's and Rolf's destinies are linked. One cannot survive without other. To save Geneva, we must save Rolf.

???

Nonna and I headed to Cleveland Clinic. Talk there.

46

SEARCH

Geneva awoke in her hospital bed to find a small crowd assembled around her: both brothers, looking stern; Julia, looking anxious; Julia's father Ralph Jorgensen; Nonna; and Peter, looking afraid. If Peter was here it meant— Geneva shot up in bed, her heart pounding like a runaway freight train. "What's happened? Where's Rolf."

Nate squeezed her hand. "Take it easy, Sis. Rolf's okay. It's you we're worried about. Dad's on his way."

Geneva looked toward Danny. "Where is he? Rolf? Have you found him?"

"No, I haven't. I'm sorry. I did some checking, though. There's a rumor going around an American is looking for international buyers for a number of crystals."

Geneva grimaced. "Cynthia, of course."

"Maybe. We have no proof. Cynthia has disappeared. And no one can find Rolf or the crystals."

Julia stepped forward, looking at Geneva. "You can, though. Can't you?"

"I won't find Rolf to have the CMU"—Geneva turned to Peter with a frown—"haul him in."

"Not even if Rolf's life is at stake?" Julia sat on the side of her bed.

Geneva stared as colors twisted and gyrated. With a snap and a sizzle, the lamp on the nightstand next to her bed went dark. "What do you mean?"

Julia's eyes were large and round. A turquoise-red fog surrounded her. Whatever she was about to say, she believed, and it terrified her. "I had a dream. Nonna, too. I know you always tell me not to take them too seriously, since they're so easy to misinterpret, but..."

"What? Tell me."

Julia gripped her arms. Her nails pinched Geneva's skin. She didn't dare protest, though, lest she interrupt Julia's confession.

"The man in my dream. It was the same man who warned me Rolf's life was endangered last time. Remember? The day we went to Coffersations?"

Geneva forced her eyes off the violet-red-turquoise haze surrounding Julia. "What did he tell you?"

"He came to warn me. Rolf's in danger. We are to find Rolf and the crystals, or he'll be killed."

Nate stepped forward. "It's a dream. One possible outcome. Danny and I can find Rolf and the crystals."

"No." Geneva watched as the water in her glass twisted into a mini-tornado. "I'm tracking him. It will be much faster if I do it, since I don't need to leave this room to use my talent. He's in the area. I sense him. The crystals, too. Promise me when I find him you won't harm him." Geneva turned her head to the others. "All of you."

Peter leaned over her bed. "Cynthia has implicated you

in her father's murder. I have orders to bring you in for questioning. You are technically not free to help us."

Geneva gritted her teeth. "You know darn well I had nothing to do with Kaitlyn's murder or the senator's."

"Unfortunately, there's evidence indicating otherwise. A few synthetic crystals were found in your apartment."

"I had nothing to do with the crystals. Someone must have planted them there. I've been framed."

"Although I admit it looks damaging, I happen to believe you. The CMU will make you an offer. We will delay our questioning in exchange for your help tracking Rolf. What do you say? Can you close your eyes and find Rolf?"

"I want your word you won't harm him. You'll hear him out and give him a chance to prove his innocence."

Peter cleared his throat. "If you can find Rolf Jorgensen, I promise we won't harm him, unless, of course, he attempts to injure you or any other innocent person. I think all of us will agree, we cannot stand by and watch him hurt you."

"He won't harm me. He loves me."

"All right. Let's give it a try then, shall we?"

"Wait." Nate grasped Peter's shoulder and turned to face Geneva. "Are you sure you're okay? You don't have to do this. We'll find him. The crystals, too, if they're out there."

Geneva locked eyes with her oldest brother. Always protective. It wouldn't do to show fear, or he'd try to prevent her from helping. "Thanks, but yeah, I'm sure."

"Okay," Peter said. "Clear out, everyone. Let Geneva prepare herself, and we'll get started."

The men left the room, leaving Geneva with Julia and Nonna. She changed into street clothes and the three of them spent a few moments meditating, which helped to focus their abilities. By the time the men returned, she was ready to begin the search.

She sat in a chair. The rest of the group gathered, some standing around her chair, some sitting on the hospital bed. Geneva took a deep breath. Her lungs inflated, and colors rushed forward to greet her. First the familiar teal and royal blue of her brothers, followed by the arctic blue of Peter, then Julia's violet energy and Nonna's green, so much like Rolf's and yet, darker. Her mind grasped the thread of color and moved beyond the hospital walls out onto Euclid Avenue, sifting, searching, and straining for recognizable energy streams.

A spot of yellow caught Geneva's notice. She drew it close for inspection. Not the blinding yellow of Cynthia Torra. She tossed it aside and another color rose to take its place, green not yellow. A bit farther, another yellow, harsher than the first. Geneva took measured breaths to slow her racing heart. *Cynthia.* Not far from the Clinic.

Her pulse slowed, but her blood chugged through her veins. There, just beyond Cynthia, a familiar green. She'd almost missed it due to the dark streaks. Rolf closed in on Cynthia and fast. He used dark energy to track her.

Geneva's eyes shot open on a gasp, causing Nate, who stood next to her, to jump.

"I found them."

"Where?" Nate asked in unison with the others.

She stood. "Hurry. We've little time. They're both on Euclid Avenue. Not far from here. We need to get going."

Nate stood in front of her. "We'll take it from here."

"Get out of my way, Nate."

Nonna's steady voice broke the silence. "If your sister isn't present when we find my grandson, it will be a dead body we encounter. Rolf's and Geneva's fates are like this." Nonna held two fingers, twisted together. "If Rolf dies, so does Geneva. One will not survive long without the other. Is this what you want?"

Nate studied Nonna a moment as if he wanted to argue, but whatever he saw made him change his mind. He looked at Peter and then turned to Geneva. "We'll need to take two cars."

Five minutes later, Geneva was heading out the door. Her legs wobbled a bit at first, but the longer she stayed on her feet, the better she felt. By the time she climbed into Julia's father's car, along with Julia and Nonna, she'd begun to feel like her old self. Her brothers and Peter followed in Nate's car.

"Take a right," Geneva ordered Julia's father, who drove. The green of Rolf's aura moved closer to the glittering yellow. "Hurry, make this light."

Julia's father floored it, roaring through the intersection. The light changed to red. A screech of tires and horns sounded behind them.

"Oh my God," Julia said. "Two cars collided behind us. Not Nate, thank God. I can still see their car."

"We can't stop. They'll have to do their best to catch up. Text them to make a right onto Chester. It looks like Cynthia's inside a building, and Rolf's closing in on her."

Julia bent over her mobile phone, texting. "Nate says we're not to confront Rolf and Cynthia without them."

"We don't have the luxury of waiting. We'll be lucky to get there in time." Geneva glanced at Nonna in the rearview mirror. Her clasped hands held a rosary. *Please let Nonna's prayers come true.* Geneva kept the yellow and green colors in the center of her mind. "There, ahead. Pull over and let us out."

"Where's Rolf?" Julia's father asked. "I don't see him."

"He's inside. He's okay. Park the car and come find us."

"I don't like the thought of you three going in there alone. Better wait until your brothers arrive."

"All right. Drop us here." Geneva kept her thoughts guarded in case Julia's father caught a glimpse of her plan. She had no intention of waiting for anyone. She had to get to Rolf before he did something foolish like try to strangle Cynthia.

"Remember, don't get close until we have help," he said.

Geneva didn't reply. She already had the car door open and was running toward the entrance of The Arcade, leaving Julia to assist Nonna. Somewhere in the building, Cynthia hid. And she wasn't alone. Energy vibrated on the psychic plane. *Rolf was with her.*

47

CAPTURE

em Alley. How fitting. Rolf gazed at the glass store windows of the shop in The Arcade, keeping himself far from the entrance to avoid being seen. No light shone inside the shop. But Rolf sensed his prey hidden in the shadowy depths. Waiting.

He couldn't stop his lip from curling. Nothing would keep him out. The dark in him demanded he fling himself through the wall and hurl energy at Cynthia before she could stop him, blotting every horrible inch of her out of existence. But he hadn't come this far to screw up. Caleb Stone warned him. If he wanted Geneva, the CMU would need to believe he loved her, which meant he needed Cynthia alive and the synthetic crystals as proof of her deception.

He closed his eyes, gritted his teeth, and drew the darkness deep inside, where it seethed and writhed before settling into a restless slumber. He needed to surprise Cynthia, and for that, it would be better to enter from the side walls of the building than the front. He'd grab her before she could drain him of energy and squeeze the life from her until she revealed the location of the synthetic crystals. Then he'd place an anonymous call to Peter, providing the location of Cynthia's hiding place, and let the CMU do the rest.

Geneva half stumbled, half ran through the antique wooden doors of The Arcade, and to the stairs, her heart playing a mad tap-dance against the walls of her chest. Would she make it in time to stop Rolf from wiping Cynthia out of existence?

She raced across the tiled floor, causing several shoppers to stop and stare. The trail of color she followed stopped at a small storefront, hidden in the corner right next to the exit doors. Gem Alley, the gold sign with fancy script in the store-front window read. *Of course.*

A cold shudder swept her small frame. Rolf would kill Cynthia if Geneva didn't stop him. She'd gotten close enough to sense the frightening force of his merciless rage. Much as she wanted to see Cynthia's comeuppance, she didn't want it at Rolf's expense.

Geneva turned to make sure no one watched and eyed the lock on the door. An older building. The lock shouldn't be trouble. The trick was not to project so much energy she blasted the door off its hinges and attracted attention. She sucked in colors, narrowed her focus, and thrust energy into the lock until she heard a crack. She grabbed the door-knob, twisted, and it swung open. She stepped into the dark interior. A single light glowed from the back of the store.

She took a step forward only to be tugged backward into a hard chest. *"What the hell do you think you're doing?"* Two arms grasped her shoulders, holding her tight. They were covered in a familiar green light.

"Rolf. Oh, Thank God. I almost had a heart attack."

"You're lucky I don't strangle you. Go, now. Back the way you came."

Rolf thrust her toward the open door. The forward momentum sent Geneva out the door to be pushed back inside by a cowgirl projecting a dazzling yellow light. "Ah, but you've only just arrived."

The room spun and twisted, and Geneva landed with a thud, knocking the air from her lungs. She opened her eyes. Cynthia pointed a gun at Rolf, who slumped against the wall. They'd both been a victim of Cynthia's energy-draining trick. "I've been waiting for you. I admit, though, I did not expect this one"—she nudged her boot against Geneva's head—"to arrive so soon."

She grabbed both of Geneva's arms and dragged her farther into the store, ignoring Rolf, who slid to the floor. The green color he channeled dwindled to a tiny, almost nonexistent, speck. Cynthia shook her head, causing her auburn curls to bounce from side to side. "We could have had fun together, Rolf. You and I would have made quite the pair." She placed her boot on Geneva's chest. "Tell me, whatever did you see in this pathetic freak show?"

Rolf didn't answer, although he lifted his head to gaze at them, his eyes twin black holes. If looks could kill, Cynthia would be a charred mass of ashes.

Geneva's heart shriveled. Had she lost him? The steady candle-flame of hope radiating in her chest the day he confessed his love to her flickered, sending fear skittering along her nerve endings. She shivered, one long, never-ending ache of a shiver. A familiar masculine voice spoke, "Think carefully before you pull the trigger."

Dad? Geneva couldn't control her gasp of recognition. Her father approached, catching Cynthia off-guard. Julia and Nonna trailed close behind him. Julia stooped to Rolf, laying a hand on his head.

"What is this, a family reunion?" Cynthia waved her gun at the new arrivals. "Get your hands off him. On the floor. All of you."

There was a moment of silent communication, and one by one, everyone complied. Geneva noticed Rolf's aura had strengthened, thank God. The dark wasn't so prominent now. And the fact she could see it was a sign Geneva's energy returned, aided by Julia, no doubt.

"All except you, Rolf. Come here."

Rolf managed to pull himself up and sway toward them. "What game are you playing?" His gaze locked onto Cynthia's. "You can't think you'll get away with this. There are too many witnesses."

"I most certainly will. When we're done, there won't be any witnesses."

"What are you talking about?"

"Everyone knows you're a dark master who's been using dark energy to kill. It won't come as a surprise to learn Rolf Jorgensen went on a final killing spree before turning a gun on himself."

Geneva stifled a gasp. "Kill me if you have to, but leave Rolf alone."

"No, Geneva," Rolf said.

"You two are so sweet it's sickening. But I'm afraid I don't have time to debate the merit of keeping anyone alive. Goodbye, my dear."

Cynthia pointed the gun at Geneva's head. Time seemed to stand still. Everything happened at once. There were shouts—her dad, Julia, Nonna, Rolf. Geneva pulled energy, but it wasn't enough. Rolf rolled, covering her. The gun fired, the sound echoing across the small store.

Blood gushed from Rolf's side. Energy in its rawest form rushed through Geneva, spilling into the room. Glass shattered, jewels flew in every direction. Someone screamed over and over.

"Grab her." Peter pointed at Cynthia. Her brothers tackled her and wrestled for the gun. Nate won.

Strong arms enfolded Geneva. Rolf's arms. "Shh, it's okay." Blood oozed from his side, staining his torn shirt. The smell of burnt flesh hung in the air.

"You're bleeding! Are you hurt?"

"I'm fine. A sting. No big deal. The bullet grazed me, that's all. Focus on your breathing. You can do it."

Relief poured through her. Sobs jerked her body from side to side, and she kissed his dear face. She couldn't stop. She sat and smoothed both hands through his thick hair and around his solid back. She gulped. "Thank God. But how is it the dark didn't protect you? Are you sure it's nothing?"

He smiled, warm and dark and delicious. "Yes, I'm sure. The dark only stops the bleeding when I'm using it. I couldn't risk using dark energy without hurting you. So I didn't. But please, go on kissing me."

"I hate to break up the party, but we need to get you both to the hospital," Peter said to Rolf. "That wound may not be life-threatening, but you're losing a lot of blood."

Nate took off his shirt and handed it to Rolf where he sat next to Geneva on the floor. "Here. Press this into your side."

A prickle of awareness slithered across Geneva's spine. She looked toward Cynthia, who watched her, a triumphant smile on her face. Blood stained her cheeks where flying glass had hit her. Geneva frowned. What did Cynthia have to smile about?

Danny held both Cynthia's hands out in front of her. Nate aimed the gun at her and examined the black velvet bag. *The synthetic crystals.*

Cynthia ignored them. Instead, she opened her palm to reveal a lone pink crystal. It drew Geneva's eye. The crystal pulsed and sparked like...like a beating heart.

A sharp pain had her grabbing her chest.

"What is it? What's happening? What has she done?" Rolf asked.

Darkness covered the room.

48

THE OTHER SIDE

R olf had never been one to beg for anything. But as he held onto Geneva's still form, he found he would barter with whatever means he had at his disposal. "Geneva, honey, please. Open your eyes. Look at me."

He leaned close so he could feel her breath. None escaped her sweet lips. He felt for her pulse. No beats moved under his fingertips. Her eyelids remained closed, as if she dreamed. *Oh God. This isn't happening.* He pushed into her mind, but her brain waves were nonexistent. A hollow sound tore from his throat, taking all reason with it. "Open your eyes, G. Please, for me. Please, I can't lose you now."

She couldn't be. She mustn't be. Raw agony ripped through him, unleashing the blackest part of his soul. The part he and everyone around him feared. It poured from every part of his being, filling the shop with deadly, dark energy. "What have you done to her?" he roared, tossing his head toward where Cynthia stood a few feet in front of him. "What is that stone? Tell me."

He had to hand it to her, Cynthia didn't flinch at the dark

energy. Neither did she move a hand to stop it. Peter and the brothers let her go, fleeing toward the door and safety.

"Rolf," Julia said.

Something in her tone cut through the rage coursing through his blood, demanding violence. He glanced back. Julia's mouth formed words, words with meaning, if his mind would translate. His gaze remained on hers instead of returning to Cynthia. Why were Julia and Nonna lying on the floor next to Geneva? She was dead. His light. His love. His reason for being. His hands fisted at his sides.

Dark energy spread within two inches of the three women. The three he cared most for in the world. Hadn't he always known one day he'd bring them death and destruction? He wanted to rage at the sky or heaven or hell. He wanted the dark to blot out everything he once held dear until he could no longer feel pain or anger or emptiness or anything.

Julia's mouth still moved, but at a faster speed than before. "Geneva won't die. Not today. Pull the dark back. Do it now. Or we won't be able to save her."

Nonna bent over Geneva, eyes closed, hands on her chest, reciting some ancient prayer. Dark energy inched forward, now centimeters from swallowing her whole.

Julia shouted at him. "Do it, Rolf. Do it now. Do it so Geneva can live."

Nonna, with her strange talent, so much like his own. Nonna, who was different than others and kept her gift a secret, like him. Nonna, who a neighborhood bully once said could pull a soul from the brink of death.

"Nonna can bring Geneva back."

Julia's words penetrated the thick fog wrapped around Rolf's brain. The first tendril of dark energy unfurled a long finger to swallow her skin. He took a step forward, his hands reached toward them, his mind focused. The dark responded. It hovered, as if reluctant to let go of its prey and receded. Rolf pulled it back, back inside into the deep recesses of his mind where it could harm no one.

"What is she doing?" Cynthia shouted. "No. No, she can't. She doesn't deserve to live. She doesn't deserve..."

Her words dropped like a switch had been flipped to end the sound. Rolf turned. Cynthia plunged to the ground. Her eyes rolled back in her head so that he could see the whites of her eyes. Her body stiffened and twitched as if she'd touched a live wire. Then it relaxed, and she lay unmoving. Nate rushed forward, kneeling over her, feeling for a pulse. "She's dead."

Rolf figured he would feel something—cold hard satisfaction, bone-aching relief, numbing anger. But concern and fear for Geneva consumed his thoughts.

Could it be? Was it possible Nonna had brought her back from death? He rushed to Geneva's side. She opened her eyes and tried to sit.

"Jesus Christ." The words were all he could manage before collecting her into his arms and holding on tight. "Take it easy, honey. It's all right. Take your time."

"She'll be fine now." Nonna gave him a warm smile and a pat on the cheek. "We'll all be just fine."

"What happened to her?" Geneva pointed at Cynthia. "You didn't...?"

Rolf looked into her eyes so she knew he spoke the truth. "No, I didn't kill her, although I wanted to."

"What..."

Peter cleared his throat. "I believe the energy in the crystal returned to its source."

Julia gasped. "Of course. That makes sense. The energy in the crystal has to go somewhere, doesn't it? When it didn't kill Geneva, it returned to the person who activated it, Cynthia."

"It would appear so." Peter laid a hand on Rolf's shoulder. "Son, we should get both of you to the Cleveland Clinic to be checked out. It's clear Cynthia possessed the crystals all along." He pointed at the Ericksen brothers and the black velvet bag. "Let's get these to the lab and have them analyzed."

Geneva's father appeared at their side, looking ten years older. "The Scarlet Heart. I never thought I'd see it again."

"Dad, are you okay? You look like you've seen a ghost."

"Your father has." Peter touched the pink crystal that no longer pulsed and glittered with energy. "The Scarlet Heart was last seen twenty years ago when your mother was killed by the intruder who made off with the crystals she and your father collected. It appears Senator Torra was the recipient. He and Cynthia had been holding on to them all these years, searching for others."

"We've checked the premises." Nate came beside them. "There's a safe in the back. Danny managed to open it. Nothing inside."

"Makes sense," Peter said. "There were only ever a few genuine crystals. It seems the Torras have used them all. Once activated, they cannot be reused. This"—he held the Scarlet Heart between two fingers—"is now just a pretty jewel."

Rolf stood, pulling Geneva into his arms with a wince. Now that the excitement had passed, his left side hurt like hell. He eyed Peter. "You no longer believe either of us a threat to society?"

Peter shook his head. "No, I don't. What I witnessed today was a man pushed to the end of his rope, who still managed to hang on and do the right thing for the woman he loves." He gave Geneva the glimmer of a smile. "And a woman who loves her man. So much so, she defied death itself. I'd say you both deserve a happy ever after."

Geneva's father came forward, holding out his hand to Rolf. "I feel the need to apologize on behalf of myself and my sons for doubting you cared for my daughter."

Rolf frowned. "You no longer believe the legend?"

Carl Ericksen grinned. "What, a dark master isn't capable of love? I think we'd all agree, any man who's willing to take a bullet for Geneva loves her. You're okay in my book, Jorgensen."

Then Julia and Nonna hugged him, the Ericksen brothers shook his hand, and Peter called for an ambulance. And Geneva smiled at him through tears of pure joy, and the world that had been spinning lopsided on its axis for most of his life, shifted, righting itself.

And Rolf knew with a certainty even the dark in him couldn't conquer, everything he ever wanted from life was right here, in this room, shining from Geneva's adoring eyes.

EPILOGUE

Six Months Later

CALEB STONE ENTERED the ancient gray church on Cleveland's Public Square and spotted an open seat toward the back, in a wooden pew hidden in shadow. A wedding ceremony was in progress, but he managed to slip inside undetected. His sharp gaze found the bride and groom, taking in their sleek forms in a single glance.

Rolf Jorgensen, dressed in a black tux, stood at the altar and confessed his deep love and undying devotion to his bride, Geneva Ericksen, who presented him with a tremulous smile. Caleb had made the right decision allowing Jorgensen to escape. These two looked at each other with the kind of tenderness and passion he could only dream about. The bride's golden hair was pulled into a soft bun on the back of her neck. She wore a set of glistening pearls and flowers in her hair. She looked beautiful, as all brides should. But she didn't hold Caleb's attention for long.

His penetrating gaze slipped past the bride and settled on her maid of honor, Julia Jorgensen. She'd arranged her dark hair as he preferred it, swept to one side, and trailing down her back and onto her navy-blue dress. She carried a bouquet of soft-pink roses, the perfect complement to the pink in her cheeks. As if she sensed his presence, she turned her head in his direction. He reacted on instinct, drawing his energy inward to avoid detection. He was a creature of night-time dreams and smoke and mirrors, a shadow of a man, more figment of imagination than flesh and blood. His fate didn't lie with Julia. And yet...

Caleb didn't move, unable to pull his eyes away. *And yet...*

The preacher asked the usual question—whether anyone should object to the marriage. Carl Ericksen stirred but said nothing. The rest of the congregation let out a collective sigh.

Jorgensen kissed his bride, perhaps lingering longer than normal wedding etiquette allowed. But of course, these two were far from normal. Even in a crowd like this, those with psychic abilities—Caleb counted twenty before growing tired—could feel the potent combination of the couple's combined talent. Apart they were powerful. United...Caleb hoped he'd never be called upon to find out how powerful a couple they were united.

The glowing bride and groom turned to face the crowd. The minister presented the new Mr. and Mrs. Jorgensen.

The congregation roared. Caleb joined in their clapping. Despite the fact he could not steal joy for himself, it gave him great pleasure to see this particular couple happy. Not because he'd played a crucial role in their happiness, which he had. Not because he grew tired of his own existence, which he did. But because it made Julia happy, which he acknowledged had become his primary reason for being.

He followed the bridal party's procession down the aisle. Julia met with her partner, Nate Ericksen, who wrapped an arm around her waist. Caleb worked to suppress the stab of jealousy to see another man's hands where his could never be.

Guests were leaving the pews now to greet the happy couple in the back of the church. It was his cue to depart. He'd promised himself he'd not linger long. Yet, he argued, what would one more minute hurt? One more minute to bask in Julia's presence. One more minute to imagine his hands on the soft curve of her waist, to pull her close and kiss her rosy lips, to run his hands through her thick, dark hair.

Stop. He must stop. He must put her out of his head. He could no longer risk lingering in her dreams. He feared he'd revealed himself during this latest escapade. *And yet...*

And yet, he couldn't stand by and watch her suffer. Not for a day, not for an instant, and not knowing her life was in grave danger. Julia may never be his, but his heart still loved her as if she were. He would warn her of this latest threat. One final time, he promised himself. And when he knew she was safe, he'd leave her to find what happiness she could in another man's arms.

Geneva and Rolf Jorgensen waved goodbye and stepped into the waiting black limousine. His sweet Julia hugged them, brushing away a tear. He drew his brows together, his forehead creasing. He longed to kiss her tears away.

The limousine pulled forward. Next to him, a girl said the couple planned to travel to Hawaii, where they'd spend a month basking in the glorious Hawaiian sun.

Time to go. The deed is done.

Caleb turned. If he stayed a moment longer, Julia would spot him. And all would be lost. But, he reminded himself, he would return to her late tonight, when she lay in her bed dreaming. One last time he'd visit, pull her into his arms, and tell her how to avoid danger. *And afterward.* And afterward, he promised himself, he'd take himself off to some foreign country—Russia or Lithuania or the moon—and stay far, far away from the everlasting temptation Julia Jorgensen presented. So far away he'd no longer die a little bit inside each time she held another man's hands, or caressed his cheek, or kissed his lips. So far away he would no longer feel this overwhelming desire and ache to make her his own.

Caleb Stone pulled his black leather jacket tight and walked to the parking lot behind the church to find his car. He never looked back. If he had, he would have gotten no rest that night. Nonna stared after him, a half-smile on her face, one wandering brown eye moving over his retreating form.

Author's Note

Sometimes books enter the world painlessly. Sometimes it takes months and in the case of Cross Waves, years, to capture the story. (The title is aptly named.)

I'm grateful to all the many editors who looked at this book, most especially Angela James for her terrific developmental edits and providing me with a clear line of advice to make this story come alive, and to Tera Cuskaden and Marin McGinnis, for their eagle-eye copy editing and proofreading.

I am also eternally grateful to my critique partners, Angie Hockman and the Pretty Little Writers (Tara Sammon, Judy McDonough, Joyce Caylor, Cathy Matuszak, and Lydia Sharp), and to all my many beta readers. Thank you for shaping this book into what it is today by reading and re-reading chapters.

My biggest cheerleaders are my family—both immediate and extended—thank you for putting up with my many mood swings (my husband, Barry, and children, Simon, Samuel, and Ella), reading my books, and cheering me on. I am so grateful for your support.

And finally, to my loyal readers for sticking with me on the long and arduous journey to publication. You are what make this all worthwhile.

Love and hugs — Amanda

OTHER BOOKS BY AMANDA UHL

Mind Waves, Mind Hackers Series, Book 1

Charmed By Charlie

A word about the author...

Amanda Uhl has always had a fascination with the mystical. Having drawn her first breath in a century home rumored to be haunted, you might say she was "born" into it. After a brief stint in college as a paid psychic, Amanda graduated with a bachelor of fine arts in theatre and a master's degree in marketing. Over the past twenty years, she has worked as an admissions representative and graphic designer, owned her own freelance writing company, and managed communications for several Fortune 500 companies, most recently specializing in cyber security. Amanda is an avid reader and writes fast-paced, paranormal romantic suspense and humorous contemporary romance from her home in Cleveland, Ohio. When she's not reading or writing, you can find Amanda with her husband and three children, gathering beach glass on the Lake Erie shoreline or biking in Cuyahoga Valley National Park.

CPSIA information can be obtained
at www.ICGtesting.com
Printed in the USA
LVHW040841121020
668551LV00001B/37